Praise for

Parting Shot

"I think her old fans and new fans alike will enjoy this story. If you haven't read anything by Mary Calmes, then stock up today! This author is simply one of the best authors I've ever read."
—World of Diversity Fiction Reviews

"I quite simply couldn't put this down! I loved every single moment!"
—Confessions From Romaholics

Old Loyalty, New Love

"…this is another book by Mary Calmes I'll be adding to my re-read and all-time favorites lists."
—The Blogger Girls

"If you haven't read this one yet, it is a must add to the TBR pile."
—The Novel Approach

"Shifters are a passion of mine, and Mary Calmes gives a new type of shifter and a freaking hot alpha male to lead them."
—Mrs. Condit & Friends Read Books

Change of Heart

"The story draws you in from the first scene and never releases its hold until the final sentence."
—Literary Nymphs

"With secondary characters that are just as strongly written and a story that runs smoothly, this engrossing story will keep the reader's attention till the very last page."
—Rainbow Reviews

By MARY CALMES

Acrobat
Again
All Kinds of Tied Down
Any Closer
A Brush of Wings (DSP Anthology)
with Cardeno C.: Control
with Poppy Dennison: Creature Feature
Floodgates
Frog
Grand Adventures (DSP Anthology)
The Guardian
Heart of the Race
Ice Around the Edges
Judgment
Mine
Old Loyalty, New Love
Romanus
The Servant
Steamroller
Still
Three Fates (Multiple Author Anthology)
Timing • After the Sunset
What Can Be
Where You Lead
Wishing on a Blue Star (DSP Anthology)

CHANGE OF HEART SERIES
Change of Heart
Trusted Bond
Honored Vow
Crucible of Fate

A MATTER OF TIME
A Matter of Time Vol. 1
A Matter of Time Vol. 2
Bulletproof • But For You
Parting Shot

THE WARDER SERIES
His Hearth • Tooth & Nail • Heart in Hand
Sinnerman • Nexus • Cherish Your Name
Warders Vol. 1 & 2

Published by DREAMSPINNER PRESS
http://www.dreamspinnerpress.com

ALL KINDS OF TIED DOWN

Mary Calmes

Dreamspinner Press

Published by
DREAMSPINNER PRESS

5032 Capital Circle SW
Suite 2, PMB# 279
Tallahassee, FL 32305-7886
USA
http://www.dreamspinnerpress.com/

This is a work of fiction. Names, characters, places, and incidents either are the product of author imagination or are used fictitiously, and any resemblance to actual persons, living or dead, business establishments, events, or locales is entirely coincidental.

All Kinds of Tied Down
© 2014 Mary Calmes.

Cover Art
© 2014 Reese Dante.
http://www.reesedante.com
Cover content is for illustrative purposes only and any person depicted on the cover is a model.

ISBN: 978-1-63216-064-5
Digital ISBN: 978-1-63216-065-2
Library of Congress Control Number: 2014939163
Printed in the United States of America
First Edition
July 2014

This paper meets the requirements of
ANSI/NISO Z39.48-1992 (Permanence of Paper).

For Lynn.
Nothing happens without you.

Lisa, thank you for reading and answering
questions and stemming the flood of worry.

Cardeno, thank you for checking on me
and staying up late and for the endless support.

Jessie, thank you for being my bright spot.

CHAPTER 1

RUNNING.

All our interactions with suspects ended the same way. I would say, hey, let's wait for backup or a warrant. I'd mention we didn't have probable cause, and sometimes I would even go so far as to point out we weren't armed because it was our damn day off! Not that he ever listened. The chase was always on seconds after I spoke. The fact that he even stopped to listen to me before acting stunned most people who knew us.

"Please," I would beg him. "Just this once."

And then I'd get the head tip or the shrug or the grin that crinkled his pale blue eyes in half before he'd explode into action, the velocity of movement utterly breathtaking. Watching him run was a treat; I just wished I wasn't always following him into the path of whizzing bullets, speeding cars, or flying fists. Since I'd become his partner, the number of scars on my body had doubled.

I considered it a win if I got Ian Doyle to put on a Kevlar vest before he kicked down a door or charged headfirst into the unknown. I saw the looks we got from the other marshals when we returned with bloodied suspects, recaptured felons, or secured witnesses, and over the years they had changed from respect for Ian to sympathy for me.

When I was first partnered with him, some of the other marshals were confused about it. Why was the new guy—me—being partnered with the ex-Special Forces soldier, the Green Beret? How did that make sense? I think they thought I got an unfair advantage and that getting him as a partner was like winning the lottery. I was the newest marshal, low man on the totem pole, so how did I rate Captain America?

What everyone missed was that Ian didn't come from a police background like most of us. He came from the military and wasn't versed in proper police procedure or adherence to the letter of the law. As the newest marshal on the team, I was the one who had the book memorized the best, so the supervisory deputy, my boss, assigned me to him. It actually made sense.

Lucky me.

Doyle was a nightmare. And while I wasn't a Boy Scout, in comparison to my "shoot first, ask questions later" partner, I came off as calm and rational.

After the first six months, everyone stopped looking at me with envy and switched to pity. Now, going on three years, marshals in my field office would bring me an ice pack, pass me whatever pharmaceuticals they had in their desks, and even occasionally offer advice. It was always the same.

"For crissakes, Jones, you need to talk to the boss about him."

My boss, Supervisory Deputy Sam Kage, recently called me into his office and asked me flat out if there was any truth to the rumors he was hearing. Did I want a change of partner? The blank stare I gave him hopefully conveyed my confusion. So it was no one's fault but my own that I was running in the slushy melting snow down the forty-seven hundred block of Ninety-Fifth Street in Oak Lawn at ten on a cold Tuesday morning in mid-January.

Arms pumping, Glock 20 in my hand, I saw Ian motion to the left, so I veered off and leaped an overturned garbage can as I headed into an alley. I should have been the one on the street; my partner was better at leaping and running up walls like a ninja. Even though I was younger than his thirty-six by five years, at six two and 185 pounds, he was in much better shape than me. While he was all lean, carved muscle with eight-pack abs and arms that made women itch to touch, I was built heavier at five eleven, with bulky muscle and wide shoulders, more bull than panther. Ian had a sleek, fluid way about him; I was all sharp angles and herky-jerky motion. We were as different as we could be, though people often commented that we had a really similar irritating way of carrying ourselves when together, an unmistakable strut. But I would have known if I was doing that, if I puffed up when I walked beside my partner. No way I swaggered and didn't notice.

The second I emerged from the trash-strewn alley, I was hit by a 250-pound freight train of a man and smashed onto the pavement under him.

"Oh!" I heard my partner yell as my spine splintered and every gasp of air in my body was trounced out of my frame. "Nice block, M!"

The escaped convict tried to lever up off me, but Ian was there, yanking him sideways, driving him down on the sidewalk beside me with a boot on his collarbone. I would have told him not to go overboard with manhandling—I took it upon myself to caution him against all manner of infractions during the course of a normal day—but I had no air, no voice, nothing. All I could do was lie on the cold, clammy cement and wonder how many of my ribs were broken.

"Are you getting up?" Ian asked snidely as he rolled Eddie Madrid to his stomach, pulled his arms behind his back, and cuffed him quickly before moving to squat next to me. "Or are you resting?"

All I could do was stare up at him, noting that he was scowling, as usual. That scowl was permanently etched on his face, and even when he grinned, the creases above and between his eyebrows never smoothed all the way. He was tense, just a little, at all times.

"If I didn't know you were tough, I'd be starting to worry," he said gruffly.

The fact that neither I nor Eddie was moving should have clued him in.

"M?"

I tried to move and pain shot through my left wrist. What was interesting was that the second I winced, his light eyes darkened with concern.

"Did you break your wrist?"

As though I was responsible for my own bones getting snapped. "I didn't break anything," I groaned, a bit of air finally inflating my lungs, enough to give me a hoarse, crackly voice. "But I think your friend over here did."

"Maybe we better get you to the hospital."

"I'll go by myself," I groused. "You take Madrid in."

He opened his mouth to argue.

"Just do what I say," I ordered, annoyed that I was broken. Again. "I'll call you if I can't make picking up Stubbs from lockup."

His scowl deepened as he took my good hand and hauled me to my feet. I went to move around him, but he leaned forward and his prickly dark brown stubble grazed my ear, the sensation making me jolt involuntarily.

"I'm coming with you," he said hoarsely. "Don't be an ass."

I studied him, the face I knew as well as my own—maybe better after looking at it for the past three years, straight on or in profile as he drove. His gaze on the ground, suddenly flicking up, colliding with mine, startled me with its intensity. He was utterly focused; I had every drop of his attention.

"Sorry."

I was stunned, and it must have shown on my face because the furrowed brows, the glower, were instant. "Holy shit," I teased. "It's a little early for spring thaw."

"You're a dick," he flared, turning away.

After grabbing hold of his shoulder, I yanked hard, fisting my hand in the half trench he wore, stepping in close. "No, I'm happy—actually, really happy. Come on. Relax."

He growled at me.

"Take me to the emergency room." I chuckled, holding on to him.

His grunt made me smile, and when I squeezed his shoulder, I saw how pleased he seemed to be. "Let's go."

He heaved Madrid to his feet—which was interesting since our fugitive outweighed him by a good sixty pounds—threw him up against the car, opened the back door, and shoved him in. It took only moments, and then he was back to facing me, stepping forward into my space, so close I could feel the heat rolling off him.

"You should never question that I'm gonna go with you. That's what partners are for."

"Yeah, but—"

"Say okay."

He never demanded things of me. Normally there was browbeating, teasing, derision—but not concern. It was strange. "Yeah, okay."

Nodding quickly, he walked around the side of the 1969 Cadillac deVille we were currently driving. Whatever was seized during drug raids or other criminal activity was what we got. The last ride had been a 2000 Ford Mustang I was crazy about, either driving—which I scarcely ever did—or riding in. It was a sad day when it became the victim of heavy machine-gun fire. The grenade tossed through the window had been the final straw. Ian kept saying it was fixable up until that point.

The *bow-chicka-bow-wow* car we were in now, all whitewall tires and green metallic paint, was a little much for the US Marshals Service. But we were supposed to travel incognito, and cruising through the worst parts of Chicago, no one gave us a second look.

"Get in," he barked.

"Yessir."

And as usual, we were off like a rocket, no gentle merge into traffic. Ian always drove like he was fleeing a bank robbery and I had learned to simply buckle up.

"What the fuck," Eddie Madrid yelled from the backseat, having lurched forward and then been hurled back in a whiplash maneuver. "Someone belt me in."

I started laughing as I turned to my partner, who was swearing at the people sharing the road with them. "Even our prisoner fears for his life."

"Fuck him," he snarled, taking a corner like he was a stunt driver getting ready to jump out.

Eddie slammed into the partial window on the passenger side of the sedan. "Jesus Christ, man!"

I just braced for impact, hoping I'd make it to the hospital in one piece.

"LEMME GET this straight," Ian said that afternoon as he led James "the Cleaver" Pellegrino to our car. "You've got a broken wrist, and you're bitching about your shoes?"

Normally doctors didn't cast broken bones until a few days later due to swelling. But because I had no intention of riding my desk until it mended, and because it was a clean break, the ER doctor had made an exception. He said that if the cast got too loose, I might have to return and have another put on. I didn't care; the important thing was that I could follow Ian back out into the field.

"Yeah," I whined, scrutinizing the plaster cast on my wrist and then, more importantly, my now scuffed-up John Varvatos cap-toe boots. Pellegrino had taken one look at me standing in the doorway when he came up from the basement, and bolted. We had been responding to an anonymous tip and found him at his cousin's house in La Grange. To keep him from making it out the back door, I dived at him. We ended up rolling over concrete before Ian had come flying around the side of the house and landed all over the guy. "They were new last week."

"And they were gonna be trashed by now anyway," Ian commented. "No way around it in the snow."

I glanced up at him. "This is why I wanted to move to Miami with Brent. Snow would be a distant memory."

He snorted out a laugh. "That guy was so not worth moving for."

I arched an eyebrow.

"And besides," he said gruffly, "you weren't gonna leave me anyway."

"I would ditch you in a second, buddy. Don't kid yourself."

He scoffed. "Yeah, right."

Apparently he knew better than to believe such an outright lie.

"You guys want me to leave you alone?" Pellegrino said snidely.

Ian threw him up against the car, and Pellegrino screamed because he landed on his chest, the same place that had recently been in contact with exposed brick.

"Shut up."

"This is police brutality."

"Lucky we're not the police," Ian reminded him, smacking him on the back of the head before his light blue gaze landed on me. "And why do you wear your good stuff to work? I've never understood that."

"Because," I answered, gesturing at him, "Dockers and a button-down and an ugly tie is not what I wanna be seen in every day."

"Well, that's great, but you ruin a ton of shit and then bitch about it."

"Hiking boots do not scream fashion."

"Yeah, but your John-whatever boots are fucked up already, and mine are still good."

"They look like shit," I assured him.

"But still functional," he teased, and the rakish curl of his lip did flip-floppy things to my stomach.

It was bad. So very, very bad. Ian Doyle was my totally straight best friend and partner. I had no right to even be noticing how the half trench coat molded to his shoulders; the roping veins in his forearms; or the way he touched me when he talked to me, sat beside me, or got anywhere in my general vicinity. How he was always in my personal space, as though I had none, was not something he was even aware of, so truthfully, it wasn't right for me to notice. But trying to pretend I didn't was eating me up alive. It was the real reason I should have asked for a change of partner, because I dreamed of being in bed with my current one.

"No snarky comeback?"

I coughed. "No."

He squinted. "How come?"

"You have a point, I guess. I shouldn't wear shoes to work that'll get ruined."

"I can get you a new pair," the Cleaver offered quickly before Ian could form a reply. "Please."

Ian smacked him on the back of the head again, opened the car door, pushed my seat forward, and shoved Pellegrino in.

"You're such an asshole, Doyle!" Pellegrino yelled before Ian slammed the door shut.

"Don't bruise him," I cautioned like I always did.

"Why the fuck not?"

I groaned.

"And for the record," Ian huffed, rounding on me. "You do not go into buildings alone. What did we say about that after Felix Ledesma?"

I mumbled something because my iPhone had buzzed with a text and I was reading.

"Miro!"

"I hear you."

"Look at me."

My head snapped up. "Yeah, fine, okay, shut up."

"No, not fine. Not okay. Every fuckin' time you take off your shirt and I see the scar right above your heart, I—"

"I know," I soothed, leaning close to bump his shoulder with mine.

He growled.

"Oh," I said, noticing the time. "You need to dump me and the Cleaver off so you can make your date with Emma."

The way his whole face tightened was not a good sign, but far be it from me to tell him that his girlfriend, though wonderful, was not for him. It would have been so much easier if she was toxic and I hated her. The truth was, she was sort of perfect. Just not for him.

"What're you gonna do?"

"When?" I was confused. "I'll process our prisoner so you can be on time for once."

He looked uncomfortable. "And then what?"

"Oh, I'm supposed to be playing pool tonight with some guys from my gym."

His face lit up.

"No." I snickered. "Bad. Your girlfriend does not want to play pool with strangers."

His glare was ridiculously hot. "How do you know?"

"That's not a date, Ian."

"Well, you shouldn't go either."

I wondered vaguely if he had any idea how petulant he sounded. "I broke my left wrist, not the right. I can hold a cue just fine."

"You should go home and go to bed," Ian said, glowering as he walked around the car to the driver's door.

"No, man, I gotta work through the pain," I teased before I got in.

"What're you talking about?" he asked irritably after he slammed his door and turned to me. "You broke your fuckin' wrist."

"But isn't that your mantra or some shit? The Green Beret code and all? Screw the pain?"

"Playing pool isn't work. You don't hafta do it."

Throat clearing from the back seat. "You know, you guys could just leave me here," the Cleaver suggested cheerfully. "Then nobody has to do paperwork at all, and maybe you guys could double date."

Ian twisted around in his seat. "I have a better idea. Why don't you shut the fuck up before I get you back out of this car, take off the cuffs, and make you run away so I can shoot you."

"Maybe you'll miss."

Ian scoffed.

"I'll take that deal. What're you carrying, a nine millimeter?"

"Again, not cops. Marshals," Ian explained. "You ever get shot with a forty caliber?"

I couldn't contain my chuckle at how contrite the Cleaver appeared.

"Maybe I'll just stay put."

"And shut up," Ian barked.

"Yeah, okay."

He turned around and gripped the steering wheel, and I realized how tense he was.

"Shooting people is bad," I stressed playfully, poking Ian's bicep.

I got a derisive sound back, but that quickly, he seemed better, the edge gone.

"Move this crate. I need to get this guy processed fast, because I really have to change."

"At least your shoes, huh?" Ian teased, the tip of his head and the eyebrow waggle really annoying.

I did my best to ignore him.

CHAPTER 2

GRANGER'S WAS an older pub downtown, close to The Loop. I had fallen in love with it over the many times Ian dragged me there. It had good cheap beer, great hotdogs, and a haphazard floor layout that sort of meandered from room to room, making it feel bigger than it really was. Ian and I normally staked out a spot between the pool tables and the dart boards where we could still see whatever game was on the TV above the bar as well as the door. Checking who came in was always important to law-enforcement types and was something that couldn't be turned off.

So I wasn't thrilled that the table where my gym cronies gathered was toward the back, but I made my way through the crowd to them anyway after stopping at the bar to get an IPA I liked.

"Miro you made it," Eric Graff, my occasional racquetball partner and one-time fuck buddy, greeted me as I reached them.

The other men and women were also pleased to see me, all except Eric's new boyfriend, Kyle, who, I was guessing, didn't love Eric's arm draped around my shoulders. I would have told him not to worry—I never went back for seconds unless either my mind was challenged or there were fireworks in bed. Neither had been the case with Eric.

Giving his arm a quick pat, I extricated myself and moved through the group until I reached Thad Horton, who was more than an acquaintance but not quite a friend.

"Hey," I greeted the pretty man who I had swam laps with many a time. He was a tanned, tweezed, manscaped twink, always quick with a smile and a kind word.

"Miro," he almost squeaked when he saw me, which alerted the gorilla standing beside him.

"Babe?" he asked, checking on Thad before focusing his attention on me. "Who're you?"

"Just a friend from the gym," I said quickly. "You must be Matt. Thad talks about you all the time."

He took my hand, clearly relieved, shaking fast. "Matt Ruben."

"Pleasure."

"Oh, are you the FBI agent?"

"Marshal," I corrected him, watching Thad grimace behind him and mouth the word "*Sorry.*"

Quick shake of my head to let him know it was no big deal.

"That's right. Marshal," Matt went on. "Thad was very impressed."

"It sounds far more glamorous than it is."

"Doubtful," Matt said kindly. "You wanna break, man? We're just starting a new game."

"Yeah, sure."

It was fine, and everyone was nice enough, but I'd made up my mind to leave when the game was over. I was bored, as was the usual with me unless either Ian or one of my very best friends was there. I really was lousy at casual interactions. When my phone buzzed a few minutes later, I leaned back against the exposed brick wall to answer.

"You're on a date," I commented.

"It's actually a group thing, and we're having dim sum."

I snorted out a laugh. Dim sum would not fill Ian up. He loved Chinese food as much as me—but noodles, chicken, and pork in large portions, not small pieces in steamer baskets.

"Fuck you, come meet me."

"Meet you? It's a date. She wants you to get comfortable with her friends."

"I don't care. I feel like hitting a ball."

Whenever he was bored, he thought about going to the batting cages. "Closed until March, buddy," I reminded him. "It's like twenty degrees outside right now, plus snow."

"What about bowling?"

"What about it?" I chuckled.

Silence.

God, I was ridiculous for even considering going. "Where are you?"

My hunger for Ian Doyle's company had gone from casual appreciation and friendship to a craving for the man himself that sat like a cold, hard stone in the pit of my stomach. Not that anyone knew; even the object of my affection would never be allowed to see how famished I was for his touch on my skin, his scent on my sheets, his breath in my ear. I hid the yearning well.

"At Torque in River North."

"That's not a Chinese restaurant."

"Like I don't fuckin' know that."

"Then what're you—"

"I told you, it's stupid."

"Are you sure it's okay?"

"Yeah, I'm sure, just come on."

"All right," I muttered, levering off the wall, "Gimme like—"

"Wait, where are you?"

"I'm at Granger's."

"Oh, I'll come there instead."

"Ian, buddy, you're on a *date*," I emphasized. "You're not supposed to bail."

"I'll just tell them—"

"Just stay put. I'll be right there."

A huff of breath and then he was gone.

I made my excuses to the group, drained my beer, handed off my pool cue, and was on my way to the door when I moved to shift around a woman and she turned.

"Jill," I said, smiling fast.

"Miro." She beamed for a second and then faltered. "Oh, is Ian with you?"

How her whole face fell, like there was nothing worse she could think of than seeing my partner, was sort of sad. "No, he's not. I'm actually going to meet him now."

"Good," she sighed, clearly relieved, and then she visibly realized what she'd said. "Oh, no, I didn't mean it like—"

"It's fine."

She exhaled sharply. "I'm sorry. I know he's your partner, but honestly the only good quality the man has is having you for a best friend."

I smirked. "You don't think that's a little harsh?"

"No, I really don't. You should have a PSA made, Miro. Something like: even though Ian Doyle is drop-dead gorgeous, just walk away, because dating him will be short and disappointing, as he's clearly holding out for someone else."

I nodded, moving to leave. "So you've given this some thought, I see."

"I wasted a month of my life thinking a US marshal would be a fun thing to have," she said, shrugging. "I may be an idiot, but he's the one guilty of false advertising."

"Well, I think—"

"And he's terrible in the sack."

It was my cue to run; it was too bad I couldn't. The crowd was too thick for me to bolt, so I plastered on a smile and pushed through. She caught my hand quickly, squeezing tight, letting me know that we were still good, before I pulled away and she was swallowed.

Outside, I moved to the curb to hail a cab, and my phone rang.

"What?"

"We're on our way to The Velvet Lounge. Meet me there."

I laughed into the phone. "Ian, buddy, I am so not dressed for The Velvet Lounge."

"Me neither."

"You're wearing a suit, aren't you?"

"No. Why?"

Lord. "Let me talk to Emma."

There was some muffled noise and then, "Miro?"

"Hey, Em," I said softly. "Are you guys going to The Velvet Lounge?"

"Yeah, we are, right after we drive Ian by his place so he can change."

I coughed softly. "Em?"

"Yes?"

"Was The Velvet Lounge a last-minute group decision?"

"Well, yeah. I'm doing some PR work for the owner, and he just called to say he put me on the list for tonight. How awesome is that?"

"So great," I agreed weakly. "But would it be okay if I borrowed Ian? My plans fell through, and I don't know if he told you I broke my wrist today, but—"

"No, he—oh, I'm so sorry," she said sympathetically. "But ohmygod, yes. Can I pretty please pawn him off on you?" Her voice had dropped to a whisper. "I swear to God, he's so bored and he's bringing everybody down."

I was certain he was. Ian did not suffer in silence. "Yeah, please. Put him on."

"I'll owe you big time. Thank you."

If she only knew how permanently I wanted to take him off her hands. "No problem."

Again there was the muffled noise of a phone being passed around. "Hey?"

"I'll grab sandwiches at Bruno & Meade. You come over, bring Chickie, and we'll take him for a run after we eat, all right?"

"Yeah?" He sounded so hopeful.

"Yeah, come on. Your woman said you can come play with me."

"I don't need fuckin' permission," he said, instantly defensive.

"Yeah, but you didn't want to hurt her feelings, which was nice," I pacified. "But she's fine, ready to have a fun night, and you're bringing all the hipsters down."

"Like I give a—"

"You'd rather be there?"

No answer.

"E?"

"I'll meet you at home."

"No, at my place, not yours."

"That's what I said."

It *wasn't* what he said unless… but thoughts like that did me no good. "Okay."

"Yeah, so, all right."

Which was his version of thank you and I'm sorry for being a dick and everything else. He was very lucky I spoke Ian. "Don't forget to bring the scoop thing, 'cause I ain't picking up your dog's crap."

He was laughing when I hung up.

WHEN I got home, the lights were on in my small Greystone, so I knew Ian was already inside. I tried really hard not to like the idea of him being there when I walked through the door, because wanting something I couldn't have was a recipe for bitterness. I loved having Ian as a partner, we fit perfectly, each playing off the other's strengths, and I didn't want that feeling to change. So I squashed down the stomach flip over seeing him in my kitchen, drinking a glass of water as he leaned against the counter.

"Just come in, why don't you," I groused.

From around the side of the couch came Ian's creature. Easily a hundred pounds of powerful muscle, Chickie appeared even bigger than he was with all the long black and white hair. I wasn't sure what kind of dog he was, and Ian didn't know either. I had often said maybe timber wolf.

"What are you doing in my house?" I asked the dog, who didn't break stride until he reached me, shoved his wet nose in my palm and danced for me, so very happy to be included.

"Thanks, M," Ian said as he drained his glass and sat it down. "You're the only one he doesn't freak out."

"It's because I know he doesn't really eat people," I said, scratching behind Chickie's ears and under his chin as he wriggled and then pranced after me as I joined Ian in the kitchen. "Maybe we should run him now, before we eat. He seems kinda wound up."

"Yeah, that'd be good," he agreed.

"Lemme change," I said, putting the bag of food down in front of Ian. He was in sweats and a hoodie, so I needed to be dressed the same. "Throw this in the fridge and see if I have any beer glasses in the freezer."

"What's wrong with drinking from the bottle, princess?" He grinned at me.

"Dick."

He started to whistle as I took the stairs to the loft where my bed, closet, and second bathroom were. It wasn't a whole second level, which I liked about the layout.

Once I was in sweats that had "US Marshal" down the side, I came back down and headed toward the front door.

"Why do you wear those?"

He lost me. "What?"

"The work sweats."

"I don't understand the question. We wear these when we train."

"Yeah, I know, so why the hell would you wear them when you're off?"

"They're sweats, Ian. Who the hell cares?"

"They're flashy."

My eyebrows lifted involuntarily. "They're flashy?"

He flipped me off, snapping Chickie's leash on and stalking to the door.

"They're *flashy*," I repeated.

"People are gonna want to see if you're a real marshal, and what if they fuck with you?"

"Yeah, that's true, because, you know, the dog won't deter anyone at all."

Again I was flipped the bird before the three of us went out the front door. Locking it behind me, I leaped off the top step of the small stoop.

"One, two, three—go!" I yelled, and I bolted away from Ian, running down the sidewalk like a crazy man and charging across the street without looking, knowing that in my Lincoln Park neighborhood the only thing I was in danger of being hit by would be a snowplow.

It was dark but the streetlights were on, and the sky was a beautiful deep blue with indigo patches that would soon be lit up with stars—though I might or might not be able to see them for the light pollution. I loved the time of night when people were sitting down to dinner and I could see into their homes for just a moment as I jogged by on my normal run. The houses blurred at the moment, as I raced toward the park with Ian and Chickie close behind.

"Miro!"

I didn't stop, and I heard Ian curse before Chickie was suddenly running beside me. Ian had allowed him to run free off the leash.

Veering right, I ran by one of the poles that kept cars off the gravel path between the field where kids played soccer and the playground with the swings and jungle gym. Chickie caught up with me again, and when I took a different route down toward the jogging path, Ian was there, hand suddenly fisted in the back of my jacket, holding on.

I slowed down, laughing, and he yanked me into him, bumping; his chest pressed into my back. We were both still moving, so he lost his balance when we collided and would have gone down if he hadn't wrapped an arm around my neck for balance.

His hot breath, his lips accidentally brushing against my nape, brought on a shiver I couldn't contain.

"Why'd you run?" he asked, still holding on, his other hand clutching the front of my jacket, his arm over my shoulder, across my chest.

"Just to make sure Chickie had fun," I said, feeling how hard my heart was beating and knowing it had nothing to do with the sprint I'd just led him on.

"Yeah, but you're cold," Ian said, opening one hand, pressing it over my heart for a moment before he stepped away from me.

I was freezing the second he moved. "Yeah, I am," I agreed quickly, patting Chickie, who was nuzzling into my side. "Let's jog back, get the blood pumping. That way we'll get warm."

Ian agreed, and we jogged together along the path, Chickie flying forward, only to come loping back, making sure Ian was where he could see him.

We made a giant loop and made it back home right before we both turned into Popsicles. Since I hadn't seen Chickie relieve himself, I told Ian he should probably walk him around the block once more.

"But I'm hungry," he whined.

"Well, I don't know what to tell you. Your dog did not take a shit, and he needs to."

Ian pivoted to look at his dog. "Chickie!" he yelled.

Chickie took one look at his master and squatted right there on the patch of grass beside the curb. Ian's expression of disgust and disbelief sent me into hysterics.

"You scared the shit outta the dog!"

"That's not funny."

I couldn't even breathe, it was so funny.

As Ian pulled plastic bags from his pocket, I doubled over, and Chickie came barreling up the steps past him—right to me—and licked my face, very pleased with himself.

"Stupid dog," he muttered as I continued to howl. "Stupid partner."

The man was cursed with both of us.

IAN TOOK off his hoodie and pulled on a zippered cardigan of mine before he came into the kitchen and watched me put together our sandwiches. I had picked them up from Bruno & Meade, a deli I loved, and what I liked about it was that it didn't assemble to-go orders. They gave you everything that came on the sandwich, all the ingredients, but the bread was sealed separately so it didn't get hard—or soft, depending on which kind you ordered—and everything else came in Ziploc bags or small plastic containers.

"You realize this is the height of laziness, right?" Ian commented as he put sliced bread and butter pickles into his mouth. "I mean, seriously, you could buy all this crap at the store and do this yourself."

"Oh yeah? The aioli mayonnaise, the chorizo salame, and Ossau you like? Really?" I asked, sliding the plate over to him. "You think I could just pop into a Jewel for that?"

He scowled at me.

"The sourdough that's freshly baked every day?"

Something was muttered under his breath.

"I got the gouda you like, and the marinated olives too."

"Are you still talking?"

"Why, yes." I smirked. "I am."

"Shut up," he muttered, grabbing a bottle of his favorite beer—Three Floyds Gumballhead, which I made sure was always there—from the refrigerator before he turned for the living room.

"And roma tomatoes are your favorite, so I made sure I asked for—"

"Yeah, fine, you're a fuckin' saint and I'm an ungrateful ass."

I cackled as he flopped down onto the couch and turned on the TV. The sounds of football filled the room. After a moment he turned around and looked at me.

"What? Need a napkin?"

"No, I have a—you're not gonna argue?"

"Why would I argue?"

"Ass," he mumbled, turning back to the game.

I joined him on the couch, sitting close like I always did, and he took some potato chips off my plate. "Go get your own," I said, smacking his hand away.

He shoved me with his shoulder and I almost dumped my plate.

"What're you doing?"

"Don't be stupid," he retorted, nudging my knee gently with his and then leaving his leg pressed against mine. "Since when don't I eat off your plate?"

He was right. I would let Ian do whatever he wanted, whenever he wanted. I was his for the taking—as were my potato chips.

CHAPTER 3

IAN LEFT about one in the morning and had promised to be back at seven to pick me up for breakfast. When he wasn't there by quarter after, I called him, but it went straight to voice mail. Since I didn't want to be late and the walk to the train platform would take too much time, I decided to drive my truck. I so seldom drove the Toyota Tacoma, I had thought on numerous occasions about selling it. But inevitably, someone needed help moving practically the moment I'd start to seriously consider the idea. And today I was glad I still had it as I headed in to work.

I was halfway there and got a call from Ian.

"Where the hell are you?" I snapped, annoyed and hungry and without coffee.

"I could say the same."

"I'm starving, asshole; you were supposed to feed me."

"Do you ever read your texts?"

"I don't have a text from you."

"Yes, you—oh shit."

"Oh shit, what?"

"I e-mailed you, I didn't text you. Fuck."

"Just tell me where you are."

"Oh crap, Kage is calling me on the other line. Hold on."

"Ian—"

"Wait," he barked, and then silence.

I had no idea where I was supposed to be driving, but not knowing where Ian was would make me crazy faster than anything.

Knowing he was somewhere I should have been too, to back him up and keep him safe, would unravel my well-constructed façade. I needed to find him.

The line went dead, and then my phone rang right afterward from a number that wasn't in my caller ID. Concerned that it might be my boss, I started hunting around for my earpiece. It rang five times before I gave up and answered.

"Jones."

"What's the rule?" The deep and gravelly voice of my boss, Supervisory Deputy US Marshal Sam Kage, rumbled in my ear

"Third ring," I replied automatically.

"What's your excuse, then?"

"I was talking to Ian."

"No, I was actually talking to Doyle, so try again."

"Well, I was talking to him before you were."

"Why aren't you with him?"

"That's a really good question."

"Pardon me?"

Fuck.

"Again I ask: why didn't you pick up your phone?"

Lying to him, about anything, big or small, was a mistake. "I can't find my earpiece."

"I'm *sorry*?"

Double fuck.

"Where is it?" Kage growled.

"It's here somewhere."

"So since I'm not on speaker, may I assume that you're holding your phone?"

No coffee and Kage first thing. FML. "Yessir."

"Stop the car and find the earpiece, Jones."

Procedure had to be followed. After pulling over before I got on the expressway, I retrieved the earpiece from the very back of the glove compartment, put it in, connected my phone, and told Kage he could go ahead and start talking.

"I'm sorry?" he asked irritably.

It was like throwing gasoline on a fire. As I banged my forehead on the steering wheel, I prayed he would just tell me what he wanted me to know.

"I need you to meet vice detectives out in the Washington Park area to take custody of Kemen Bentley, a missing witness who was supposed to have testified against Taylor Ledesma, his former lover, before he escaped protective police custody. He got caught in a task force run by vice, the FBI, and the state police. They were cracking down on underage girls and boys working as escorts, and he was there in one of the hotels they raided."

"Yessir."

"Doyle is on site."

"Roger that."

"Make sure he texts or calls you from here on out." He hung up without another word, as was his way.

I called Ian.

"Shit."

"That was fun," I said, making sure he couldn't miss the sarcasm.

"I fucked up."

"Yeah, you did."

"I was tired."

"He only calls you because Doyle is before Jones in his phone."

"I know."

"Use your phone correctly."

"Fuck. Yes, fine. I will."

I felt better. "Okay."

"I didn't have breakfast, you know," he complained. "Or coffee."

"Whose fault?"

"Stop being mad."

"I'm not mad; I'm just annoyed. And I hate not knowing where you are. It's like when you go off on your missions and… but you know that."

"I do," he husked.

"Yeah, so," I began, realizing how miserable I sounded. "When you're actually *here* and you disappear—that's fucked up, Ian."

Heavy sigh from him. "It won't happen again."

"I'm your partner. I should always know where you are."

"Yes."

"Okay." I smiled into the phone. "Now, about food. We'll get some after we take custody of the witness."

"So you're not gonna be pissed all day?"

"Who cares if I am? You don't have to ride with me."

"What? No. When we get back to the office, your car stays there."

"Maybe I wanna drive today."

"No." He didn't like me on the phone in the car, even on my earpiece, because he didn't think I was a good driver. Having me even a bit distracted annoyed the hell out of him.

"You don't get to just say no, Ian. Your word isn't law."

"It's not?" He was baiting me.

"Fuck you."

He snickered. "You want pizza for dinner? I really want pizza."

"We haven't even had breakfast yet."

"Yeah, but I like to plan, you know that."

I did know that. "Maybe Emma wants to go out."

"But no deep-dish," he said, blithely ignoring me. "I want hand-tossed."

"No one eats that in Chicago."

"I do."

"You don't count."

"I do too count."

Yes, he did. He counted more than anyone to me.

"I'm your partner; you gotta take care of me."

All the words that came out of his mouth that he didn't actually hear? They were astounding.

"Beer or wine?" I asked, trying to restore normalcy on my end.

"Oh for fuck's sake," he groused. "Wine? With pizza?"

So much disdain in his voice. "Fine, beer it is."

"How far out are you?"

"Like twenty minutes, if I wasn't about to be in morning traffic."

"Okay," he sighed. "I'll get with the guys from vice."

I snorted out a laugh.

"How old are you?"

"No coffee," I reminded.

"Yeah," he agreed, almost sadly.

"What's with the tone?"

"Nothing."

"*Something*," I said confidently, because I knew him too well, every nuance of his voice categorized and memorized. He couldn't hide anything from me.

"It's too late to rethink your lot, M. You're stuck with me."

"Where's this coming from?"

"Just, you know… I'm not easy."

"*Oh* buddy, I *know*."

"Shut up."

"And I wouldn't dream of getting a new partner."

"Okay," he said hoarsely, and then he hung up.

The drive should have taken maybe twenty-five minutes, but this was morning traffic on I-90 East toward Washington Park. I'd be lucky to be there before Christmas.

By the time I reached where the raid had gone down, I was more than ready to stretch my legs. Climbing out of the truck, I went around to the trunk of the deVille and opened it. As it was a work car, we both carried keys for it. I took off my jacket and my suit blazer, put on my tac vest, and eyed the raid slicker. SOP said it had to go on, but it was freezing, and my parka with "US Marshal" across the back was at home. But I could imagine getting shot because no one knew who I was and what Kage would say, and worst of all, what he would do to me and what my new job description would be. He was not to be messed with.

After putting my blazer and jacket both back on, I pulled the raid slicker on over that, then removed my badge from the chain around my neck I'd worn out of my house and clipped it to my belt.

"Miro!"

Glancing around, I found Ian dressed in a long-sleeved T-shirt with "US Marshal" emblazoned down the arm, his vest, khaki cargo pants, and a baseball hat.

"Dressing down today, marshal," I teased, closing in.

He shrugged. "Yeah, well, we both were supposed to, but since I dropped the ball, I guess I'll be doing all the heavy lifting today."

"You poor thing."

"This is what I'm saying."

"At least I should stay clean today," I quipped, reaching his side but not getting too close. All I wanted was to grab him, so I kept my distance on purpose.

Except... moving quickly with that fluid way he had, he stepped right into my personal space. "You said you weren't mad."

"I'm not," I said, my voice thick.

"Then act like it."

"Okay," I said at the same time a man came flying out the front entrance and started racing across the parking lot.

It happened so fast. I saw the men chasing him, made out the letters "FBI" on their raid jackets even from a distance, and took off, sprinting around the cars to intercept who I figured was a fleeing suspect. I ran a long route, circumventing the other pursuers, and emerged to the right of him. Hurtling into his path, I clipped him on the shoulder and we went down together, rolling, sliding over snow and gravel until a car halted our momentum.

Winded, gasping, I choked as the man shoved me off and tried to scramble away, crawling on hands and knees.

"Freeze, asshole," Ian bellowed, running up to us, his Glock leveled at the man's head. "Don't fuckin' move!"

I heaved for breath as the man was swarmed, shoved facedown onto the asphalt, and searched for weapons. Checking my wrist, making sure the cast was still intact, I realized from the twinge of pain that shot through it that I needed to take it easy on the tackling until I was back at 100 percent.

"Put your hands up," one of the agents yelled, coming around the back of the Toyota Camry we had rolled up against, his gun leveled at me.

"The fuck you say!" Ian yelled before he drove the man back, lifting him up off his feet and pile-driving him over the trunk with a forearm in the guy's throat. "That's a fuckin' deputy US marshal you're pointing your goddamn gun at!"

Lots of movement, and I was hauled to my feet as four state police officers pulled Ian off the agent and crowded around him until he holstered his weapon.

"How 'bout a thank you for catching your suspect," Ian snarled.

I pushed into the crowd, grabbed hold of his vest, and shoved him backward until we were free, only the two of us outside the throng of troopers.

"Hey," I said softly, my hands on his sides, slipping to his hips without thought.

"Fuck you!" he shouted at them all. "You don't draw a gun unless you know what the fuck you're supposed to be shooting at!"

He was furious, and it was only because I could bench-press more than he could, having muscle on him where he had height on me, that I could hold him still.

"Hey," I said again.

His blue eyes flicked sideways and met mine.

"Thank you for having my back."

"Always," he grumbled. "You know that."

And I did.

"You're bleeding."

I shrugged. "Every time, you know that."

"Is your wrist okay?" he asked, grabbing hold of it, turning it over in his hands, checking even before I could form an answer.

"It's fine."

"Stop doing shit like that," he said crossly, letting go, seemingly reassured that the plaster was holding together. "Wait for me."

"I will."

"Miro!"

"I promise," I replied, chuckling. "Don't fuss."

It was always weird walking into someone else's investigation, but since the feds were in charge, it wasn't as bad as it was just dealing with Chicago PD or state troopers. Sometimes there was a lot of posturing, and I always wanted to tell everyone to whip 'em out and I'd get my ruler and proclaim a winner. Ridiculous.

The special agent in charge, the one running the task force, apologized for his man pulling a gun on me and then waited for Ian to return the sentiment.

"What?" my partner asked irritably.

He shook his head and walked us to the hotel room where the missing witness perched on the bathroom counter, his feet in the sink, looking bored.

"Mr. Bentley," I greeted him.

"Sweetheart, do you know that you're bleeding?"

I shrugged, walking into the room before Ian. "Where ya been, Kemen?"

He flashed me a beautiful smile, all perfect white even teeth and dimples. The boy, all of nineteen, was stunning, warm mocha skin and huge green eyes. I understood why he'd been kept, but I grieved for the loss of his childhood.

I remembered his file. He'd been sold by his mother for drugs when he was only ten, then changed hands several times until Taylor Ledesma saw him dancing at a club and took him from the guy who was selling his ass for three hundred a night. Kemen became Ledesma's sole property and prized possession. The good part was that never again was he raped, gangbanged, or passed around. The bad part was, he had no freedom. He was not allowed outside of the waterfront penthouse apartment.

"I won't testify," he said curtly. "Taylor Ledesma was decent to me. I explained that to the police and I'm telling it to you guys. I won't."

"That was smart, what you did," I commented casually.

When his focus shifted to me, I could tell I had piqued his interest.

"Because Ledesma conducted all his business in Spanish, you decided to learn the language so you'd know what the hell was going on."

"Yeah, sure, made sense, right?"

"Yeah," I agreed. "And Ledesma never made you leave the room when he conducted business—how come?"

Kemen swiveled to face me, stretching all the tight muscles. "He liked showing me off to men who would never have me. He got off on it."

"Makes sense. So then what happened?"

"There was a raid on his home. The FBI showed up, and they took me into custody but then handed me over to Chicago PD when they thought I was underage."

"And then once they found out you were eighteen, they put you into protective custody after you agreed to testify."

Suddenly his feet were of paramount importance, as much focus as he was giving them. "I changed my mind."

I put a hand under his chin and tipped his head up to recapture his attention. "And you gave the detectives watching you the slip."

"Yes." He inhaled, rubbing his cheek in my palm like a cat. "But I wouldn't run away from you, marshal. Absolutely not."

I let my hand drop away. "You've been on the run for six months. Are you ready to stop?"

"I'm still not going to testify."

"The man wants you dead," I informed him.

"So you say."

"So everybody says," Ian promised. "We'll take you to our office so you can hear the wiretaps. Now get down and turn around."

"Oh honey, whatever you say."

Ian scoffed as Kemen slid off the counter, every movement graceful and fluid, pivoted like a dancer, and put his hands behind his back. Long, lean muscles covered his compact frame, and really, pretty didn't do him justice. But where I differed from others was that I saw a kid, and they saw a piece of meat.

"Man, you look like shit," Ian said abruptly.

I glanced at him and he gestured at the mirror. I looked.

It was a surprise: my left cheek scratched, bruises darkening along my jaw, and my lip split. But the worst part was my brand-new distressed leather shearling-lined bomber jacket was shredded under the now-tattered raid slicker.

"Aww shit," I muttered.

"You're more upset about the jacket than your face, aren't you, baby?" Kemen sympathized, looking at me like I was pitiful. "I know. It was pretty this morning, huh?"

"It was," I sighed.

"Are you serious?" Ian asked, his gaze darting between me and our wayward witness.

"Are you?" Kemen demanded. "That jacket is hot."

"*Was* hot, apparently," Ian snickered.

"Heathen," Kemen pronounced.

"Let's go," I grumbled. Ian cuffed him, and I opened the door.

Gunfire in the hall stopped me, and several state troopers rushed forward, weapons drawn. They were prepared to go out, but to me, the balcony I'd glimpsed when we came in was the better option.

"What?" Ian asked.

I tipped my head toward the glass door.

"No."

"Yes." I nodded. "Come on."

"Fuck, okay. I'm right behind you."

Moving fast, we were at the sliding glass door when the gunfire spattered again and I heard yelling behind us.

"That's not—" Kemen gasped. "—for me, is it?"

"It is," Ian and I said at the same time.

"Pimps don't normally come after their meal tickets with semiautomatic machine guns," I continued, sliding the door open and peering over the side.

"And?" Ian asked.

"We can hang down and drop; from this floor to the third, there's a lot of room sticking out. We can't miss it."

"Okay," he agreed, tipping his head at me. "You go and I'll lower him down."

I knew him better than that. I'd get there, he'd drop Kemen, and then he'd run off into the firefight without me. "No, you first, I'll cover you."

He tensed for a fight. "Listen, Miroslav, you should go first because of your wrist."

"No, it should be you because of my wrist," I corrected him. "You're stronger right now. I don't wanna drop him."

The gunfire got louder and screaming joined the shouting.

"Now," I barked, cutting off any further protest.

Shoving Kemen at me, Ian walked to the edge of the balcony, checked the distance, climbed the railing, scowled at me, and then lowered himself down. Only his hands were visible for a moment, and then I heard him hit the balcony below us.

"You okay?"

"Yeah, it's only like maybe six feet when you're hanging. Just a quick drop."

"Easy," I said to Kemen. "You next."

"No-no-no," he said, panicking suddenly. "I can't go off a balcony."

"Please, this is not a big deal," I said, picking the smaller man up and slinging him over my left shoulder like he weighed nothing.

"You're not even uncuffing me?" he squeaked.

"Nope." I chuckled, walking to the edge, leaning over, and letting him slip.

He screamed for the second and a half before he was in Ian's arms.

"You two are insane!" he shrieked as I flipped over the railing, held on for a moment with my one good hand, and then let go.

Ian braced me when I landed, hands on my hips again, like the night before, his chest pressed to my back.

"Thanks," I said, smiling from inches away.

"Your ideas suck," he said grumpily. But the bitching was affectionate, and I got that before he shoved his face down into my shoulder. He needed just a second.

"All better," I taunted.

"Ass," he proclaimed before spinning me around to face the locked balcony door. More gunfire echoed above us, and because I didn't like the idea of drawing attention by shooting the lock or the glass, I got out my wallet.

"What are you doing?" Ian whispered.

"These doors are cheap," I said, sliding my Visa between it and the frame. "Good ones slide into a groove so you have insulation and more security. Cheap ones like this meet up flush, and there's only a tiny catch on—" I heard the click. "—the lock."

"Where the fuck did you learn to do that?" Ian squinted at me.

"Misspent youth," I said, straightening and sliding open the door. "You knew that."

"I know some of it, but clearly not enough."

"That was hot," Kemen said, flirting with me.

Pulling my gun, I went in first, checking under the beds and in the bathroom and the closet before motioning them in.

Ian pushed Kemen ahead of him and locked the balcony door behind them. He sat Kemen down on one of the two double beds as I went to the door, where I flipped the security lock and waited as he called for backup.

I took my first breath when I heard sirens.

Kemen and I glanced up when we heard pounding over our heads, followed by short bursts of gunfire. He turned slowly to me.

"What happened?"

"Someone recognized you. Maybe one of the girls, maybe one of the pimps, or maybe even a cop, but whoever it was, they knew who you were and put in a call to Ledesma."

He started shaking.

"Are you getting it? Is this starting to sink in?"

Silently, he nodded.

"If you're gonna stop being an asshole and stay with us and trust us, we'll take off the cuffs."

He mouthed the word yes, making no sound.

Ian took them off, and the second he did, Kemen wrapped both arms around my left, attaching himself tight.

"You're gonna be okay."

He was quiet and didn't move.

Minutes later, there was a knock at the door.

Moving sideways so I wasn't in front of it in case bullets came through, I lifted my gun. Ian stood on the other side mirroring me.

"Federal marshal," Ching yelled from outside.

"Hey," I shouted back, which wasn't protocol at all. "It's Miro and Ian."

Ching's groan came through loud and clear. "What are you supposed to say, asswipe?"

"I forget," I ribbed as Ian chuckled.

"Fuckin' Jones," Ching groused, but I could hear the amusement in his low voice. "Becker, Sharpe, me, and Kohn are out here. This floor's secured, but nothing else, so you guys stay put."

"Yessir," I said, chuckling.

"The balcony, Jones?"

"I think it's the best way to leave a room," I apprised him. "Don't you?"

That time I could hear more than just him laughing.

WHEN WE finally got the all clear, we put a Kevlar vest on Kemen, put a jacket on over that, and with us all dressed the same, all in the same jacket, exited the hotel. Kage stood in front of at least a dozen reporters shoving microphones in his face as we walked by. I didn't realize until we were moving through the crowd how many policemen, news crews, and bystanders had gathered around the hotel. It was a zoo.

It was good press for the police sting. There was a real deficit of places teens could be sent if they weren't bad enough to go to a juvenile detention facility and home wasn't an option. We needed more programs to rehabilitate them and get them off the street. I didn't know what the statistics were, but I did know that a lot of the girls, and boys, who got out of a life of prostitution got sucked back in. And a lot of them, like Kemen, were confused and mistook the shelter a pimp offered for love. He related pieces of his life story to us on the ride over to our office from the hotel. I knew most the facts, but hearing him flesh out the details was grueling. Even Ian squirmed a bit.

Once we got to the office, we put Kemen in a holding cell and went back to our desks to start the arduous reporting process. Ian started making the calls to vice to let them know they could pick up Taylor Ledesma. The process to indict him was ready for round two.

I took my jacket off, wincing at the scrapes on it, and put it on the back of my chair. Ian was right; I needed to invest in some crappy clothes for work.

"Coffee," Ian moaned as he dropped into the chair at his desk that butted up to mine. "I told the kid that we'd bring him back something."

"Okay." I chuckled. "Let's go."

We put our badges back on the chain holders we wore when we weren't in the field and walked the two blocks to our favorite breakfast diner, arguing the whole way about the e-mail Ian had sent me earlier in the morning. He finally passed me his phone and told me to make it forward so that when Kage called him, I would get an alert as well. I didn't think it could be done from Ian's phone—I thought only our boss could do it—but I fiddled with it just in case. When he got a text message from Emma telling him she'd made dinner plans with friends for them, I passed it back to him.

"No pizza for you, buddy," I said, nudging him with my shoulder.

"What?"

I ordered three specials and talked to Rosa, my favorite waitress, as Ian texted Emma. I got Kemen a huge orange juice, and Ian and I both even bigger coffees with two shots of espresso in each. We would definitely be awake after drinking that.

"What's Bastille?" Ian asked when we had our food and were sipping coffee on the way back to the office.

"I know what Bastille Day is," I threw out.

"No, it's a restaurant down on Rush."

"I have no idea. Why?"

"That's where Emma has us going tonight."

"Oh, nice," I said, taking another sip of the elixir of the gods. "Damn, that's good."

"I just want pizza."

"Stop whining, it'll be fun."

"I don't like French food."

"You've never had any French food, so how would you know?"

"I just do."

"Way to be open-minded."

"I don't wanna go," he muttered.

"Just drop it."

But he didn't. Instead, he complained on the walk back, on the way up the elevator, down the hall to the holding cell to pick up Kemen, and finally to the conference room where the three of us sat and ate.

"Bastille is nice," Kemen offered as he took a sip of his orange juice before he started in on his Mexican omelet. I passed him the guacamole and salsa, and Ian forked over the sour cream when he had what he wanted. "I've been there a ton of times."

"There, ya see," I said between bites, "Kemen says it's nice."

Ian made a jacking-off motion.

"You did not just do that." Kemen sounded horrified.

"That's funny."

"What is?" I asked Ian, ignoring our witness.

He shrugged. "It's just, whenever a witness is younger than you— or a woman—you use their first name. Older than you and a guy, you use their last. Do you realize you do that?"

I had never actually thought about it, but it was sort of nice that Ian had. That the things I said were noticed.

"They serve fusion Vietnamese-French," Kemen said out of the blue.

We both turned to him.

"At Bastille," he retorted, annoyed with us. "It's called a conversation. We were having one. Hello."

Ian made a retching noise in the back of his throat.

"Ohmygod, don't ever do that again when I'm about to eat," Kemen said dramatically, eyes wide. "Holy crap, he's disgusting."

"Eat your food." I said, trying not to laugh.

"And this omelet is ridiculous," he passed judgment. "Who eats this much food in one sitting? It's the size of a pound cake."

Ian said something back, but he was chewing.

Kemen asked me for the translation.

"He said it's the Wednesday morning special."

"You guys shouldn't eat like this," he warned. "Nobody should."

"You're gonna eat it."

"No, darling, I'm going to pick at it. I'm not going to eat it all. Who eats like this and doesn't have a heart attack?" he asked, making a face as he watched Ian hoovering it down. "Oh dear God."

His horrified expression was the best part of my morning.

THAT EVENING as I cleaned up after dinner, putting the remaining five slices of deep-dish spinach pizza in my refrigerator, I replayed a conversation I'd had with a very handsome man who'd cornered me after my shower at the gym. He'd been very clear as he leaned into my space that he would love to eat dinner with me, but more importantly, he'd like to take me home.

"We could have a really good time."

I had no doubt, but I could not have been any less interested. There'd been no one since my ex, and it wasn't that I was pining over him—it was simply that whoever I dated I had to introduce to Ian. And if I wasn't going to introduce them to Ian because it was just a one-night stand—what was the point? Besides, no one turned me on enough to want to jump into bed except for my very straight, very unavailable, partner.

The whole thing was a mess. I needed to get laid. As soon as I met someone I couldn't keep my hands off of, I'd be all over this insane obsession with Ian.

My phone buzzing with a text startled me, I'd been so lost in thought. I was not surprised to find Ian wanting to know where I was. It was a big part of the problem for me, his constant attention, even though I would've bet my life that he didn't realize what he was doing. The fact of the matter was, though, that Ian was as possessive of me and my time as he was of my stuff. It was too bad it didn't really mean a damn thing.

Ignoring the text, I finished cleaning up and left the plate and wineglass I'd used on the wooden dish rack to air dry.

When the phone rang minutes later, I answered.

"Are your fingers broken along with your wrist?"

"You're on a date, dumbass," I informed him. "Focus on the people in front of you and stop trying to talk to me. Endeavor to make a good impression."

"I can't."

"You can't what? Focus?"

"Yeah."

"And why not?"

"'Cause now we're heading over to Ethan's house to have drinks and maybe play board games."

I had to process that. "What?"

He grunted.

"You don't like board games. You like video games."

"Yes, I know."

"Tell them you like to shoot stuff."

"I'm starving."

I stifled a laugh. "What did you eat?"

"I dunno."

"You don't know what you ate?"

"Nope. The whole menu was in French."

"You didn't eat sweetmeats, did you, because I think that's brains."

"No, I think it was fish."

"You hate fish."

"Yeah, I know that too."

I coughed. "You realize that Emma is doing her damnedest to integrate you and her friends because she cares about you? And you're being an ass about the whole thing?"

"Maybe she should care less about group stuff and more about her and me stuff."

"But she knows you guys work when you're alone, and now she needs to see how you fit into her life with her friends and family."

"Yeah, okay, what're you doing?"

He shouldn't have cared right then. "Ian? I'm hanging up."

"No, really. What're you doing?"

He was like a dog with a bone. "Cleaning up."

"Cleaning up what?"

"Dinner dishes."

Silence.

"Ian?"

"You had pizza, didn't you, you shit?"

I laughed. "Well, yeah, but I had deep-dish that you hate."

"I don't hate it."

"Yeah, but you don't love it."

"I love it more than French food."

"Because you have an undeveloped palate," I criticized.

"Who cares?" he said harshly. "I love… pizza."

"I know."

"And Chickie."

We were going to talk about the dog now? "Get off the phone."

"Go walk him."

"I'm sorry?"

"Chickie. I thought I'd be home by now to take him out, but I'm not, so—go walk him."

"Screw you. I am not the dog walker."

"He'll pee in my apartment."

"Like you'd notice."

"What the hell is that supposed to mean?"

I huffed. "I will not be baited into fighting with you on the phone. I'm hanging up."

"You're contractually obligated to walk the dog."

"I'm really hanging up now."

"You promised to take care of Chickie."

"When you're deployed, yeah."

"He's your responsibility too."

I hit the End button and he was gone.

I turned off the lights and collapsed onto the couch, sore from the day's events. My phone rang and I let it go to voice mail three times before I answered.

"Oh for fuck's sake, what?"

"What if it was an emergency?"

"The only emergency is that you're bored out of your mind."

"Why don't you wanna walk the dog?"

I sighed deeply.

"What?"

"That guy I hit today and my wrist—man, I'm beat."

"Oh," he said, his voice soft, rumbling. "Why didn't you tell me?"

"It's no big deal. I'm just gonna lie here and watch TV until I get sleepy."

"Okay."

"So try and have fun."

"Yeah, I—you're fine, right?"

"Course."

"You're sure?"

"Absolutely."

"Okay," he said and hung up.

I never made it off the couch.

CHAPTER 4

WHEN I got out of the shower the next morning, I heard movement in my kitchen, so I moved to the railing at the end of my bed—there was just enough room there for me to walk—and yelled down that I was armed.

"Yeah? And?" came back the snide reply.

"You could ring the doorbell like a normal person," I mentioned, smiling in spite of myself when Ian walked out of the kitchen directly below me and into the living room where I could see him.

"But I have a key," he countered.

"Which you're only supposed to use when I'm not here."

"You're never not here."

I sighed. "Which if you think about, is really sad. I need a vacation to some tropical paradise so I can get laid."

He squinted up at me. "Why can't you just get laid here?"

The question, asked so innocently as he stood in the middle of my townhouse, was like a punch in the gut. Because I *could* have sex, right there, on the couch... bent over the couch, on the floor, or even better, in my bed. I could get laid anywhere in my home... if Ian were gay. I could. But I wouldn't, because he wasn't.

Christ.

"Well?"

"I need a vacation," I muttered, turning away since I was in a towel and nothing else. "And why're you dressed like a lumberjack?" I shouted, wanting to make sure my voice carried.

"Why're you yelling? I can hear you fine."

There was no winning.

"Just tell me why you're dressed like that," I prodded.

"Homeland Security raid at that youth halfway house in Schaumburg. We have a lead on that girl, what was her name?"

I stopped halfway to my closet, having to make new clothes choices. "It's Lucy, isn't it?"

"Yeah, that's right. Lucy Kensington. She skipped out before she could be taken into custody by marshals in Lubbock," he said as he clomped up the stairs. For a Green Beret, Ian walked really heavy.

"I thought you were supposed to be stealthy."

"I'm bringing you coffee, don't be a dick."

I chuckled as I grabbed a pair of briefs from my armoire, my low-rise jeans, a T-shirt, a Henley, and a pair of socks. "She's the one who's supposed to be testifying against some cult leader there, isn't she?"

"Yeah," Ian answered, reaching the top of the stairs and walking over to me, a mug in each hand. Instantly he grimaced.

"What?" I asked as I took the one he offered me.

"You have bruises all over you," he remarked before taking a sip of coffee. "And between that and the cast on your wrist, you're a fuckin' mess, man."

I shrugged. "I knocked down a moose yesterday, you saw me."

"I guess," he said irritably, frowning, reaching out to touch my shoulder. "Gross, why're you slimy?"

"It's lotion, ya heathen. You have to take care of your skin, use moisturizer on your face, or you're gonna look like a saddle when you get old."

"Uh-huh," he said, obviously placating me. "Is your wrist better today? You sounded like it hurt last night."

"It did, but it's fine now. Go away while I get changed." The coffee was good, he'd used the Kona I kept in the freezer instead of the French roast I had in the pantry.

He pointed at the clothes in my hand. "You can't wear those jeans to a raid."

"What?" I asked, drinking down more hot coffee. He was good about adding the right amount of cream so I could still taste it but drink it fast.

"I've seen those jeans on, and they're way too tight. You can't run in them. This is not *Starsky and Hutch*."

I stared at him until he groaned, muttered under his breath, and went back downstairs. But he was right; all I needed to do was ruin a two hundred dollar pair of jeans sliding over asphalt. Returning to my closet, draining the mug as I did, I refolded them and picked something else to wear. Once I was changed, I brushed my teeth and then started putting product in my hair.

"Done yet, princess?" he demanded as he strolled into the bathroom.

I glared at him in the mirror. "Do you think I just roll out of bed and my hair looks this good? This is art."

"It looks like you woke up and ran your hand through it."

"I know, and that takes *time*. Each strand has to stand at a different angle or it doesn't work," I explained to my ignorant partner. "All the pieces have to be in the right place."

"Or what?"

"Or it's not sexy."

"You're plenty sexy," he yawned, snatching my empty cup off the counter before walking out. "Now, can we go before we're too old to do our job?"

It was as good as it was going to get. I flipped off the light and walked to my bed so I could sit down and put on my harness boots.

"Corduroys?" he said like he was in pain.

"You didn't notice in the bathroom?"

"I didn't look in the bathroom," he said dryly.

"Well, I'm sorry, but I don't own a pair of Wranglers like you do," I informed him. "Or Levi's for that matter."

"There's nothing hotter than button-fly, my friend."

He had a point.

"But really, your fuck-me jeans would not have gone over well."

I ignored him, and when I stood up, he winced.

"What now?"

"How much did those boots cost?"

I lifted my foot to check the bottom. "I dunno, three, four hundred."

"Please take them off. I know my black leather combat boots are in your closet somewhere; just wear those. I beg you."

"These are boots."

"No, they're not," he cajoled. "C'mon."

"I have a pair of Antonio Maurizi wingtip boots that I could—"

"I don't know what those are, but I can't imagine they're any better than what you've got on your feet right now. Just change 'em."

"I have the biker boots that—"

"No, *I* have your biker boots from that Saturday we went out to the farmers' market."

"Oh." Funny that I hadn't even missed them. "Do you have the Dolce&Gabbana distressed-leather biker boots or the—"

"I have no idea what I have. They're soft, that's all I know."

I had to think.

"Miro!"

"Yeah, okay," I muttered, sitting back down and pulling off the boots as he stalked over to my closet, rummaged around, and came back with his beat-up military-issue combat pair. They were worn but still in great shape, and most of all, stupid as it was, they were Ian's and so I loved wearing them. And they fit like a glove.

"God, I should move in," he grumbled, oblivious as I stopped breathing. The things that came out of that man's mouth would be the death of me. "Imagine how much faster this would go in the morning if you didn't have to think: should I wear the Antonio-whoever shoes instead of the—"

"Antonio Maurizi," I yelled as he took the stairs.

"Like I fuckin' care!"

I followed him down minutes later, and when I went to the hall closet and pulled out my chester coat, he stopped me.

"Grab your uniform parka and let's go."

"Yeah, but—"

He growled, so I grabbed what he wanted, made sure I had my badge, gun, ID, wallet, keys, and phone, and then went out ahead of him.

After he locked my front door, he shook his head like I was exhausting and charged down the front stoop.

"Why're you mad at me?"

"Do you have any idea how long it takes me to get ready in the morning?"

I grinned wide. "That's because you're naturally gorgeous. I have to work at it. Getting this level of pretty doesn't come easy."

"Get in the car!"

I was still chuckling when I got in and told him I needed more coffee.

"If you didn't take so long in the bathroom, you could chug down more caffeine."

"Yeah, well, again. I need time to look this good."

He pulled away from the curb like he was driving the getaway car in a bank heist, and instantly I had to grab hold of the dash.

"Jesus, Ian."

The wicked smile was not lost on me.

LUCY KENSINGTON looked like she belonged on the cover of a romance novel in which the heroine is one of the sweet plucky virginal ingénues who the hero falls head over heels for. In reality, she swore like a sailor and went after Ian with a knife, trying to dig out his heart as quickly as possible.

I was guessing she was normally handled more delicately, because she screamed in indignation when he disarmed her, put her facedown on the concrete, and cuffed her. She called him a lot of foul names I'd heard and a few I hadn't—a real achievement—until the shooting started. Once we were all under fire—Homeland Security, local police, and us pinned down in the courtyard of the halfway house—she shut up, curled into a ball behind Ian, and apologized to both of us over and over.

"I'm so sorry," she sobbed, her cheek against Ian's broad muscular back. "But I wouldn't have made it this far if I wasn't a total bitch."

"Well, we're here to take care of you," Ian said, trying to soothe her as the *rat-a-tat-tat* of AK-47 fire echoed in the small space.

If I lived to be a thousand, I would never understand the mentality of people firing at law enforcement when they entered their building. Yes, we were stuck now, but reinforcements would come to surround the building, and then there'd be nowhere for them to go, either. There was no way out. Even if they took hostages, it all eventually ended badly. There was no scenario in which they won. All they had to do was think logically, just for a moment.

"And Javier."

"I'm sorry?" I had been zoning for a moment, but her comment caught my interest.

"My boyfriend, Javier—Javi," she explained. "Abel Hardy's after him too. He's the guy we were running away from. He's why we left Texas."

"And where is Javier?" I asked, not really even wanting to know.

"He was in our room on the third floor."

Of course he was. We were in the courtyard on the first floor, outside the building. It only made sense that Javier was inside, all the way up on the third. Murphy's Law and all that.

"I already told the marshals in Lubbock," she began patiently. "That if Javi and me didn't get taken in together, that I wasn't gonna testify. That's why we ran away, because they wouldn't listen. But you will, right? You're different than the Texas marshals." I glanced over my shoulder at her. She was gazing at us with her big cornflower-blue eyes like we were angels straight from heaven.

"So you and Javier were together when—" I searched my memory. "—the drug bust went down."

"And we saw Mr. Hardy shoot all those people. Yeah."

"How many?"

"Five. There were three men and two women. They were those tourists that went missing. It was all over the news in Lubbock."

I nodded.

"You and Javier were there?" Ian wanted to make sure.

"Uh-huh," she replied innocently. "He told me to be quiet, but I was so scared—kinda like now, but at least y'all have guns. We didn't have nothin'. I was sure Mr. Hardy was gonna kill us too, but then the police came, and then the marshals."

"And you and Javier got separated?"

"Yessir, we did."

I could see how it happened, how it was reported that Lucy saw it all without mention of her boyfriend.

"So you'll get him, right?"

Fuck.

"Right?" she pressed.

"Javier what?"

"Valencia," she sighed. "Isn't that pretty?"

We both nodded before Ian turned to the Homeland Security agent who had been crouching down beside us the whole time.

"Who're you?" I got around to asking.

"Agent Gerald Spivey."

"Okay, Agent Spivey." Ian sighed. "Marshal Jones and I are going in after another witness, so we need you to secure this one. Do you understand?"

"Yessir."

"Great." Ian puffed out a breath before he turned to face me. "Don't get shot in the head."

"Ditto."

The troopers covered us as we ran for the building, and then Ian counted and I had his back as he kicked in the door and we went in. That was as far as we got. Apparently SWAT had come in through the back and they were there, already having breached the interior, fanned out along the corridor, all of them encased in body armor.

"Marshals," the SWAT commander greeted us tersely.

"Lieutenant," Ian returned. "Is this level secure?"

"Affirmative, all threats have been neutralized."

I didn't even want to know how many people were dead.

"We're going to the third floor now. Is there a witness here to secure?"

"Yessir." Ian nodded.

"Follow us up."

"Do you have snipers on site already?" I asked.

"Negative. We have no higher ground. As this is a residential area, our purpose is containment. No one leaves the grounds that could be considered a threat to private citizens."

Translation: anyone running from the halfway house who was armed would be shot dead. He had twenty men with him, and even though I could tell Ian wanted to be in the middle of the team, I grabbed hold of his forearm and held him still as they filed by.

"What are you doing?"

"They go first, then us."

"You think I don't know that?"

"Then stop tensing up like you're getting ready to run. Just wait." I finished talking and let him go.

"I'm waiting," he retorted, clearly annoyed.

I moved in behind him, my mouth to his ear. "Don't disappear; stay where I can see you."

He leaned just enough so he could feel me there, at his back. "I always do."

"You *never* do."

"Okay."

The rear guard ran by, and Ian bolted after him with me following close.

When marshals searched, we yelled, we announced ourselves, we barked out orders like "freeze," "get on your knees," and "put your hands where we can see them." A SWAT team just moved. With us, if you fired, you still had a chance. We would call out what we were, "Federal marshals, put down your weapons!" With SWAT, if you were stupid enough to fire on them, they fired back and that was it. I was pleased that there was no gunfire in the stairwell as we made our ascent, none on the second floor we searched to make sure the witness hadn't run, and none when the SWAT team began pounding up more steps to the third.

Ian and I trailed behind, sending down a lot of other scared civilians after radioing ahead that we were sending them out of the halfway house. They'd need protection too.

By the time we made it to the third floor, SWAT had already swept it, hyperefficient, leaving two men to guard the stairwell as the rest of them breached the door to the roof. Half of them were outside already, and I could hear gunfire being exchanged. More kids huddled in the hall and peeked out of rooms.

"Javier Valencia!" Ian yelled.

From the second to last door on the right, a kid stepped out with his hands raised above his head. "Please don't shoot!"

"Federal marshal," I shouted. "I need to take you to Lucy."

"Lucy?" he asked hopefully, taking a step forward.

Another kid grabbed his arm to stop him, whispered something, and Javier froze. "How do I know you're a marshal?"

Turning slowly, I reached down and lifted my parka so he could see the badge on my belt. "I'm sorry the marshals in Texas didn't listen to you and your girlfriend."

He raced down the hall to us and didn't stop until I lifted a hand to slow his approach. I was surprised that he slowed but walked right up against my open palm.

"It's okay, kid," I said gently, putting my hand on his shoulder as he started to shake.

His face scrunched up like he was ready to cry, and I understood at that moment that both he and the girl he loved were younger than they looked. "Is she okay?"

"She's fine. Let's go see her."

"All of you," Ian yelled, making sure his voice carried. "Let's go."

Seeing Javier trust us was all the rest of them needed. They poured out of the rooms carrying purses, backpacks, and messenger bags. Ian went first, passed the two SWAT guys stationed at the top of the stairs, followed by the kids, thirty counting Javier, and I brought up the rear.

Even moving as fast as we were, the story came out, the kids explaining in staccato bursts of information. The gunmen were friends of the guy who ran the house. They were just supposed to be passing through, but that was a month ago. They were making homemade bombs, dealing drugs to fund the operation, and stockpiling weapons. No one knew what they wanted, but they had called themselves environmental extremists.

"But they sold drugs, man," one of the kids said. "That's not right. Right?"

He seemed honestly confused.

"No, it's not," I agreed, reminding them to stay together, remain in single-file formation, and to hurry up.

We made good time and were met at the bottom by a throng of uniforms. We waited along with everyone else for SWAT to subdue the gunmen on the roof. None of the common areas were safe until they did which meant that entering the courtyard or going out the front was off limits.

There was smoke on the roof and minutes later we were given the all clear.

Chicago PD corralled the kids and loaded them onto a prison transfer bus while Ian walked Javier back to Agent Spivey and Lucy.

She squealed when she saw him; he rushed forward, and there in the middle of everything, they were passionately reunited. I doubted either of them could breathe with how tight the lip-lock was.

Once Ian pulled them apart, Javier looked around and said absently, "I don't remember that guy." Ian and I both saw him at the same time, one of the kids we brought down from the third floor—and he was carrying a handgun.

Before I could yell a warning to the officer loading up the second bus full of kids, Ian holstered his gun, flew forward, and tackled the guy from the side, hitting him hard, making a hole in the middle of the line. Ian landed all over him, wrestling him to the ground as several uniformed police officers ran forward, weapons drawn, shouting out orders for Ian to freeze and put his hands on top of his head.

"Federal marshal!" I yelled, bolting toward my partner, terrified for a second that they were going to shoot Ian even as they started lowering their guns after seeing the back of his parka.

When I turned back to check on them, Lucy and Javier were smiling at me.

"You see," Lucy said brightly, "We're already helping."

I put them both in the car, started it up, and turned on the heat so they could snuggle in the backseat and stay warm while I got out again to wait for Ian.

Ian passed off the gunman and joined me at the car where I was leaning against the roof.

"What?" he sniffled, squinting at me.

"What's the procedure, Ian?"

"When?"

"You see a guy with a gun: what're you supposed to do?"

"Oh for crissakes."

"What," I repeated firmly, "are you supposed to fuckin' do?"

"You yell 'gun' and pull yours." He was exasperated and I could hear it in his voice.

"Uh-huh," I agreed. "And what did you do right there?"

"He was in line with the other kids, Miro," he defended himself. "You know what would have happened. He would have grabbed the kid in front of him, and then we would have had a hostage situation or worse. What if he put a gun to one kid's head and then got on the bus with the others?" His voice started rising the more agitated he got. "Then what?"

"Then what? I dunno. You're the psychic," I volleyed.

"Why're you being stupid?"

"So now I'm stupid, but you're the one who didn't follow protocol."

"Are you serious?"

"Yes, I'm serious. What's wrong with you?" I insisted, feeling my face get hot. "All he had to do was look up and see you running, and he could've shot you in the head."

"I have my vest on."

"Which does nothing for your *head*, you stupid prick!" I roared, banging my fist down hard on the roof. "What'd you say before we even went into the stupid building—"

"Listen—"

"No! Fuck you! What'd you say?"

"I said 'don't get shot in the head,'" he answered woodenly.

"That's right! Don't get shot in the head! And then what do you do? Huh? You fuckin' almost let it happen to you!"

My heart was pounding, I was shaking, and my whole body was freezing even as my face was on fire. I couldn't stop imagining the guy turning and firing and Ian going down. It was on a continuous loop in my brain.

"Miro."

I needed distance, and now. I spun around, charged over to the side of the building, and bent over, hands on my knees, trying to breathe, to not hyperventilate.

He was there in seconds, hand on the back of my neck, squeezing gently. "Sorry. I'm really sorry. Forgive me, I didn't even think."

I had to concentrate on getting the air in and out of my lungs.

His fingers slid up my nape into my hair, and the slow stroking calmed me as he bent over beside me. "Next time we'll both run, and I'll have you close enough to cover me. 'Cause I don't want some perp to grab anybody, but the tackle would have been all right if you were close enough to shoot him if he drew on me."

I nodded.

"So, yeah, that was bad, and if you could leave that out of your report so Kage doesn't chew my ass off, that'd be good."

I lifted slowly, finally finding the silver lining in my day.

"Aww, come on," he pleaded as I grinned at him before heading back to the car. "You really gonna do me like that?"

I was silent as I got in the car, although, no, I would never hang my partner out to dry. But there was a difference between the truth and what I would let him *think* I would do.

When he joined me, sliding into the driver's seat, he leaned his forehead on the steering wheel and groaned.

"Can we please leave now, Marshal Doyle?" I asked.

"I said I was sorry."

"Yes. Yes, you did."

He started the car; I leaned back and got comfortable, putting on my seatbelt and closing my eyes.

"I'll buy you breakfast."

"Not hungry," I sighed deeply.

"I'm hungry," Lucy said from the backseat.

"I can eat," Javier seconded.

"Fuck," Ian said miserably.

Served him right. "I hate to be scared," I muttered.

"Yeah, I know that, don't I."

Yes, he did.

"Are we gonna eat?" Lucy continued.

"Are you guys buying?" Javier wanted to know.

"He is," I said, offering Ian and his wallet up on a silver platter.

I OFTEN thought that the reason some members of law enforcement went rogue was because of the enormous amount of paperwork they had to do, to be legit. It was exhausting. But even though it was more work, I typed up a full report on what Ian did in the moments after we secured our witnesses, saved it, sent it to him—and then redid it before I submitted it to Kage. It was fun to watch Ian go pale as he read through it.

"Oh fuck me," he whined.

What was even more perfect was when, moments later, Kage threw his door open and he called Ian and me in to give us the news about what the dispensation was on our two runaways. Ian slunk in behind me, stood in front of our boss's desk with me, and listened as he explained that Lucy and Javier would be transferred to Oregon since Chicago was no longer safe for them. Marshals from the Portland field office would be there by the end of the day to take the two into custody.

When he was done and excused us, Ian stayed where he was.

"Something else?" he asked Ian sharply.

I covered for him. "We just wanted to make sure that the two of them are going in together. We wanted to let Lucy and Javier know for certain."

Instant glower from my boss. "You brought them in as a unit, Jones, so that decision was already made in the field. They'll absolutely be entering the program together."

"Thank you, sir," I said cheerfully, turning to leave.

"You're dismissed, too, Doyle."

I made sure I moved fast since now Ian knew I'd fudged the report, and was halfway across the room when I pivoted back and saw Ian close the door behind him.

Jaw clenched, he started after me.

I darted out into the hall and hit the elevator button, debating on whether to pop back to holding to talk to Lucy and Javier. I had already promised them they were going into witness protection together, and they had believed me, but one more reassurance couldn't hurt. I had explained that, just as my boss said, intake was based on field decisions.

"You fuck!"

The elevator dinged at the same time and I ducked inside with fifteen or so other people, turning to smile at him as he charged forward. The doors closed right before he reached me.

I'm sure everyone heard the yell as the car started its descent.

"I don't know what's with that guy." I shrugged and got many smiles and some laughter from the back.

Downstairs, I got off; our office was up on the twenty-fourth floor, so it was never a fast ride up or down. Out on Dearborn Street, I glanced around at the concrete, steel, and glass buildings and decided that since it was so close to lunch, I'd walk over to the food trucks and get a sandwich from the Vietnamese one I loved. Crossing the street, I headed down, realizing I'd been in such a rush to get away from Ian that I forgot my parka and I was shivering.

I debated going back, but it made more sense to grab lunch first even though I'd be suffering from hypothermia by the time I got there.

"You're such an asshole!"

I had enough time to glance over my shoulder before I was grabbed from behind.

"Get off me!" I laughed, the protest covering the gasp of pleasure of having Ian's arm thrown over my shoulder as he yanked me back into him. He was so warm, the heat from his body pressing against mine, wedged tight, the feel of his chest and abdomen indescribably good, as well as his breath in my ear as he whispered the threat against my life.

"I'm not afraid of you," I said, drinking in every brush of contact.

"Why would you do that?" he persisted, still pulling on me, tightening his hold, barely letting me walk.

"To teach you not to scare me," I said softly, slipping my hands under his open parka, sliding them up his sides.

"Yeah? You feel like you taught me a lesson?" he teased, bumping into me as we moved awkwardly, our hips and chests grazing, each of us stepping into the other's space, trying not to falter, trip or be tripped as we shuffled.

I ducked my head to try and spin and pull away, but he countered, and I ended up with him plastered to my back, his left arm around my neck, his right hand on my abdomen.

"Miro?"

I shuddered. I couldn't have stopped the sensation from rolling through me if I tried. It was too much; I was overstimulated from just that much contact.

"Ya cold?"

Oh dear God yes, go with that. "Yeah, I'm fuckin' freezing."

Instantly he let go and started pulling off his parka.

"Oh no, then you'll be freezing," I hedged, walking backward a few steps before whirling around and jogging down the street. "Let's just go fast!"

He caught me easily, hand closing on my bicep, tugging me to a stop. "I have a sweater on, all you have is that knit thing. Just take the jacket."

"It's a Henley," I informed him as he shoved the coat he had already taken off at me.

"Whatever." He snickered, shaking his head as he looked at me. "Just put it on. We'll get food and go back and finish the mountain of paperwork."

The jacket was warm, and best of all, it smelled like Ian. When I shoved my hand in the right pocket, I found a pair of gloves I'd been missing since November. "Hello?"

"What?" he asked as we walked.

"These are mine."

"You gave those to me."

"I did not."

"Well, give 'em here, 'cause I'm freezing."

"Oh for crissakes," I said, unzipping the parka.

His grin was pure concentrated evil as he stopped me.

"Nice."

"I hope we're only walking as far as the food trucks, though."

"We are."

"Okay, good, because seriously, it's like eight out here."

"It's more like twenty-five," I corrected him.

"And the wind off the lake?"

Maybe he was right.

Once we were back in our building, riding the elevator up, we got shoved all the way into the corner. I stood in front of him and was surprised when he took hold of my hip and leaned me back into him.

"I'm *freezing*."

"Sorry," I sighed, the feel of his groin pressed to my ass making me light-headed.

"It's okay," he mumbled against the back of my neck before I felt his forehead there. "I'm warming up a little."

Fucking Ian. I was going to get a hard-on in the elevator because he was too damn close to me. I really needed to go out and find someone to sleep with. Maybe I would go back to the gym after work and find that guy I'd blown off the night before and—

"Are you listening?"

"What?" I fixated on his right hand up under the parka on my hip, the feel of his stubbled chin brushing my ear, and his breath on my cheek. Everything else was lost.

"I said, remember we gotta get out on time today."

"Why?"

"Because we gotta go over to Emma's."

"What are you talking about?" I asked, looking over my shoulder at him.

"Her brother's birthday party?" He tried to jog my memory.

"No," I said simply.

"You can't say no," he told me. "It's my girlfriend's brother."

"Which is exactly why I don't have to go," I said. "She's *your* girlfriend."

"And you're my partner and my buddy. It's in the friend thing."

"Contract?"

"Yeah."

"No, it's not."

"I think you didn't read the fine print."

"I think you're delusional if you think I'm spending an entire evening with—"

"If I gotta go, so do you," he insisted, like it was all decided.

"Not true, actually."

But he smirked at me, all cocky with the crinkling laugh lines and the curling lip and when his head went down on my shoulder, I gave up.

"We're supposed to be there around seven."

I was never getting laid.

CHAPTER 5

THE DOOR was open when I reached Emma Finch's loft in the Gold Coast District early that evening, and that was lucky because over the music and talking, no one would have let me in. Moving through the crowd in the huge space with its wide open floor plan, I found the hostess in the kitchen.

"Miro!" she announced happily, taking the bottle of pinot noir and bag of Kona coffee from me before hugging me tight.

"Why do you sound relieved?" I chuckled.

"Is the coffee for me?" She sounded hopeful.

"Yes, ma'am."

"See," she said to the women clustered around her. "He's a keeper."

"And pretty too." One of the women leaned on the counter to meet my gaze. "What kind of name is Miro, because I'm thinking Greek, but you have very eastern European features."

"What does that even mean?" Emma asked her friend.

"He's got those great Slavic cheekbones and the long nose."

I laughed. "I'm Czech, actually. Miro is short for Miroslav."

Emma's eyebrows lifted. "Miroslav? Really?"

My grunt made her smile.

"But Jones?"

"Longish story," I informed her, glancing around for my partner.

"Well, I'm so glad you're here." She sighed, drawing my attention back before she handed me two bottles of Newcastle. "Go find him, please. The last I heard, he was playing *Call of Duty* and killing everyone, and then Dennis came over like ten minutes ago and said that he changed the game because his girlfriend wanted to play *Grand Theft Auto* or something."

"That's all right up his alley," I said, taking a sip of beer. "You know that."

"He needs to learn to not be so competitive."

"Yeah, okay." I snickered. "You get right on that."

She turned me around and shoved me forward. "Go play."

A few people were dancing, more standing around, but I didn't know anyone so I moved toward the back of the loft where I knew the game system was. I'd been in Emma's place a few times, not often, but enough to know the layout. On the fifty-five-inch plasma screen, two cars were racing. The expressions on the faces of the people sitting around on the area rug-covered concrete, couches, and loveseats were not amused. No one was having a good time. Ian had one wireless controller and Emma's blond-haired, blue-eyed frat-boy-handsome brother, Dennis, had the other. You could feel the tension in the room; the big dick contest was on.

I moved into the space, nodding at a few who smiled at me before reaching Ian and standing beside his chair. "What you don't know," I told Dennis, "is that he drives like this in real life all the fuckin' time."

"Finally," Ian muttered, sounding annoyed, letting his head fall back so he could look up at me. "Where ya been?"

"Had to get pretty," I teased, grinning.

He surveyed me.

"What?"

"You look the same."

"It's the clothes, idiot."

"I guess."

I would not have the fashion conversation with him again. He had two distinctions in his own wardrobe: clean or dirty.

"Miro." Dennis breathed out my name before he paused the game and got to his feet to shake my hand. "You made it."

"Hey, man, happy birthday. Your sister stole your gift," I said, ratting her out, passing Ian his beer as he rose beside me. "So hit her up for the wine."

"That's okay," he said, squeezing my hand tighter. "I just hoped you'd show up."

"I know why." I cackled, reaching behind me and giving Ian a quick smack on the abdomen. "You want me to leash my dog."

"No, I—"

"Fuck you, M," Ian said even as he shoved me sideways and tossed the controller to one of the guys sitting on the couch.

"Oh, you're done?" Dennis asked him innocently, as if that wasn't what he wanted all along.

"Yeah, man," Ian said, his voice dropping low into the raspy growl that happened sometimes. "*So* done."

I smiled at Dennis as Ian took hold of my bicep and tugged me after him.

"How come you changed outta my boots?"

"Not stylish enough for this outfit," I patronized.

"Got it."

I snorted out a laugh. "You have no idea why I changed at all, do you."

"No."

I shook my head. "I really gotta take you shopping. You have a woman to impress now."

"I don't think clothes are gonna fix it."

"Fix what?"

"Nothing," he said, draping an arm over my shoulder. "Come on."

We returned to the kitchen, where Emma was still holding court.

"You give someone else a turn, sweetie?"

"Course," he answered sharply, squinting at her.

I grabbed his sweater and pulled until he stood next to me, shoulder to shoulder. "Be nice."

"I'm always nice," he grumbled under his breath.

"It's an alcohol-to-blood imbalance," I instructed Emma as she smiled at me. "When there is more beer in him than blood, you'll notice an improvement in tone and mood."

As she chuckled, a guy I didn't know moved up beside me.

"Hey, Em," he greeted softly.

"Oh, Phil, you made it," she said quickly, her voice catching.

"Of course," he replied, his attention quickly landing on Ian and then shifting back to her.

Something was up, but when I turned my head to check if my partner noticed, I found his focus elsewhere. He was far more interested in the man who had just come in the front door.

"What?" I asked, leaning in close to him.

He dipped his head, his face in my hair as he murmured in my ear. "Is that guy dealing over there?"

Leaning back, I found the man in question, passing out tiny baggies of goodies for Dennis's guests. "Are you fucking kidding me?"

"Oh Miro," Emma said suddenly, sounding edgy, nervous. "I meant to ask when you came in—how is your wrist feeling?"

"Roland!" One of the women standing beside Emma squealed and then slipped around the hostess to bolt over to the man.

"He's fine," Ian answered for me absently, his eyes never leaving the stranger who had passed Emma's friend what looked like something wrapped in foil. "That's acid or Molly, fuck him."

"You strapped?"

"Course."

We both turned around to lean on the counter, and I surveyed the room, taking note of the front door.

"Ian." Emma whimpered behind me. "Please. This is Dennis's party. I'm the one who insisted on inviting you."

"Really," he said, lifting his foot and rucking up his jeans so he could reach down into the biker boot he was wearing. "So your brother didn't even want me here."

"No, Dennis just—it was fine as soon as I told him Miro was coming."

He chuckled as he raised what I called his SIG Sauer P228 semiautomatic and he said was an M11, to shoulder level. Whatever name it went by, wielded by Ian Doyle, it was deadly accurate. Reaching into my back pocket where the badge normally clipped to my belt was, I pulled my ID and lifted it high. What was interesting was that it was me, and not my partner with the gun, that the man saw.

"Sir," I directed. "I need you to lace your fingers over your head."

He finally saw Ian and took a step back.

"And get on your knees!"

He glanced from Ian to me.

"Now," I commanded even as I saw him decide.

Turning, he bolted.

"Fuck," I swore, realizing that because I wasn't carrying—it was a party, for crissakes—I had to do the running and tackling. I couldn't be proper backup; Ian had to be mine.

The front door was crowded with party guests coming in, which accounted for him running toward the balcony. Maybe. The choice really didn't make a lot of sense. But when he darted, I shoved my ID at Ian and then was right there on Roland's heels. People started yelling, screaming, and I saw the blond man cross his wrists over his face before he went straight through the glass patio door.

I didn't even think to slow down.

Following fast, I used him as a shield against the glass flying toward me, got my hand on the back of his overcoat, and hung on as he hit the railing and sailed over.

Flipping backward, I saw everything in a slow-motion arch: the dark night, the snow falling gently through it, the lights of other buildings and street lamps, and finally, thankfully, the fire escape.

When we went over the side, we switched places so I was falling first, propelled through the icy air. Grabbing for anything with my one good hand attached to the working arm, I reached out and caught the ladder as Roland slammed into the railing and then tumbled over onto the platform, winded and gasping for breath.

The way I was hanging was bad: all my weight held only by my right hand, but that was why we practiced those damn dead lifts. Pulling myself up, I got a foot on the railing, pushed, twisted, let go of the ladder, and flung myself forward onto a slow-rising Roland. There was no air left in his body after I crashed on top of him, driving him facedown under me. It was loud and bracing, everything shook and rattled, and if I didn't wake up the people in the apartment I faced as well as those directly below, I would have been surprised.

As if on cue, a light went on in the apartment and I had a shotgun pointed at my head through the glass.

"Federal marshal," I yelled, both hands held high, chest heaving.

The man lifted his head, which was a good sign because it meant he wasn't aiming anymore, not that he had to, as close as he was with the weapon in his possession. "Show me your badge."

"I can have my partner bring it up," I offered.

He squinted and then leaned close to the window and glanced down at the man unconscious under my knees. "That's Roland Morris."

"I just arrested him for drug possession," I explained.

The man studied my face as I began shivering with cold and my quickly ebbing adrenaline.

"You have a broken wrist."

And I did, but it was a strange time to notice. "Yes."

"You carrying?"

"No sir."

He scrutinized me a second before leaving suddenly.

When my phone rang a second later, I answered. "Hey," I said before I coughed. "Everything all right up there?"

"The fuck should I know, I'm in the elevator!"

"Why're you mad?"

"Why am I mad?" he yelled. "You jumped off a fucking building!"

"Ian—"

"What the fuck?!"

"C'mon, what's the big deal? You jumped off a balcony the other day."

"That was different and you were right behind me!" He was indignant and really loud.

"Technically—"

"Shut up! Shut the fuck up!"

He was furious, and I was starting to worry. Normally I could tease him out of any mood. "Ian, it's—"

"Jesus Christ, Miro!"

"Listen, if I'd had my gun, I would have let you do the jumping."

"I wouldn't have done it!" he barked.

"The hell you say," I retorted. "You would have done it in a heartbeat."

"Fuck you, Miro. I'm not that reckless!"

I scoffed. "I'm sorry, have we met?"

The line went dead as a window opening caught my attention. Shotgun man was back, but this time he had the gun under his arm and he was holding out a blanket for me. He then flipped open a badge and I saw a Chicago PD shield.

I took the chenille throw and wrapped it around me in relief. "Miro Jones, US Marshal."

"Henry Bridger, narcotics."

"Oh," I sighed, chuckling. "Can I interest you in a drug dealer, Detective, and all the paperwork that goes with it?"

"Yes," he said, grinning at me. "You most certainly can."

"I'll go to the precinct with you."

"Lemme get changed."

"Okay."

"Does your partner have your coat, too, or you wanna borrow one of mine?"

"He'll bring it down with him."

"Where the hell were you?"

I pointed up.

"I thought marshals only put people into protective custody or chased down fugitives."

"Oh, no, Detective, we're full service."

"I'd have you come in, but—"

"He could wake up, I know," I agreed, taking the Glock he passed me. "I carry a 20 loaded with 40 caliber, but this 34 is sweet."

"The GTL 22 attachment is nice, right?"

I nodded, lifting it, testing the weight. "I should get a light for mine too."

"You have to get a special holster, though."

"True," I said, a little unsteady as I stood up. "If my partner wants in…."

"I'll buzz him up."

"Thanks. What's the number?"

"I'm in 801."

Eighth-floor apartment. God, I really didn't need my boss to get even a whiff of this. I could only imagine the comments from the others, from White and Sharpe—Sanchez's replacement—Dorsey or Kowalski—all of them lived to give me crap. But worst of all would be the explanation: *why, yessir, I did jump off a balcony*. The idea was about as appealing as a tooth extraction.

"Jones!"

The yell came from the alley below.

Leaning over, I looked down at Deputy US Marshal Ian Doyle and waved.

"You fuck!"

I shushed him.

His shoulders fell and his head tipped as he glared up at me.

"801," I called. "Come help me."

He ran, tearing down the alley, and disappeared around the side of the building. I took a seat on the bench beside me and then checked on Morris to make sure he was still breathing. Minutes later, still shivering in the night air, I heard the one-man wrecking crew at the window.

"Hey," I greeted my partner as he climbed out onto the fire escape.

"Ten fuckin' years off my life," he growled, squatting down in front of me, taking my face in his firm, callused hands.

"Not dead," I confirmed.

He checked me over roughly, huffing out a breath as he turned my head right and left, finally lifting it before sliding his hands over my throat, chest, down my sides, and across my abdomen. "Anything hurt?"

"Everything," I admitted, hoping my confession would hide the hiss of pleasure over being manhandled.

"Are you sure you're okay?" He was clearly scared and the emotion deepened his voice, his gaze concerned as it held mine. "You're all flushed."

I cleared my throat, easing free of his clutching hands. "Yeah, I'm good."

"What can I—"

"After we book this guy, can we eat?"

Ian's smile, the way his eyes warmed and his gaze lingered, sent my stomach into a familiar tumble. The look of blatant ownership never failed to send blood rushing straight to my cock. And the man had no clue.

I had thought when it was new, us as partners, I was reading too much into the way I would glance up and fall into his smile, catch him glancing my way, or feel the weight of his stare on my back. No other man who didn't want to fuck me had ever reacted that way, would look right back at me, unwavering, before softening—happy, it seemed, to simply be in my space. But he did. Ian did. And it was a constant source of both unease and pride.

IT TOOK a couple of hours, the paperwork. We sat at Bridger's desk and he typed into the computer as Ian wrote out what he saw and I recorded what I had witnessed. Other people at the party were still being questioned, and as Bridger made more notes, I turned so I could scrutinize my partner.

"What?"

"Do you have a plan to make up with Emma?"

The glare was another of my favorites, used when the glower or squint wasn't enough. "Make up with her why?"

"You busted her brother."

He glanced at Bridger, who nodded, before returning his attention to me. "I'm not the one who invited a drug dealer to my house."

"Yeah, but you could have given her, and the others, fair warning about what you were doing. You could have gotten them out before they got swarmed by policemen."

"Yeah," Bridger agreed. "Man, you better make with the groveling."

"I was doing my job," he defended himself.

I shook my head.

"Is he kidding?"

"Sadly, no," I told the detective.

Bridger whistled low and went back to typing.

"What else?" Ian prodded begrudgingly.

"I think I'm crippled," I complained, my body starting to cramp from sitting so long.

"That's what happens when you jump off buildings," a new voice growled.

Fuck.

I winced and lifted my head slowly, which did nothing to lessen the intimidating presence of the man I didn't want to face. At six four, covered in hard muscle and in possession of the coldest pair of steel-blue eyes I had ever seen, my boss, Sam Kage, was not the kind of man you messed with. And it wasn't just me who walked on eggshells around him. Ian was a badass Green Beret, an Army captain, but he didn't mess with our boss either. There was something about him: a fierceness, a tenacity, so that you knew he would get you, hurt you, make you pay. And while I had only witnessed that resolve applied to criminals, I didn't want to tempt fate.

"I didn't have a gun," I hastily explained. "We were at a party."

All the men in my life squinted at me like I was an idiot.

"So I went after the suspect to tackle him," I rambled on.

"Where were you?" he asked Ian.

"Securing the scene, sir."

Kage moved closer to me. "You do it again, Jones, and I will bust your ass to court duty until you die."

I coughed. "Yessir."

"Go to the hospital and get checked out."

"Yeah, but—"

"Before tomorrow or your ass is sitting home," he barked. "Until further notice."

Shit. "Yessir."

His attention moved back to Ian. "You keep letting him get hurt, and I'm going to start questioning your decision to be a marshal, Doyle. Maybe this job is too tame for you. Can't keep your head in the game without the threat of imminent death?"

"No sir," Ian said sharply.

"Sorry?"

"I said, no sir."

Kage grunted. "When I added to my original five-man team, with Ching, Becker, and then you, Kohn, and lastly Jones, I figured you'd all be with me a good, long time."

Ian kept silent.

"But if your plan is to not actually watch out for your partner, I can find someone who will."

The muscles in Ian's jaw clenched.

"We're a team, Doyle."

He cleared his throat. "Yessir."

Kage turned to Bridger. "Let me know what else you need from my office, Detective."

Bridger nodded, taking the card from Kage with a sharp inhale. It made sense; the man was really scary. His height, the powerful build, the icy stare: all of it gave you the impression that if you fucked up, you'd be gone. I certainly never wanted to be in a position to test him.

"What floor is homicide on now?"

"Fifth," Bridger answered quickly. "May I ask why, Marshal?"

"I need to speak to one of the detectives I'm supposed to be meeting here."

"Which one? I can call up for you; check if he's here this late."

"He is, because, again, we scheduled a meeting. And it's Duncan Stiel."

After a moment, Bridger chuckled. "Oh, you mean the billionaire's boyfriend?"

Big. Mistake. Ian *wished* he could scowl with such icy contempt. Bridger actually swallowed.

"No," Kage said flatly. "I mean the highly decorated homicide detective."

Bridger coughed.

"Fifth floor, you said."

"Yes."

"I can find him myself."

Bridger remained silent.

His gaze landed back on me. "Hospital."

As though I would disregard a direct order from the man. "Yessir."

Kage glanced at Ian and then turned and strode out of the room. People scuttled out of his way as he moved down the corridor we could see through the glass windows on the far side of the room.

"He's sort of intense," Bridger commented. "That's gotta be loads of fun."

"That's true," Ian agreed. "But lemme tell you, when you're stuck somewhere, there isn't anyone you'd rather have either coming for you himself or insisting someone else get off their ass and ride to your rescue."

"Yeah," I said, chuckling. "The term 'moving heaven and earth,' that was made for him."

"It was," Ian agreed. He glanced at Bridger. "Is he done? Because we have to make our second trip to the hospital in so many days."

"When'd you break that?" Bridger asked, tipping his head at the cast on my wrist.

"Two days ago."

"Holy shit. How?"

I repeated his motion but tipped mine at Ian.

"Oh."

"Fuck you, M. Let's go."

I started laughing and Bridger widened his eyes.

"So all you marshals are a little on the scary side."

"Hell yeah," I said as Ian hauled me to my feet.

"And you all gotta have the same haircut? Even your boss?"

Kage's cut was basically military, above the collar in the back and around the ears. Ian's was shorter since he still served in the Army Reserve. My hair was longer and thicker and I put product in it to make it messy and stand up. But we had a dress code that our immaculately put-together boss vigilantly enforced.

"We have to all look alike so the bad guys can't tell us apart."

"Uh-huh," Bridger said, nodding like I was nuts.

In the elevator, I found I was a little light-headed.

"Hold on to me."

Putting a hand on Ian's shoulder, I followed him out of the police station.

"Don't jump out of any more open windows," he ordered when I stumbled.

"Tired of getting in trouble with the boss?" I baited him.

"Keep pushing it. I think that'd be a wise decision."

I was being an ass. "I'm sorry. I promise."

"C'mere," he huffed, putting an arm around my waist as he walked me to the car.

AT THE hospital, I realized it was after nine and I was not a little hungry, but a lot. There was a 24/7 diner across the street, and after a few minutes of prodding, begging, and whining, Ian begrudgingly got up and left to get us both some food.

The nurse who saw me while he was gone, Arlene, was nice. She checked to make sure my pupils weren't dilated, moved on to my reflexes, and was concerned about the cuts and contusions. I explained that those were old.

"Old?"

"From earlier."

Arlene was confused until I explained that I'd just been there two days ago. Once she had my chart, she checked the cast on my left wrist as I explained how I was actually Spider-Man.

"You know, most people who break bones take it easy for a few days afterwards, Marshal."

"Yeah, I know."

"Are you sure?"

"You think I have a concussion?"

"Among other things."

"Why ya say it like that?"

"Because there's obviously something deeply wrong with you," Arlene snapped.

"It's his brain," Ian said as he walked in with a tray of shakes, burgers, onion rings, shoe-string fries, and bottled water.

"The diner let you take that out?"

"The food?" He was confused.

"The tray, idiot."

"Like anyone's gonna say shit to me."

Arlene promptly scolded him. "You can't have that in here."

He pushed back his jacket so she could see the badge on his belt.

"That doesn't mean anything to me," Arlene said flatly.

"I'll give you my shake if you drop it."

The shakes were huge, so it worked out fine. He and I drank the chocolate and she had the strawberry.

She drew blood, listened to my heart, and took my blood pressure, and when I was wheeled back from Radiology after being X-rayed, Ian was lying on my bed, watching a basketball game and finishing up the fries.

"We should go get dessert after this," he said before belching.

"Did you call Emma?" I asked, waving him off the bed so I could get in.

"Didn't have to," he said, holding out his iPhone to me, not taking his eyes off the game.

Putting it on speaker, Arlene and I listened to Emma Finch break up with my partner. She was hurt, angry, and even though it turned out that neither she nor her brother were going to jail, there would probably be a ridiculous amount of community service performed.

"That's how she breaks up with him?"

I made a face. "I can probably fix it up," I apprised Arlene.

"Don't do that," Ian said, and both the nurse and I turned to him. "It's fine."

"You're grieving inside," Arlene offered.

"And you're in shock," I added.

"Nope," he grunted. "But I could use a beer."

I turned to Arlene.

"You shouldn't have any beer," she said, voice firm.

"Gotta take a piss," Ian announced before he got up and left the room.

"He's super," Arlene said sarcastically.

I was still laughing when the doctor finally showed up fifteen minutes later. After three long hours, I was discharged after midnight with a bill for tests and procedures that would have made me gasp if I didn't work for the federal government. The staggering amount was completely covered since it had been incurred during the performance of my duties.

"Remind me never to get hurt when I'm not at work."

Ian wasn't listening; the only part he cared about was that I was cleared to return to work the following day. I ended up being none the worse for wear for having sailed through the air without a trapeze or a net.

"I can have a beer." I chuckled.

He threw an arm around my neck and tugged me close. "You scared the fuck out of me."

"I know."

"Don't."

"Okay."

"You're the solid part of this."

Of *us*, he meant—I was the solid part of us. And I knew that too.

"You gotta be you, and I'll be me."

"Agreed," I said, smiling as we got on the elevator.

"And so we're clear," he husked, turning to meet my gaze. "She's fucking Phil."

I squinted at him, because I'd obviously missed something. "What?"

"Emma," he said with a slight smile. "She's been fucking that guy Phil who was there tonight. This is just a nice excuse to kick me to the curb."

"No."

He nodded.

"I don't believe you."

"Why would I lie? It puts me in a bad light since obviously I wasn't enough for her."

"Wait," I grumbled, tugging on his shoulder, getting him to turn to face me. "How do you know this?"

He shrugged. "I know."

"That's bullshit. You don't know."

He passed me his phone. I took it as we got out of the elevator and headed toward the front door. On his camera roll were several pictures of Emma at dinner with the man I remembered seeing at the party, however briefly. They leaned close, held hands, and left the restaurant Bravo together. The next grouping was in a cab, then outside his Greystone, and finally through a window, catching them clinging together. No intuitive leaps needed.

"We never said it was exclusive," he informed me as we reached the street and he rounded on me. "She's *technically* not cheating on me, but I don't want to sleep with someone who's sleeping with someone else."

"Of course not."

He shrugged. "It is what it is."

"But she could just be honest."

He took a deep breath. "I'm okay."

"Who took these?"

"I did."

"You stalked your own girlfriend?" I asked, taking hold of him.

"I was gathering intel," he defended, stepping in closer so my arm went from being stretched out to folded against me, my hand flat on his torso.

"To show who?" I managed to get out, minutely aware of the rippling abs under the soft cotton, fighting to not curl my fingers into the material.

"You," he said, smirking, crowding into me as people leaving the building pushed by us.

Before I thought about what I was doing, I slid my hand up over the solid muscled chest, the shot of Demerol making me braver than normal. "Let's go get a drink."

"No," he yawned, leaning down and pressing his forehead into my shoulder for a second before lifting free. "Let's go get some pie."

Pie sounded better. "Okay."

"We'll get it to go and eat it on your couch."

"You really like my couch," I sighed, because I loved that he liked being at my place.

"I do," he admitted. "It's a good couch. I've never had a nightmare on it."

That was a very good thing.

CHAPTER 6

WE STOPPED on the way back to my place, picking up pumpkin pie for me and chocolate cream for him and then clothes for him for the morning. He fell asleep halfway through *Die Hard*, and I covered him up. When the movie was over, I got up to rinse dishes, and he was completely stretched out when I got back, throw pillow under his head, dead to the world. Amazing how vulnerable he looked when he was sleeping. I wondered how Emma could bear to be parted from him.

I took his phone with me when I went upstairs. It was a small townhouse with a loft above the main floor at the top of the stairs where my bed stood along with a nightstand and a vintage industrial lamp. I'd found that lamp in an abandoned building when I was fifteen and kept it with me ever since. Even moving between foster homes, I managed not to lose it, certain that someday both it and I would have a home.

On the other side of the stairs was my bathroom and my closet, and that was it. Everything else was on the first floor. What was nice was that I could lie on the end of my bed and look down into my living room. At 750 square feet, the Greystone was tiny, but I didn't need a lot of space. It was mine—I owned it—from the reclaimed barn-wood flooring in the living room to the Philco fridge and polished concrete in the kitchen to the Kohler waterfall showerhead in my bathroom. I had made it my sanctuary. All the accents were mine, black and white photographs of friends and places I'd been, colorful framed artwork hanging on every available wall, and the distressed wood ladder in one corner that I put plants and more picture frames on. I had open shelving in the kitchen to display Fiestaware and Pyrex my friends collected in college that I originally got stuck with but now loved. It was compact, like living in a bungalow, and I liked the feel. I had opted for a picnic table instead of a traditional one, so I never had to worry about chairs and was always surprised how many people loved the idea of sitting on a bench to share a meal. It was a warm place and completely low maintenance at the same time. Compared to the spartan dark-floored gray-walled white-trimmed converted warehouse space Ian lived in, mine was cozy. He always said so.

Stretching out on my bed, I pulled up the pictures of Emma and Phil on Ian's phone and started deleting them one by one. When his phone rang and I saw her number, I answered.

"Hi," I greeted solemnly.

"Miro?"

"Yeah."

"Are you okay? I've been calling all night and Ian hasn't picked up."

"I'm fine."

"I… okay, well, is Ian with you, because—"

"He's passed out. He had a rough night."

"Don't you have that backwards? You're the one who went off my balcony."

"He knows you're sleeping with Phil, Emma."

"I'm sorry, what?"

"I'm deleting the evidence off his phone right now. It's not healthy for him."

A long pause. "I never noticed him," she finally said.

"Well, he's trained to go undetected, so that makes sense."

"I guess."

I coughed softly. "Was there something else you wanted to say to him?"

"Yes. No." She sighed. "I don't know. I shouldn't have left the voice mail."

"He played it for me."

"Of course he did. I would have known you were lying if you said he didn't."

"Sorry?"

"Please, Miro, he tells you everything. You're the other half of him."

"I wouldn't go that—"

"And really, since we're being honest, I could barely stand him when you weren't around."

"What are you talking about?"

"What am I—are you serious?" She laughed harshly. "He speaks when you're there, Miro. He laughs, he interacts."

"I—"

"And when you're not, he's closed up. Winnie and Val had no idea he could laugh or smile until that time you met us out at the bowling alley."

"And so what, you decided to keep him but have Phil on the side?" I asked, trying not to sound accusatory.

"It was never exclusive between Ian and me."

If I was ever lucky enough to have Ian Doyle in my bed, I would make damn sure he knew he was the only one welcome and wanted there. He would never get away once I had him.

"And he's a shitty lover, Miro. You should warn any girl who goes near him," she said angrily, her voice dripping with disdain. "He's completely selfish."

I ignored her. "Is there anything of his at your place or vice versa?"

"You should have advised me that his job is his number one priority, that he would leave in the middle of the night without so much as a phone call to go off on some mission, and be gone for a month."

"I asked you a question."

"And then show back up and expect to get laid."

It sounded liked Ian. "Emma?"

"No! I have nothing of his at my house, and he always scoured his apartment when I left to make sure I didn't forget anything." She was furious, and I could hear the wounded tremble in her voice. "There's nothing that's not *his* in his place. He would never allow that."

But that wasn't true.

I'd lost count of the number of my T-shirts he'd taken. My University of Chicago hoodie had been appropriated, as had my red cashmere scarf and, apparently, the boots I'd forgotten about. But I'd never given it a second thought. We swapped things; it's what partners did. I had a sweatshirt of his from West Point and his Burberry wool cashmere peacoat I had borrowed eight months ago and never returned.

I also had a military field jacket that he'd left at my house the last time he got home in the early morning hours. I remembered the knock on the door at 1:00 a.m., excusing myself from the guy all over me on the couch—Wayne something—and opening my door to find my bruised and beaten partner standing unsteadily before me.

"Oh shit," I gasped, not sure where I could touch and not hurt him.

"I have a concussion," he announced. "You gotta take care of me."

I held out my arms for him. "Of course."

He staggered forward and gave me his weight, head down on my shoulder, arms wrapping me up tight.

"That's an Airborne insignia," the guy I would no longer be fucking choked out. "Holy shit, man."

All I knew was that my partner was Special Forces. I never delved, it wasn't my place. "You can go," I said quickly, more content to have the man I wanted leaning on me, almost asleep on his feet, his breath puffing over the side of my neck, than I wanted to have sex with a guy I'd known for a couple of hours.

"Whatever, man, fuck you."

The slam of the door jolted Ian, and he clutched at me.

"It's okay. Let's get you upstairs. You can have my bed."

"No," he moaned, "the couch. I dreamed about the couch."

It was an overstuffed two-piece microfiber sectional sofa. There was nothing remotely interesting about it, but he started stripping as he walked—hat, jacket, belt—and then flopped down on it, toed off his untied heavy combat boots, and shucked his pants, followed quickly by his socks. He shoved one of the many pillows littering the couch under his head, sighed deeply, and stopped moving. After a few moments of admiring the long, muscular body stretched out before me, I covered him with a chunky cable-knit throw.

I picked up after him, put all his clothes in the washer, and sat down to read. After twenty minutes or so, he woke up, moved over, put the pillow in my lap, and lay back down.

"Supposed to watch me," he mumbled before he fell asleep again.

And I wondered at that moment why he was at my house instead of with Emma, but it didn't bother me enough to question him, not enough to call her and have her come over and collect him. I wanted him right where he was, solid and in one piece.

"*Miro?*"

"Sorry," I said quickly, embarrassed that my mind had been wandering, her voice bringing me back to the present. "And I'm sorry things ended like they did."

"It's fine, I'm already over it."

I hoped that was true. "Bye, Emma."

"Good-bye, Miro. You were actually my favorite part of knowing Ian Doyle."

It was sad, and I was still thinking that when I looked up and found him standing at the top of the stairs. "Speak of the devil."

He grunted. "What're you doing?"

"Deleting pictures off your phone," I informed him.

"You get 'em all?"

"I did, yeah."

"That's good." He yawned softly. "Healthy."

"Like you would know from healthy," I grumbled.

"Hey, I forgot to grab something to sleep in. I need pajamas or shorts or whatever."

"Check my closet," I directed, placing his phone on my nightstand. "Top drawer of the armoire. Take your pick."

He was shirtless, so I got a nice view of the washboard abs, muscular chest, and the obliques shown off by the worn jeans as he moved around the bed. I could also see a myriad of scars from knives, bullets, and—my favorite—a bull whip. A corrupt warlord in some little cesspool of the world had actually flogged him. I had been horrified when he explained the evidence left behind on his skin, but Ian being Ian just shrugged. I tried not to let my mind drift to the horrors visited on him when I hadn't been there keeping vigil. As far as I could tell, the people who were supposed to have his back hadn't been very good at protecting him or… the opposite was true and they were fantastic and whip scars were simply the tip of the iceberg of what *could* have happened. Not that he talked about it. I only knew about the incident with the whip because he'd confessed it to me late one evening when he was very drunk. I'd wanted to touch him then, and I wanted to touch him now. The desire to slide my hands over his hard muscular frame, to have those thick arms wrapped around me, and to lick every inch of his sleek olive skin was a constant craving. I was ready to taste him, have him, and keep him the second he gave the word.

"Gross, dude, there's thongs in here," he called out from the other side of the wall.

Shit.

He was rummaging around in my stuff and that was my mistake. Nothing killed heat like comments on your fucking underwear.

"Just grab something and get out," I yelled, sitting up, needing to change clothes myself.

"Don't be so fuckin' sensitive." He chuckled, keeping up the running dialogue. "I'm sure guys love it when you wear froufrou crap like this."

"I have a gun," I warned instead of screaming. I so needed a vacation far away from him.

"Is this leather?" He snickered evilly.

"Going for the firearm!"

He was back, walking toward me in sleep shorts that hugged his crotch as he walked, outlining the long cock I had seen many a time. He was not modest around me—gym, home, hotel rooms when we were on stakeouts—he didn't care. Getting naked in front of me was not an issue for him.

"Don't shoot," he teased as he brushed by my bed to reach the stairs, tousling my hair in the process. "I just wanna sleep."

"Take your phone," I grumbled, hating the playful touch, tossing his phone to him.

"Hey."

He was stopped on the stairs leading down, so all I could glimpse of him was from the chest up. "Thanks for not dying."

"Go to bed."

He snorted. "Going."

Moments later the lights went off on the first floor as I was on my way to the bathroom. Once I was ready for bed—teeth brushed, changed into pajama bottoms and T-shirt—I walked back to lie down. When I clicked off the lamp on my nightstand, the whole townhouse plunged into semidarkness. The moonlight streaming in from the skylight as well as through my window made everything various shades of deep, rich blue. It reminded me of my partner's eyes, which of course, didn't help me sleep at all. When I turned around on my bed and crawled to the bottom, I could see him sprawled out below me. It was nice that one of us was getting some rest.

CHAPTER 7

THE DOORBELL woke me earlier than my alarm was set for, so I got up, stumbled down the stairs, passed Ian as he headed for the loft, and crossed toward the source of the chimes, bleary, only half-awake, smelling the coffee and wondering how that was possible. I opened the front door before the why filtered through my brain.

"Hey."

Everything hurt, and having Brent Ivers on my front porch was not helping. My ex had left me six months ago for a job and a new life in Miami. At the best of times, the sex had been fun and we laughed often even though, at his request, it had never been exclusive. At the worst of times, at the end, showing up at his place and finding other men there when we were supposed to be having dinner or going to visit his family had been painful. When he left, it had never crossed his mind to ask me to go, to transfer, and it never occurred to me to say anything but good-bye. Chicago was the first place I'd ever felt safe, the only place where nothing bad had ever happened, and my work and my partner were there. I wasn't going anywhere.

"It's freezing out here, babe. Can I come in?" Brent asked, bringing my attention back to him.

I squinted. "What are you doing here?"

"I missed you."

"Bullshit," I said, calling him on his crap. "What's the deal?"

"Seriously," he whimpered, "lemme in."

Stepping aside since it didn't seem like he was leaving, I closed the door behind him as he whirled around to face me.

"Damn, you look good," he said huskily, crowding me.

I moved away, putting space between us.

"What's going on?" he snapped irritably. "Since when can't I touch you?"

"What the fuck are you doing here?" I countered.

"I'm in town on business, and I thought I'd stay with you while I was here."

"M!" Ian boomed from the railing beside my closet. "I need to borrow underwear!"

"You know where it is!" I yelled back. "You were in there last night!"

"What the fuck is he doing here?" Brent snarled, visibly startled by my partner's loud voice. "Did he sleep here?"

"What the hell is he doing here?" Ian thundered, his volume apparently set on air siren.

It was too much noise for before I even had coffee. I grunted and slipped around Brent, padding across the wood floor to my kitchen.

"Miro?" Brent shouted, following after me as I heard Ian pounding down the stairs. "What the hell is going on? What's Ian doing here needing underwear?"

It did look suspicious, but that shouldn't have mattered. Not to Brent. "The bigger question is why in the world you would think you could just show up here for no good reason," I said gruffly, pulling a mug from one of the hooks over my sink before going to make my coffee. It smelled heavenly.

"I thought we were good," he explained, stepping in close to me as I poured.

"You want some?"

"When have you ever known me to turn down your coffee?"

I passed him the steaming mug, advised him that the cream was where it always was, and went to get another mug as Ian strolled into the kitchen.

"Pour me some too," he ordered instead of asking, striding to stop beside me in unbuttoned dress pants that showed off a pair of my white briefs.

"There's no hazelnut creamer in here," Brent commented as he searched my fridge.

"That's because you're the only one who drank that shit," Ian said snidely. "All that's in there is half-and-half now, take it or leave it."

"Why are you here?"

"Why are you?" Ian volleyed.

"Miro?" Brent snapped, slamming the door of the antique refrigerator before facing me. "What the hell is going on?"

"Listen, I—"

But Ian slipped in front of me, cutting off my words as he advanced on Brent. "Did you move back?"

"No, I'm only—"

"So you thought what," he said, reaching Brent, his scowl dark as he drilled two fingers into Brent's collarbone.

"Owww," he complained, trying to peer around Ian. "Miro, make him—"

"You thought you could just come over here like nothing happened? Like you didn't fuckin' bail? Just stay here while you were in town, save on a hotel room, and get laid in the process?" Ian growled. "Is that what you fuckin' thought?"

"Back off," Brent warned.

"That's bullshit," Ian informed him, voice rising, body tensing for a fight. "So you need to get the fuck outta here before I put my foot up your ass."

"Miro!" Brent fumed, whipping around Ian and charging over to me. "What the hell?"

"Go already. It's not a good idea for you to be here."

"But my mother wants you to visit," Brent protested.

"That's low even for you, dickhead," Ian said, bumping me as he moved close, his body heat making me realize how cold the house was.

"I'll see you around, Brent," I lied, stepping around him to reach my fridge, needing the half-and-half, not liking the taste of black coffee the way Ian did. "You take care."

"God, Miro, I'm so sorry I hurt you. I had no idea you were this damaged."

"Get out," Ian ordered. "You saw him, you can use that later to rub one out, but that's all you're gonna get."

"I should kick the shit out of you," Brent snarled at my partner.

I scoffed as I poured, then opened up a drawer for a spoon. "Bye, Brent."

He was gone moments later, and Ian slammed the door behind him.

"What did I tell you about opening your door for strangers?"

I chuckled as he joined me in the kitchen and leaned against the counter as he began sipping his coffee. "You're right. I promise to be more vigilant."

"And don't fuck that guy, no matter what."

"Yeah, okay."

"No, look at me."

I gave him all my attention.

"I'm serious. He doesn't deserve your time."

"Thanks."

He held my gaze, and we were silent until he muttered something under his breath.

"What was that?"

"I said, you need to listen to me."

I was about to say something else when his phone buzzed from the coffee table in the living room.

He went to get it, answered on the fifth ring. As I watched his body language, he drew himself up into a rigid stance like he was waiting to hear something, like he was waiting for orders. And because I could connect the dots, I knew what was happening even before he put the phone down and strode back over to me.

He cleared his throat. "I won't be able to go with you on transport duty this morning. I have to leave."

"What do you mean, leave?"

"I mean like leave, leave."

"What?"

He stepped closer, laid his hand on the counter beside me.

"Tell me now."

After clearing his throat, he said, "I have to go."

"Go where?"

"I can't say."

"Can't or won't?" I pressed.

"Can't," he ground out.

I took a quick breath. "Okay, so you're off to God knows where to do God knows what."

"Yeah."

It was always a possibility.

Because Ian was in the Individual Ready Reserve while working as a US marshal, all the Army had to do was call him up and say "we need you for this mission, get your gear," and he was gone. Officers served at the pleasure of the president at all times, so the Army didn't have to bother with a contract to bring Ian back. Basically, they put in a call to the marshals and said "we're taking him, will send him back later," explained—if they could be bothered—what the mission duration was, plus thirty days for debriefing and out processing and leave time. What it all boiled down to was, when they called, he went.

"Will you be able to call me?"

"I'll try," he answered sincerely.

"It would be good, so I don't worry, yeah?"

The muscles in his jaw clenched.

"You think I'll get Becker while you're gone, or Kohn?"

"Maybe Kohn," he offered, and when I groaned, his smile came fast, the heavy laugh lines around his eyes crinkling. "Be nice to him."

"Maybe he won't shoot himself this time."

"It was a ricochet."

"Still… his bullet, his gun," I reminded him.

He lifted his brows like, yeah, maybe.

"So you gonna call Kage from the road or you want me to tell him?"

"I can ride in with you and talk to him."

"No. It'd be better if you just left, don't you think?"

It would be easier on both of us that way. Normally we would stand around not saying anything, him leaning on something—wall, desk, window—needing to go but not leaving, and I would cross my arms and drink him in, memorizing every detail, imprinting his face and body on my mind.

"Yeah, okay," he agreed roughly.

"Where are you flying out of?"

"Scott Air Force Base, it's close to Belleville."

"And how're you getting out there? That's like a five-hour drive."

"I have a flight out of O'Hare."

"Okay."

His eyes were locked on mine.

"Call me when you get wherever you're going and then when you're on your way home."

"I'll try."

"Remember, body armor is your friend."

"Absolutely."

"Okay," I mumbled. "You should leave me your set of keys for the car, too, in case it gets sold at auction while you're gone."

The service sold the cars and other items seized during drug raids, and those being used in the field were all available from a catalog.

"Here," he answered, retrieving them from his pocket and putting them on the counter. "Thanks for not offering to drive me to the airport."

That had been a disaster the last time, with me sitting in the car gripping the steering wheel and him fiddling with the contents of his backpack. "Sure. I have the spare set for your place, so I'll grab your mail and pick up Chickie."

"Thanks."

"Course. Your wolf is in safe hands with me."

"He's a husky."

"Crossed with a wolf and a malamute, yeah, I know." I teased him, thinking the whole time, *God, he's beautiful.*

Stepping into me, he hugged me tight, the guy clench, just for a moment. But when he went to pull away, I tightened my hold for a second, turning my head so I could inhale the scent of his skin and nestle my face in his hair.

He shivered, and since I didn't want to freak him out, I let go. "Okay, buddy," I said, smiling. "Be safe."

His eyes searched mine. "You too."

"I only have to watch for ricochets," I teased.

"Don't go in buildings without backup or jump off any balconies."

"I won't."

"Okay," he husked.

"Okay," I echoed and patted his shoulder one last time. "Bye."

He gave me a trace of a grin before he turned and left, walking out to the living room to collect the rest of his stuff.

I made myself busy even as I felt my chest tighten and my throat go dry. Loading the dishwasher became very important.

"I'll see ya soon," he called from the front door. "Go drop off Chickie before you go in. You know my dad takes him during the day."

"Yessir," I said, tracking him as he hit the front door, smiled warmly, and was then gone.

Telling myself he would be okay, he always was, I went upstairs to get ready for my day. And first I had to stop and pick up his werewolf.

IAN'S APARTMENT was a pit. It was small, it had jalousies on every window, and the walls were made of cement. It was like living in a giant cinderblock. It was fortunate there was no carpet in the entire place, otherwise his wolf would have torn it up. When I opened the front door, he came at me, snarling, growling, all flattened ears and snapping jaws. I knew why, of course. I was walking into his territory instead of him coming into mine.

"Knock it off," I groused, scowling as he bore down on me before I smiled and crooned, "Chickie Baby."

The whimper of happiness as he realized it was me before the dancing began was very cute. He was no longer a bloodthirsty predator; he was a big cuddly puppy.

"Stupid dog," I greeted him, not even having to bend to pet his massive head. His back reached my hip. "Who else would be stupid enough to come in here?"

He wriggled next to me, finally taking my hand gently in his jaws to get me to pay more attention to him. Squatting down, I scratched behind his ears as he licked my chin and shoved his nose in the side of my neck.

"Come on, doofus. Let's take you outside before we get in the car."

I grabbed his leash from where it hung beside Ian's bike on a peg on the wall. The apartment was such a bachelor pad, with things like an ironing board hanging on brackets in the entryway. The extra light hanging beside his bed belonged at a construction site, the shatter-resistant utility kind on a long cord with a hook at the top. It was lucky the man was gorgeous, because otherwise he'd never get a woman to spend more than a few minutes there.

I drove from his place in Hyde Park out to Marynook where his father lived and stopped in front of the small single-story postwar suburban tract residence with the big front picture window. As I walked up the gate and opened it, Ian's father stepped out onto the porch and lifted a hand in greeting.

"Miro," he called out as I let the leash go and Chickie streaked to the older man.

Down onto one knee Colin Doyle went, and I watched the dog slow himself so he didn't barrel forward and knock him over.

"I was expecting my son," Colin said as I walked up the stairs.

"I know." I smiled. "But he got called away, sir."

"Oh," he sighed, his eyes meeting mine. "When?"

"Early this morning."

"He didn't call me."

"I'm sure he will," I lied. I was the only one Ian would even consider getting word to.

He scoffed. "I don't know about that. The only reason he sees me at all is because of this dog."

I opened my mouth to argue.

"And you, Miro."

"That's not true, and I didn't do—"

"You're the one who suggested it. You're the one who said, maybe let your dad take care of the dog instead of hiring someone to go to your place and walk him."

"Yeah, well." I shrugged. "That might not have been me doing you a favor since he eats his weight in food every day."

He chuckled. "You did me a huge favor, Miro, and I'll always be grateful."

"He shouldn't have told you."

"It would have been nice if he hadn't. I could have pretended that he came up with it all on his own."

"I'm sorry."

"You have nothing to be sorry about."

"It was no big deal."

He locked me in place with his ice blue gaze, so similar to his son's, the difference being the lack of the heavy laugh lines at the corners. His father didn't have those. "It meant a lot to me, Miro."

I nodded.

I knew the history between the two men only vaguely. The little I did centered around a divorce, after which neither son nor mother heard from Colin Doyle again. He had shown for her funeral, though, twenty years later, which was the last time Ian had seen his father before we ran into him downtown. Ian and I had been partners for two years at that point. I had stopped when his name was called out, but Ian had not.

"C'mon," Ian had growled, his hand tight on my bicep, trying to move me.

"That man called your name, idiot," I said, waiting as he reached us, his smile wide, hand extended to me.

"Hello," he huffed as I took his hand. "Colin Doyle, good to meet you."

I was trying to figure out who the man was. Cousin? Uncle? "And you, sir."

"I'm Ian's father."

"Oh," I replied, stunned, having no clue that my partner of two years had family in Chicago. Turning to Ian, I waited for an explanation.

Arms crossed, muscles in his jaw clenching, my partner was stone silent.

"How are you, boy?" Colin asked softly.

I elbowed Ian in the arm.

"Fine," he muttered.

"It's wonderful to meet you," I said softly, covering his dad's hand with my other. "Would you like to join us for lunch, sir?"

"I would love that," he rasped, and I saw the quivering hope on his face. He was, in that moment, breakable. "If it would be all right with Ian, that is."

I looked at my partner, daring him to say a word.

"It's fine," he mumbled.

The restaurant was one of our favorites, a Greek place close to Centennial Park. We got a booth in the back, and I was going to sit across from Ian and his dad, but Ian shoved me into the booth first and then slid in beside me. His knee bumped mine under the table, but instead of moving away, he stayed close.

"So Miro," Colin began, having learned my name on the walk over. "What is it you do?"

"I'm a deputy US marshal, sir, like your son."

"You're a marshal?" Colin asked Ian.

And he had begrudgingly answered, as well as every question after that. But each one had to be dragged out, until Colin got up to use the bathroom and I rounded on my partner and shoved him out of the booth.

"What the fuck?"

I was on my feet in front of him in seconds, poking him in the chest, which was like trying to prod a piece of granite. "How dare you treat your father that way!"

"It's none of your fuckin' business, Miro," he insisted, his tone icy. "And after what he did to my mother, you—"

"What'd he do?"

"I'm not gonna—"

"Did he beat her?"

"No," he snapped.

"Drink?"

"I don't want to get into—"

"Gamble? Cheat on her?"

"Miro, you—"

"Did he hit you?"

"No, he—"

"Abuse you?"

"What're you trying to—"

"I wanna know what he did."

"He fuckin' left!" he whispered harshly instead of yelling, leaning close so only I could hear him clearly. "One minute he was there, the next he was… you don't even know."

I studied him.

"What?" he demanded angrily.

"He left you guys."

"Yes."

I squinted at him.

"She was never the same. She never laughed again."

Not even for her son? It sounded infinitely selfish to me. Wasn't the one parent left over supposed to do the work of two? Wasn't that how it worked? Not that I had any experience with any kind of family, but that was my understanding.

"Okay," I said, nodding, sitting back down and sliding into the booth.

After a moment, he joined me, careful the second time not to touch me.

"I bet he's sorry," I said slowly, "if you ask him. I bet he is. He seems sad."

"I don't care if he's—"

"You're back," I said jovially, greeting Colin, cutting Ian off. "Which is good, 'cause I'm starving and I wanted to order tabouli salad, but I wasn't sure if you liked it."

"I'll try anything," he said cheerfully, and I saw the furtive glance at Ian. Between that and the way he fiddled with his napkin and bit his bottom lip, I could tell Colin was terribly nervous.

"So where do you live now?" Ian finally asked.

"In Marynook," he answered. "It's in Avalon Park."

The entire lunch conversation was slow and painful and stilted, but we made it through, and when Ian got up to take a phone call, Colin leaned across the table and patted my face.

"Thank you, son," he said, and since it was the closest I'd ever had to paternal anything, I smiled back.

When Ian returned, he wedged in close to me, no longer perching on the tiny piece of upholstered bench so he didn't have to touch me. We were plastered together from shoulder to knee.

His father got up to make a call of his own, and as soon as he walked away, I turned to Ian. "You okay?"

He made a noise before he let his head fall forward, a motion he repeated often, the only tell he had that he wanted to be touched. I slid my fingers up the nape of his neck and gently pushed into the short, thick coarse hair.

"You're doing really well."

He grunted before he put his forehead down onto his folded arms. I gave his neck a last squeeze and let go.

"Don't invite him to the game with us," he directed.

I chuckled. "Okay."

That day had been an icebreaker, and they weren't close, but at least they had talked after that, upon occasion. Then when we had busted a large drug-trafficking ring that also dabbled in dog fighting and the wolf/malamute possibly husky hybrid had been discovered in one of the pens, Ian had taken one look at the predator and seen a kindred soul. The problem of what to do with Chickie Baby, as Ian named him, every day had been answered by me. His father was retired, had a huge yard, his wife worked days at a law firm, and the kids were all out of the house. When I suggested it, his father jumped at the chance to do something, anything, for Ian. And it turned out that Chickie was a great big puppy who only wanted love and attention. Unless you were trying to come up fast on Ian or break into his place. I shuddered to imagine the consequences of those two actions.

"Miro?"

"Sorry," I said quickly, whipped back into the present. "Okay, so I'll be here as close to six as I can be, sir."

"You have my number. If anything happens and you can't get him, call me."

"I will," I promised, turning and leaving the porch. Chickie caught me at the gate, stepping around in front of me, the whimper very sweet. "I'll be back, buddy," I said, petting him before he shot back to the porch when Colin called him. I waved from the car.

AT THE office, I had just made it to my desk when Kage walked up beside it, looming over me.

"Morning," I greeted him. "Did Ian call you?"

"His CO called me so I'm clear that he'll be gone for an indeterminate amount of time."

I nodded even though that news made my stomach do somersaults.

"And you," he said. "Where's your doctor's clearance?"

"In your inbox, sir," I apprised him. "I went, I swear."

He tipped his head at my arm. "And the wrist is good?"

"Cast should be off in six weeks, but it's fine, really. I mean, I went off a balcony last night, so we know I'm—"

"Perhaps the smart thing might be not reminding me of that."

It certainly might. "Yessir."

When he left, I finally took a breath. I missed Ian already.

CHAPTER 8

SOMETIMES YOU went looking for one thing and found another. For instance, while my partner—the man I was secretly pining for—was away on a mission for the US Army, one of the many things I'd been doing was fugitive transport with my fellow marshals. That Tuesday, six weeks later, I was trailing after Mike Ryan and Jack Dorsey as they, with a whole contingent of state and local police, took Casey Dunn out to Northbrook where his body-dump site was.

Dunn was a cleaner for a Ukrainian arms dealer, took care of all the man's enemies and put them in the ground under an auto salvage yard. As a stipulation of the agreement before he went into witness protection for rolling on his boss, he had to show the authorities where all the bodies were. They weren't just interested in the body that Dunn's brother, who testified against him, had seen him bury the night he followed him from their family home in Schaumburg. They needed a lot of murders to pin on Ivan Tesler; nothing in single digits would do. The thing was, when we arrived at what Dunn said was the second to last of the graves, all of a sudden he started screaming.

"I don't kill women!" he shouted, and the way he moved, quickly behind me, shivering hard like his skin was crawling with ants, I got the idea that he was seriously freaked out. He had not been expecting to find the lady there.

It took three days after that to clear Dunn, and during that time, they examined the body as well, discovering startling similarities to other crimes committed by a known assailant. The problem was twofold. First, crimes—as in plural, and that was never good. Second, the problem with adding the newest kill to the list of victims of Craig Hartley was that the man himself was locked up and had been for the past four years. The thought process was predictable; there were three possible scenarios: Hartley had a partner, there was a copycat, or he himself was communicating with someone on the outside.

It was not my job to do any of that detective work. But since I was the only one this particular serial killer would speak to, I was on loan to the FBI and met them out at the Elgin Mental Health Center.

I met Special Agents Eric Thompson and Debra Rohl there, along with the local team of agents I already knew headed up by a man I had been working really hard not to see—Cillian Wojno. It was what came of sleeping around. Every now and then, you found yourself in uncomfortable situations with people you used to bang.

We did our best to ignore each other; we didn't shake hands, just managed the head tip of acknowledgement before he followed the others into the interrogation room and I waited on the other side of the two-way mirror. They wanted to see if Hartley would speak to the new team without me, as it would make their job far easier. I hoped he would, but I wasn't optimistic. I was, after all, the one who'd saved his life even though he'd shoved a very expensive chef's knife into my side. The only reason I'd lived was that the tip had slid off one of my ribs on the way in and slowed the entry. I had nearly bled out in his kitchen, but even then had the presence of mind to stay in front of him so my Chicago PD ex-partner Norris Cochran didn't have a shot. I'd wanted Hartley to pay for what he did to all the women and their families, not die from a gunshot wound to the head.

It was a whole big procedure of manacles and leg shackles when Hartley was finally brought in. It would have been considered overkill, but between his genius IQ, superior strength, and the fact he had been one of the top cardiothoracic surgeons in the country five years prior, they weren't taking any chances. As always, I watched as the people in the room reacted to him.

He didn't look like a monster. In fact, at six two, with a golden tan that was his natural skin color, a carved physique, and bright green eyes, you first thought boy next door, not cold and calculating serial killer. That had been everyone's mistake, and nineteen women had paid with their lives.

As he took a seat, he scanned the room, eyes flicking over everyone before they settled back on the face of Rohl.

"Good morning, Dr. Hartley."

He quirked his right eyebrow but didn't speak, and I saw him fold his hands together.

"Will you speak to us?"

Nothing but a slight scowl and a pursing of his lips evidenced his disappointment. He had been expecting to see me and I wasn't there.

Rohl cleared her throat. "As I know you have access to a television and newspapers, you are no doubt aware that a body was found in Northbrook and that the attack mirrored one of yours in several ways."

No reaction. Beyond the coldness in his gaze, it would have been hard for anyone to tell he was even listening.

"We were wondering if you had any thoughts on who might have perpetrated the crime."

Silence.

"We're prepared to offer you some concessions, privileges, if you could lend us your insight, Dr. Hartley," Rohl said, smiling at him.

I had been a brand-new police detective when I'd encountered the man who now sat so composed on the opposite side of the table from the agents. It was strange to see him so frigid. At no time, even before I suspected him, had I been treated that way.

"Doctor?"

He smiled, but it didn't hit his eyes, and he turned to look over his shoulder at the guard standing stoically behind him. "I'm ready to return to my cell."

Thompson turned to Wojno, who in turn gave a nod to his partner standing beside the mirror. He tapped it, and I walked out of the viewing room to join the guard on this side of the door.

"I'm up," I told him.

"Sorry about that," he commiserated.

"Thanks," I said. He unlocked the door, and I slipped inside, waiting there for either Rohl or Thompson to acknowledge me.

"Miro," Hartley greeted me, his smile wide, his eyes glinting as he stood.

The guard moved forward fast, hand on Hartley's shoulder, baton out, ready to make him retake his seat.

"It's all right," Rohl rasped, visibly fighting down her fear at having the man looming over her. Her instinctive response had to have been to run. Thompson was so startled that when he'd leapt to his feet, he'd knocked over his chair.

Craig Hartley was a scary man, even more so because of the calm so easily shattered with fierce, decisive movement.

The guard stepped back warily, not replacing the baton, holding it ready instead. Thompson didn't retake his seat, just stood there watching Hartley as he stared at me like I was the second coming.

"I was hoping you were here somewhere," he sighed, gesturing for me to come closer like it was a table at some restaurant somewhere and not a maximum security interrogation room at a prison for the criminally insane. "I haven't seen you in almost two years."

"Yeah, not since you helped with the Lambert killing," I said from where I was.

"You were pleased with my observations," he reminded me, squinting, shifting from one foot to the other. "I read that Christina Lambert's killer died in prison. Was he raped first?"

I cleared my throat. "I have no idea."

"It would have been just desserts. There's no excuse for rape; that's what seduction is for."

Hartley had killed first and then mutilated his victims, turning them into what he'd described as art. It had been hard for me to see anything beyond the blood and exposed tissue, muscle, and bone. What had been clear was that Hartley had never caused his victims a moment of pain. Women went from his bed to sleep to death. It was how Norris and I had finally caught him. The recurring description we got from people was that they had seen a beautiful blond man, a gorgeous man, Prince Charming in the flesh. Once we started cross-referencing dates, times, and places, a pattern emerged, and we made daily visits to him, poking, prodding, trying to trip him up. His hubris had allowed it, so certain that neither Norris nor I was as smart as him. But he'd allowed us in the last night, given Norris permission to look around as I watched Hartley cook in the kitchen.

It was my fault; I'd turned my back on him and seen the Tahitian pearl ring with the diamonds sitting in a dish on the ledge above the kitchen sink. It was like being struck by lightning—that moment when I made the connection to why that ring looked familiar and where I'd seen it before.

I knew that particular piece of jewelry, had seen it a hundred times, and had always thought that the expensive bauble looked lovely adorning Kira Lancaster's ring finger. It had been on prominent display in the photo we were given when she went missing. The token of affection had been an anniversary gift from her husband, and Hartley had taken it as a trophy after he slept with and killed her. He had given the ring to his sister, and it came out later that she had been over the night before. As she was doing dishes, she had slipped the ring off, placed it in the dish, and then forgotten it there. The simple act had unmasked her brother for the monster he was.

I saw the ring, and as I'd turned and looked over my shoulder, he'd rushed forward and pulled the knife from the block beside the sink. His arm went around my neck and I couldn't pull my gun from that angle. My yell brought Norris, weapon drawn, screaming for Hartley to get his hands off me. Two things came out of that day: I saved a killer and lost a partner. Norris didn't want to ride with a man who had no concern for his own life, and I decided that there were better ways for me to serve and protect other than being a homicide detective.

"Miro?"

I looked up at Hartley, brought from my memories by his use of my name, which I allowed, much to the chagrin of almost everyone. "Sorry."

He was charmed, and it was evident by his smile. "Nothing to be sorry for."

"But I should be paying better attention."

"I almost killed you and you saved my life anyway. I won't ever be able to make things right between us until I get out."

I nodded and grinned at him. "So never, then."

He took a breath.

"Yes?"

"Never is such a long time," he said softly, his gaze moving from me to Rohl. What was frightening was how quickly the warmth leeched out of his eyes once they were off me. "Would you mind getting up so I can speak to Marshal Jones?"

She rose quickly, and I moved forward, taking the seat in front of him. Immediately he sat and leaned close, looking me over, finally meeting my gaze.

"You look tired, Miro. Not sleeping well?"

"I'm fine," I muttered, fiddling with the manila folder Rohl had left in front of me. "Can we talk about the situation in Northbrook?"

"Whatever you want to talk about is fine with me."

"But it's your thoughts that we're interested in."

He coughed softly. "Did you get the Christmas card I sent?"

"I did, thank you."

He seemed pleased, his eyes softening, his smile widening. "Go ahead and ask me anything."

I loosened my tie, which had him riveted. "So we both know you're way too smart to have an accomplice."

"It doesn't seem likely, does it?"

"No," I said with a smirk. "And the copycat thing?"

He snorted. "Tell me, did he have my clean lines?"

"No, not at all." I rolled my shoulders, trying to dislodge the familiar tension there. Visiting a man who had shoved a knife into me carried with it a certain amount of stress. "But that brings me to our final question, Doctor."

"Of course, but first may I ask after Detective Cochran? How is he?"

"I don't know," I answered honestly. "I haven't spoken to him in a very long time."

"Because of me," he almost purred.

I tipped my head back and forth. "Sort of."

"You chose me over him, that's why."

"That's a bit simplistic, Doctor."

"Is it?"

"I think so," I said, tired all of a sudden. "But tell me, do you have an admirer on the outside?"

He studied me a moment. "I would very much like to see you more than only when you need an answer about something."

I leaned back in my chair. "Are we negotiating?"

"Yes," he said flatly.

"Marshal," Rohl warned from behind me.

"He's talking to *me* right now," Hartley reminded her icily before his gaze returned to mine. "So?"

"What do you want?"

"What are you offering?" he asked softly, seductively.

I thought of what I could actually do and not need to give myself the Silkwood shower when I got home and added to that. "Once a year."

"Every six months," he countered.

"Done," I said, because *that* was, in fact, my limit. The most time the prison allowed was thirty minutes in maximum security. I could go there twice a year, for a total of an hour. I could. "Now tell me about your admirer."

"I'll say who, but not how."

"Okay."

"And you should relocate my sister and her family, Miro."

I met his stare. "Why's that?"

He shrugged. "I have more than one follower, and many of them blame her for my arrest."

"She's your sister," I reminded him.

"She left the ring for you to find, Miro."

"It was an accident; we both know it was."

"It doesn't matter," he sighed, mapping my face, the study almost unnerving.

I turned in my seat, but Thompson was already on his phone.

"We're on it," he snapped.

I pivoted back to Hartley. "The name?"

"What will people think?"

"That I came here with these people and saw you and then we found this guy."

"And I'll be a snitch?"

"I caught you; it follows that I would catch him. Don't you think?"

"But then you'll have a bull's-eye on your back," he said sharply. "I can't have that."

"Well, however you talk to them all—make sure I'm okay."

"As long as you keep your word."

"I thought you were in my debt."

He looked like I'd hit him.

"Aren't you?"

Quick nod.

I inhaled quickly. "I'll show. I promise." He was a serial killer, and normally they didn't do well in captivity. Someone always had a question for him—they needed insight, answers—and I was the carrot they dangled to get him to play ball. Someone would always be there to remind me of my commitment to the law, and therefore, to seeing Hartley.

He swallowed hard. "Clark Viana has a home in Highland Park."

"What does he do?" Rohl asked.

"He's a stockbroker."

"And how will we know he's our man, Doctor?"

"He keeps trophies in his wine cellar."

"Okay," Rohl huffed, and suddenly the whole room was on a phone, no longer caring about me or the good doctor.

Since they were all busy talking, no one noticed when Hartley reached out and took hold of my tie. The guard, from where he was standing behind Hartley, couldn't see what was going on, but that was okay. I wasn't scared. I had, in fact, never been frightened of him, and that had become the basis for our ongoing relationship. That and the fact that he'd tried to kill me and failed.

"I'll find out how you're getting messages out," I promised.

His grip on my pale blue tie with the red circles was light; if I leaned back it would have slid over his curled fingers. "Someday, Miro Jones, I will possess you, and you will be my greatest work."

I nodded.

"You might not believe me now, but you will."

"I'm sure," I said as he slowly opened his hand.

"There will come a morning when you'll open your eyes and I'll be there with you," Hartley whispered, the middle finger of his right hand inches from my face.

"Not fuckin' likely," I grunted, leaning back, the tie running through his hand like water before I stood up. "We'll save your sister and her family."

His smile made his eyes glimmer. "The things you think I care about, Miro."

I moved through the crowd of agents to the door.

"Do take care of yourself," Hartley added.

I knocked on the heavy steel door.

"I'll see you in July when it's hot."

"Yes, you will," I agreed as the door opened and I slipped out.

Looking back in at the room, I watched Hartley as more questions were fired at him, but he went silent, facing them with dead eyes until finally the guard announced it was time for him to be returned to his cell.

I was suddenly ridiculously thankful that I'd driven and didn't have to wait on the FBI agents so I could leave. I thought about the last time I had made the trip out to Elgin.

That day I had felt the bile rise in my throat and bolted down the hallway as I pulled my phone from the breast pocket of my suit jacket. There was only one person I wanted to talk to.

"Hey," came the gravelly voice over the line. "You almost done in there?"

"Why? Where are you?"

"Outside."

He was there. All I had to do was reach him.

"You drove out?" I asked as I was buzzed through the inner door and then the outer one, leading down the corridor that separated solitary from general population.

"Yeah. I figured you needed backup."

"I do," I agreed, speeding up, wanting out, needing out. "I'll be hungry after, I always am."

"Why?"

"'Cause I barf."

"I would too."

"Okay," I said, my voice cracking as I was allowed through another three doors. Each one had to open and close before the next could. And while the security measures were impressive, I could barely breathe. "I'm almost there."

"Miro?"

I dragged in a breath. "Yeah. I'm here."

The line was silent as I passed through another two doors. I didn't see the warden, which was fine. He was probably waiting to say good-bye to the feds. I was just a marshal; he saw us all the time.

Ending the call, I collected my gun, badge, and keys on the other side of the metal detector and jogged to the front door. Hitting the panic bar, I was outside on the steps moments later. Not stopping, I rushed down the stairs and vomited into the trash can. Moments later I was passed a bottle of water and napkins and a hand pressed between my shoulder blades.

"You okay?"

I nodded, still bent over, shivering.

Ian rubbed gentle circles on my back and then, because I was sweating, pushed my hair out of my face as I straightened up. "You're gonna be okay. Rinse out your mouth and I'll get you some pancakes. Breakfast cures everything."

But it wasn't eggs or toast or hash browns I needed, it was Ian.

I needed Ian.

That was almost two years ago. And today, as I crashed through the last door to the outside and ran down the same stairs and heaved up my spleen, he wasn't there.

No grounding touch, no rough caress.

No rumbling voice.

No cocky grin that said he could make it better by sheer force of will.

I missed him, and some days it felt like my chest was full of pins every time I took a breath. And on even worse days, I had to talk to a serial killer because I was the only one he liked well enough to converse with.

My breakfast and lunch were all gone in one shot, my stomach left clenching as I made sure I was done before I moved.

"What the fuck, man," a guy who passed me moaned. "That's fuckin' gross."

"Shut the hell up," a woman snapped at him, closing in on me with a tub of baby wipes in one hand and a toddler on her hip. "Here you go, shug, clean yourself up."

It was nice. I thanked her profusely, and when I reached my car, I smelled lavender fresh. I'd left a bottle of water in the front seat, which was good, because I needed to rinse my mouth out. Gargle. I toyed with the idea of either running home or to the office to get into my locker. In either place there was a toothbrush and toothpaste.

As I contemplated where I was going, my phone beeped, and I saw Kohn's name appear on the display.

"Hey, I—"

"Where the fuck are you?"

I cleared my throat. "I'm out at Elgin."

"That was this morning?"

"Yeah, why?"

"You're with me today and we're on transport. Hurry up and report to the office so we can get our assignment."

"I'm on my way."

"Good," he said and hung up.

IT HAD been a roulette wheel of partners since Ian was away, and today I had self-proclaimed metrosexual Eli Kohn sitting at Ian's desk when I got to the office.

"Hey, Jonesy," he greeted me cheerfully.

I flipped him off.

"So grouchy first thing this morning. You must need coffee?"

I needed my partner back. That's what was missing and making me foul. "You're with me?"

"Always, baby."

I shook my head as he cackled.

Kage filled the doorway of his office and notified us that we were on transport this morning and retrieval in the afternoon. Kohn walked over and took the piece of paper Kage held out.

"Remember, gentlemen, not getting updates makes me cranky."

I knew that firsthand. Kage liked to know where we all were. Not checking in got you sent home without pay. "Yessir."

"Jones."

I stopped moving and gave him my undivided attention.

"The feds said that you were invaluable to their investigation, though they felt that your methods bordered on misconduct."

I coughed.

"They said that you flirted with Dr. Hartley and that he extracted a promise for you to see him twice a year."

"I think that whatever they heard, or didn't, has no bearing on their case."

"Agreed." He clipped the word. "You did good work today."

"Thank you, sir."

"How does it feel to have the cast off?"

I flexed my hand for him. "You have no idea."

He nodded quickly, retreating back into his office but leaving the door open like always. I caught up with Kohn in the hall.

"You know, you and Doyle make the rest of us look good."

I missed Ian too much to take any crap about him. I was in defense mode. "What're you talking about?"

"You guys jump off balconies."

"That was just the once," I said snidely, stuffing my scarf into my quilted black jacket, hoping it didn't get much colder.

He grabbed my right bicep, stopping me so he could step in front of me. "I was there for the first one, but I heard that the second time, you flew."

"That's not how I remember it."

"Tell me how you remember it, then."

Easing my arm free, I explained about jumping off Emma's balcony after the drug dealer as we walked. By the time we got to the elevator, he was staring at me like I was insane. "What?"

"Are you kidding?" he said dryly. "You don't follow people off balconies, Jones."

I scoffed, pulling my phone out of my coat pocket as it started buzzing.

"You're not the Green Beret, ya know. Your partner is."

"Yeah, okay," I placated him, grabbing his wool and cashmere toggle coat and holding out my phone so he could see the text from the Chicago PD homicide detective our office was working with. "Rybin says that he and Cassel will meet us at the safe house in Brookfield so we can take custody of our witness to transport her to court for her deposition."

"Why are you getting a text from a detective and not someone on our team?"

"You know White gives out our numbers to the detectives he's working with."

He shook his head. "That's not protocol."

I scoffed.

"Shut up."

"Mr. I took time off my last security detail to go bang some girl before picking up dinner."

"One time!"

I did my best Sam Kage impersonation. "Perhaps you need an extended vacation, Mr. Kohn, so you can get all the fucking out of your system."

"Crap," he groaned. "You would have thought Ching would have warned me that he was on his way over from the safe house."

I snickered. "Ching lives for that shit, you know that."

"I know it now," he said, exasperated.

I couldn't help laughing.

"And that Kage impression is kinda creepy."

We rode the elevator down in silence and when the doors whooshed open, Chris Becker stood there with his partner, Wes Ching.

They made an interesting pair, Becker, the ex-University of Kentucky linebacker, and Ching, his smaller though decidedly more aggressive partner. Becker was one of those guys women watched when he walked down the street, a confident stride and easy smile. Ching was quieter, and, people thought, the saner of the two, until he kicked down a door and charged through. After a raid it was always "That black guy and the Asian guy, what the fuck was with them?" Of course that was only if Kage wasn't around. If he was, you could bet no one said a word about any member of his team. It wasn't healthy.

When Becker saw us, the cocky grin instantly appeared. "Morning, ladies," he teased, waggling his thick brown brows.

Kohn flipped him off.

"What's wrong with you, you havin' your period?" Ching asked loudly.

I smiled at all the women in the hall getting on the elevator. "Make sure you all report that bullshit to Supervisor Kage upstairs."

"Fuck you, Jones!"

Kohn pointed at Becker before turning to follow me down the hall. "Asshat," he grumbled.

"Yes," I agreed. "But when Becker's coming through the door after your ass, you like him, right?"

He grunted.

That was a yes.

In the car, Kohn started complaining. "Let's take mine. This is like going back in time."

"It's vintage."

"It's shit," he confirmed. "For fuck's sake, Jones, there aren't even any air bags in this."

I changed the subject, because I had to drive. I had a whole thing about other people driving; it was only because Ian was such a dictator about it that I gave in to him. "So what witness are we transporting?"

"Nina Tolliver," he said, grinning. "And I heard you like her, so that's good, right?"

"I don't make judgments," I lied, flat out, because of course I did. I was human, after all. "And I don't like her like I wanna pick out china patterns with her. I just think she's a good person who totally won big in the 'I married a psycho murdering scumbag' department."

Drew Tolliver had started out as muscle in the Corza crime family and worked his way up and up until he was a major player in prostitution, drugs, loan-sharking, protection, and guns, and his newest addition right before the feds busted him was assassinations. His wife had been blind to all of that. What she did see, the day he stopped beating only on her and started in on his twin boys, age seven and a half, was that he was a bad man.

"I can't imagine being a prisoner in my own house," Kohn said thoughtfully. "It was smart to send her kids off to boarding school. I mean, sucks for her not to see them, but at least they were safe."

"Yeah," I agreed. "And it gave her time to get a new hobby."

The amount of incriminating evidence Nina Tolliver had collected on everyone who came to their home was staggering. By simply leaving her laptop on in the living room when men dropped by to see her husband and turning on a web camera no one ever noticed, she got hours of damning footage. Murders were planned, people were named, and every face was captured, so there could be no doubt about who was talking, who was giving orders, and who was carrying them out.

Then, to get away, she'd begged him to take her along on a trip to Atlantic City, and he'd relented. "She's really brave," I interjected, because it had to be said. "And it was brilliant to freak out on the plane with an air marshal. They took her off in cuffs."

"Yes. Brilliant."

"And now she gets to finally be with her kids in a safe, secure place."

"As soon as she testifies," he reminded me. "Which the first part of is her deposition."

"Which she does today." I sighed. "So let's get her there so she can put her husband away for life. The quicker she starts this process, the faster he rolls, and guys even higher up the food chain can be put away."

"You know her husband doesn't deserve to go into the program."

"WITSEC doesn't judge; it depends on what he saw," I said sagely.

"Yeah, I know. It just sucks."

THE SAFE house in Brookfield was not federal, but a Chicago PD property, and as such, it lacked many of the amenities that usually came with ours. It was a small ranch-style suburban tract home with a huge basement. It was older, had only radiators for warmth, and basically reminded me of one of my least favorite foster homes, down to the pink tile and frosted glass sliding doors in the bathroom. There were some missing ceiling tiles in the kitchen, so if you were cooking, you could glance up and observe spiderwebs above you. The whole place gave me the creeps. It smelled like Pine-Sol and mold. I was glad protection rotation only came around every three or four months. Sometimes marshals did transport, sometimes protection, sometimes relocation. They moved us around so we stayed sharp. It was also supposed to make it impossible for anyone to ever be able to say with any kind of certainty which marshal would show up for what duty.

It was why Topher Cassel, Joshua Rybin, Ted Koons, and Keith Wallace, the four Chicago PD detectives there when Kohn and I showed up, had no idea who was going to walk through the door. They probably didn't expect the *GQ* model Eli Kohn resembled. Between the clothes, the three hundred dollar haircut, and his lean and muscular build, they probably thought someone was screwing with them.

"Hey," Kohn greeted, pulling his badge from the breast pocket of his stand-up collar trench coat. "Lemme see yours, gentlemen."

They brought out badges for him, which were basically redundant since we were only there because we had clearance to be. After we all shook hands, I turned to talk to our witness.

Nina Tolliver was a tiny woman. It was the first thing I thought. Her long brown curly hair hung to the middle of her back, and it was held away from her face with an octopus clip—which I recognized because I had roommates in college, four of them, all women, and the bathroom had been littered with everything from rubber bands to lacquered chopsticks. None of my annoying, loving friends had hair as long as Nina's, though. So to be saying something as I walked up to her, hand out, I commented on it.

"Damn, woman, you got a lotta hair."

And that fast, instead of the obvious apprehension she had for the police detectives, I got a warm smile. She looked good in her navy Ann Taylor suit.

"I'm Nina Tolliver," she said, like I didn't know. Like maybe we were having a normal conversation. "And you are?"

"Miro Jones," I answered, smiling back.

She tipped her head. "Miro?"

"It's short for Miroslav," I explained like I always did. "It's Czech."

"I like it," she said, and I recognized that along with the interest I was getting, the genuineness, I was also seeing concern.

"Are you scared?"

She shook her head.

"Then what?"

"You two came alone?"

"No. There are two other marshals here somewhere. Maybe you haven't seen them yet."

"I don't think so."

"Gotta be," I scoffed. "I promise you, we always transport in fours, not twos."

Her brows furrowed. "You're wrong. You're the only marshals I've seen today."

It was instant—the roll of my stomach, the shiver of dread, because I knew, right then, at that moment, that it was me and Kohn and Nina, and that was all.

I glanced to Kohn and he gave me a quick nod, understanding what was happening as much as I did.

"Oh Lord, I gotta pee," he announced loudly, and all four detectives laughed as he darted out of the room.

"I like the running shoes," I said, pointing at them. "They really set off the outfit."

She shrugged. "I figured I'd carry my heels with me for the deposition, but I'm probably overdressed anyway. It's not court today, not yet."

"Right," I agreed, realizing that now would be the perfect time to kill her, before the bright lights of the media circus. The calm before the storm, just a federal prosecutor and the defense attorney listening to what she had to say. "So we have some time. You want some tea?"

"That would be great," she replied softly.

"I'll make you some tea," I yelled after Kohn before pivoting to face Nina again. "Take me to the kitchen if you would, please, madam."

She graced me with a smile, and I was about to follow her down the short hall, but I remembered that I was acting and had to make sure it all appeared real.

"You guys want any?" I offered the detectives.

"No, man, we're good," Cassel answered.

Grabbing Nina's arm, I walked her directly through the living room, into the kitchen, and stopped at the back door, where I waited.

"Hey," one of the detectives called out to Kohn. "You all right in there?"

It was obviously to gauge where Kohn was, and in that instant, I heard the chirp of a sensor.

"Fuck!" came the yell as I heard feet pounding across the floor.

"Check the kitchen for the other one!"

Hurling open the sliding glass door, I drew my gun and shoved Nina through. "Keep up with me when I run," I ordered loudly.

"Yes," was all she said.

We scrambled down the back stairs, bolted across the yard, and I hopped the small chain-link fence that separated one piece of property from the other, and then helped Nina over, lifting her easily. I was surprised that I didn't have to urge her on, to follow me, but she was very focused on survival. She wanted to live, kept chanting it, telling me as we ran.

"I have boys," she repeated as she hiked up her skirt. "They need me."

Through the neighbor's obstacle course—a Jack Russell terrier that came streaking out through its doggie door to greet us, swing set, patio furniture—we ran as I pulled my phone from my pocket and called my boss on his private line.

"Jones?" he rumbled.

"I'm running from the safe house in Brookfield with Nina Tolliver. I'm not sure if Kohn got out or not. He was creating a diversion for me and the witness by going out the bathroom window. I have two detectives in pursuit. I think White and Sharpe are down somewhere on the grounds. I'm headed to George's diner two blocks away because it's the only place I know around here. Send backup now."

"Copy that. We're en route. I'll be on-site in twenty, Jones."

He was basically thirteen miles away, which could take him either twenty minutes or an hour. It all depended on traffic, even with a flashing blue light on top of his car. I-55—we never referred to it as the Stevenson Expressway—was the quickest way. "Okay."

"Don't die."

"Yessir."

And he was gone as Nina and I hit the street and ran. With her skirt around her ass and her running shoes on, she was flying. With my longer legs, I was still much faster, so I slowed to keep pace with her, but both of us were running for our lives.

A car closed in behind us, and a bullet hit a trash can beside me. I shoved Nina to the ground, turned, saw the threat, and fired. Cassel, who had come around the car to shoot me, went down as I put one in his shoulder. But Rybin, using the car as a shield, shot over the hood and caught me in my right shoulder, just off the edge of the second-chance vest I wore under my shirt. I absorbed the shock, feeling pressure and pain. Nina's scream scared me as I fired back, putting shots in the hood and shattering the windshield, enough to make Rybin dive for cover.

"Come on!" I yelled at her.

The sirens terrified me, because the men chasing us could also call for backup. I could have been a rogue marshal who drew down on them. I could be trying to kidnap Nina. The scenarios were endless, and so because of that, I didn't stop to wave down a police cruiser. We ran on toward Ogden Avenue, gun in one hand, the other pressed to my shoulder. Not that it was helping, there was blood seeping through my fingers.

A car came up fast beside us, and my first thought when Nina screamed was that she'd been hit. But the fact that she was able to run by me, followed by searing, smothering pain in my upper chest, let me know that it was me who took the bullet. It was at the inside of the shoulder joint and above the neckline of the damn vest, on the left side this time.

Time slowed and I was scared for a second, worried that I couldn't protect her, knowing I was hurt. It was strange, that clarity in the midst of all the adrenaline.

"Are you—"

Her voice, the tremor in it, snapped me back into the moment. "Don't stop! Run!"

I passed her and she followed me, the two of us running behind a frozen yogurt place, then between two buildings. We lost them because the alley was too narrow for a car and they had to circle back around. Grabbing Nina's hand, I ran headlong into the street, horns and yelling greeting us as cars came to squealing stops to avoid running us over.

It always looked so easy in movies or on TV. People dodged cars like it was nothing. It was why I normally ended up yelling at the screen. Ian wouldn't go with me to movies anymore; instead he made me watch them at his place. He said I got too invested in the action and needed to learn to distance myself emotionally. I was working on it.

Nina was amazing. If I had to handpick a civilian to run from armed gunman with, I could not have chosen any better. She listened better than anyone I had ever met.

Safe on the opposite sidewalk, I stumbled forward, my vision blurring for a moment. I was losing too much blood too fast and had to make a change.

"Follow me," I barked at her after catching sight of a man standing in the doorway of an automotive repair shop.

Charging over to him, Nina staying right with me, I yelled for help.

People always surprised me. Instead of turning tail, running inside and rolling the big bay doors down from the ceiling, he waved at us to hurry. When we got close, he stepped aside so I could run past him, Nina right behind me.

I lost my balance, fell to my knees but twisted sideways, shoving Nina behind me, shielding her between my body and a parked car, my back plastered to her front. I heard her gasp.

"I need to see how bad you're hit," she ordered. "Take this off so I can check."

"Not until I've assessed all threats."

"Yeah, okay," she said, her breath catching, "but maybe you could hold the gun with one hand and let me take off the coat and then change hands?"

"What?" I was having trouble following her among the dizziness, darkening vision, and sharp, throbbing pain. I really needed to remain conscious.

"Just—let me."

It was difficult to maintain my focus as she reached around my chest, unzipped my jacket, and pulled at me roughly, divesting me of my ruined piece of outerwear.

"Oh God," she moaned, her face scrunching up. "You're really bleeding. This T-shirt is soaked and—I thought this vest was supposed to fucking do something!"

It did, just not everything. It wasn't body armor.

"Move your arm. I need to check and see if it came out the other side."

I ended up transferring the gun between hands as she'd suggested.

"Oh Jesus," she cried, which gave me an even better idea of the amount of fluid she was looking at. "Miro, your collarbone is—and your shoulder, I—you're losing too much blood!"

The man and five other mechanics crowded in around us even as I held my gun on them.

"It's okay," the man who let us in soothed, lifting his hands, turning his head right and then left, jerking it up both times, clearly signaling to the men. The others stepped back before he took a step forward. "You running from the cops?"

"Yes," Nina cried, her bottom lip quivering. "And they shot him! Twice!"

"Yeah, I see," he murmured before he reached behind him, pulled a shop towel from his back pocket, and wadded it up. "I'm gonna throw it over to your girl, okay? Don't shoot me."

"He's not going to shoot you!" Nina shouted, her voice rising fast. "He's a US marshal, for crissakes! He's trying to save my life!"

He startled as I felt a throb run through my chest, making me shudder with the effort it took to hold the gun up. I was starting to worry that I was going to pass out and wouldn't be able to protect Nina. If it were only my shoulder, I wouldn't have worried. The bullet had gone in the back of my right shoulder and exited from the front. The through and through was good, the blood running down my bicep to the crook of my elbow to my forearm was not so great, but still probably not life threatening. The one in my chest was another story. I wasn't sure about the damage there and it was unnerving. If I was going to die, I wanted to talk to Ian first.

"You're a marshal?"

Shit. Had to focus. "Yeah," I said, leaning sideways so he could see the badge on my belt.

"Lemme come to you, marshal."

I lowered the gun because I was quickly losing the ability to hold it up.

He moved fast, rushing forward and shoving the towel against my shoulder, near my throat.

"Fuck."

"Lado!" he bellowed. "Bring me clean towels from the back and call 911!"

"No," I said, turning my head to look at Nina but not able to catch her eye when she was in motion. She had gotten up and moved around in front of me, took her suit jacket off, and wadded it up so she could push it against the other hole in my shoulder. "Nina, get my phone and call my boss."

"How do I know who—"

"It says boss," I said, having trouble focusing before I met the gaze of the man who took over for her, now holding both his towel and the ruined suit jacket to both sides of my shoulder.

"This looks more glamorous in the movies," he informed me, smiling gently.

"Right?" I coughed, chuckling.

"I'm sorry, man, I thought maybe you'd kidnapped her or the two of you were running from the cops."

"We are," I said, laughing and groaning at the same time.

"Hurts, huh?"

"Yeah."

The phone was suddenly against my ear, Nina pressing it there gently.

"Hello?"

"Where the hell are you, Jones?" Kage growled angrily.

I looked up at the man keeping me from bleeding to death. "Where am I?"

"You're close to Ogden and Maple at Chaney and Sons Restoration."

"Okay," I said, letting my head drop forward. "You hear that?"

"Yeah, but Brookfield is like the auto shop capital of the world, I need a landmark."

"Landmark?" I asked.

"The Flower Pot Garden Center is next door."

"Boss?" I asked, because talking was fast becoming a real chore.

"I heard him. We'll be right there. Where are the detectives who were chasing you?"

"I dunno. God willing, not outside preparing to come in, guns blazing."

"That's not funny, Jones."

"I—" The sirens sent a ripple of fear through me instead of inspiring the relief they normally did. "You hear that?"

"Yeah. That's me."

I nearly passed out. "Okay. I'll wait here and bleed, 'kay?"

"Just don't die. I haven't lost anybody yet today, let's not start with you."

"Yessir," I said and hung up just as my phone rang. "It's gonna be okay," I swore to the kind Samaritan and Nina. "I promise."

"What?" Kohn asked from the other end of the line.

"Oh thank God, hey, buddy," I winced.

"Now I'm your buddy? Since when?"

"Where the fuck are you?"

"I'm in a shed in a civilian home on Vernon Avenue."

"You okay?"

"I got scraped up going out the window, but I'll live. I really don't want to shoot the raccoon that's in here with me, but if it charges, I'm gonna. I mean, it could have rabies."

I winced because it hurt to laugh. "Please shut up. Call your boss now, he's almost to me."

"I did already," he said quickly. "You sound weird. What's wrong?"

"Shot."

Silence.

"Eli?"

"Don't fuckin' call me Eli, you're not gonna die."

"Okay," I said even as my vision started going darker around the edges.

"I'll see you in a minute," he rasped, and I heard the words "federal marshal" on his end before the line went dead. He was safe, I was relieved.

"Oh shit, Miro, sit up," Nina commanded even as I slouched to the cold concrete floor. "The ground is gonna suck out all your warmth. You gotta sit up and lean on me."

But there was no way. I wanted to rest. Nina was safe because of me, and Kohn was safe because he was in a potting shed or a tool shed being hunted by a rabid woodland creature. The very idea made me chuckle.

"Jesus, Miro, you're so cold."

But I wasn't anything anymore.

"Federal marshals!"

I made a noise of relief as there was the sound of gunfire close by, like *right* outside. Several shots followed by two more. It was important to warn Nina, to get her down, but when I tried to speak there was nothing.

"Jones," I heard Kage say in his guttural growl at the same time I got a big hand on my chest. Amazing the amount of warmth in my boss's palm, I could only imagine what being wrapped in his arms would be like. "Don't die."

Lord, I really was out of it. I liked my boss, but I was only carrying a big blazing torch for one man. And Jesus, this would piss him off when he found out.

"Boss?" I managed to choke out.

"Don't talk, Jones," he snarled, and then I heard him yell. "In here!"

"Kohn's in a shed."

"He was. Dorsey and Ryan picked him up."

"Tell Ian I—"

"You can talk to Doyle your damn self. Hold on and shut the fuck up."

I was going to argue, but I passed out instead.

CHAPTER 9

I WOKE up with one IV tube feeding me, one pumping me full of antibiotics, one keeping me hydrated, and the last one keeping me comfortable. That same morning, the drugs and the catheter went bye-bye. I was glad to be rid of both. I had never been a fan of being incapacitated or drugged up and fuzzy. I like being 100 percent in control at all times. I had too many bad memories of being at someone else's mercy.

It was two days later. Once I was awake, the inquest guys showed up: the federal ones, the Chicago PD ones, my boss, his boss, and the boss of the four detectives who tried to kill me and Kohn and Nina Tolliver. The chief of police was there as well, and the state's attorney, his assistant, and a stenographer. It was a lot of people, but my room was big.

Apparently they had already questioned Kohn and Nina and had been waiting for me to wake up and corroborate everyone else's stories.

"How did you know you were in trouble?" the federal investigator asked.

"As soon as Nina Tolliver said that Kohn and I were the only marshals she'd seen, I knew there was a problem." I glanced at my boss. "Are Sharpe and White dead?"

Quick shake of his head even as the muscles in his jaw clenched.

"No?"

"White's in a coma two doors down from you, and Sharpe went home yesterday."

"What's the prognosis on White?"

"He simply needs to wake up," he assured me.

I nodded, and the investigator was going to speak again but I asked my boss another question. "Are Cassel and Rybin dead?"

"No. Both are in federal custody. You wounded Cassel, and we caught Rybin at the airport trying to flee the country."

"And Koons and Wallace? Are they dead?"

"Yes," he said flatly.

"And they shouldn't be," their boss snapped. "They were shot in—"

"They were told to drop their weapons and get on the ground," Kage informed the man icily. "They returned fire."

"We only have your man's word for that," he argued.

"Yes," he agreed, and I was glad that I was not on the other end of the hostility in the stare. "Becker and Ching are highly decorated marshals, and they've been cleared by both my department and yours."

"Yes," the investigator admitted before settling his attention back on me. "Now, Marshal, what happened after you and Mrs. Tolliver left the house?"

I went through the whole thing piece by piece for them, leaving nothing out, including the kindness of the auto-body shop owner, Kohn calling me from the shed, and how I heard several shots fired and then return fire.

"That had to be those two dirty cops firing on Kowalski and Ching," I finished.

"We don't know that they were dirty," their captain chimed in again.

"True," I said frankly. "Maybe Tolliver had someone in their families kidnapped. Maybe they were coerced."

He opened his mouth to rebut.

"Unless you've already checked their financials and there's money moving around in there," I reasoned. "And if so, then dirty is the appropriate modifier, sir."

"It is," Kage said dryly, his tone frosty. "The history of deposits shows years of bribes. Your department is riddled with corruption—as usual."

"Are you forgetting that you yourself were a police detective, Marshal Kage?"

"No," he replied, his voice full of gravel. "I had a dirty partner myself, but my captain knew, as well as IAD. Seems that you had no clue what the hell was going on in your own goddamn house."

He was not a word mincer, my boss, and when the arguments erupted, I really wasn't surprised. The reality was, however, that my boss's boss, Tom Kenwood, was the man with the most clout in the room, and when the chief deputy spoke, everyone shut up.

Kenwood crossed the room to stand at my bedside. "You did well, Jones. Rest and return to us as soon as you're able. You saved a high-profile witness with comprehensive records detailing the Corza family's illegal activities. Without your heroic actions that day, we would have been back to square one in our case and two children would have been missing their mother. Your actions are a credit to the service, as well as to your supervisor and team."

"Thank you, sir."

Kenwood lifted his head and met the gaze of the chief of police. "We are launching a formal federal inquiry into these two men and the entire department," he announced. "The attorney general is informing the mayor this morning and a special investigator will be appointed."

No one said a word.

He turned to Kage. "I want to see White and talk to his wife, and then Sharpe."

"Yessir."

Everyone cleared out except Kage. I noticed Chief Deputy Kenwood waiting for him in the hall. Leaning over, he put a hand on my unhurt shoulder. "When you're up to it, you need to call Doyle's father. Something about a wolf?"

I smiled. "Yessir."

"I'll talk to you in a week, Jones."

"Not before? I could die of boredom."

"Watch Netflix," he advised.

I nodded.

He strode out, and in the hall, he fell into step beside his boss before they disappeared. Glancing around, I located my phone on the rolling table beside my bed, plugged into an outlet. It listed six missed messages from Ian's father and one from Ian himself, which I wished I had been awake to take.

"Jesus Christ, Mary, and motherfucking Joseph!" I jolted as Catherine Benton stormed into my room, both her volume and perfume bracing.

Following her in, Janet Powell shouted even louder. "What the hell did you do to yourself?"

"I told you he was really hurt," Aruna Duffy shrieked, rushing by both women to reach me, grabbing my hand, and dropping gracelessly down on the bed beside me. She had never been a sweet delicate flower, even though at five six and 110 pounds she used to resemble one. Now, at seven months pregnant, eating everything in sight, bigger than she'd ever been, she was no longer certain of her own strength.

"I thought you wore body armor?" Min Kwon, rounding out the four, asked as she rushed around to my other side. "How did you get shot, chagiya?"

"It's like a condom, Min, holes happen," I said, lifting my chin so she'd lean down so I could kiss her. From the use of the endearment, I knew she was really worried.

She snorted as I kissed her cheek before she turned her head and kissed mine. Aruna was next, and then Janet. Catherine had the binder that had been sitting on a shelf beside my bed open. I'd had no idea what it was until I saw her perusing it, but understood as I watched her flip pages that it was my chart.

"Put that down."

Her shushing noise was sharp.

"You shouldn't be snooping," I scolded.

"Uh-huh," she said, still reading, kissing me absently before straightening up. When her head snapped up and she nailed me with her dark brown gaze, I almost flinched. "Your wrist is broken too?"

"That was before," I defended. "It's all healed up now."

She grunted and kept skimming, the enormous five-carat diamond in the platinum setting on her left hand catching the light as she flipped pages. "Hit the call button," she directed Min. "I need to talk to the nurse."

"What are you guys doing here?" I asked the women who had been my family since my freshman year at the University of Chicago.

"Aruna's your emergency contact," Min explained gently, as was her way. She was kind and logical and the heart of our little group. She was also a cutthroat litigator who you really didn't want sitting across from you in a courtroom. I watched her in court the last time I visited her, and she was damn scary. "And so after they let her know what was going on, she called us."

I rolled my head to look at Aruna.

"What? I'm not supposed to call them?"

"You scared everyone for no reason."

"No reason, my ass," Catherine flared, showing off the weight of the three-inch binder with both hands. "This is serious, Miroslav."

Good Lord, she used my given name.

"We got here as quick as we could," Janet explained.

Aruna was the only one who'd stayed in Chicago, the only one I saw on a regular basis. Catherine was in Manhattan, Janet in Washington DC, and Min in Los Angeles. But I still talked to all of them once a week. We all knew exactly what was going on with each other. So even though I hadn't physically seen Catherine in six months, Janet in eight, and Min in four, it didn't feel like that because they were all still such a big part of my life.

"I was here yesterday," Aruna explained, patting my hand, her green-gold eyes warm as she stared at me. "That's why you're in this room."

I squinted at her. "What room was I in?"

"A small one," she enlightened me, flipping her long straight brown hair over her shoulder.

"And what did you do?"

"I asked them if they wanted to be on the news tomorrow."

"You work for *20/20*," I reminded her. "You don't do the local news here in Chicago."

"As if they wouldn't die to have me do an exposé on how hospitals treat wounded heroes."

"I'm not a hero."

"You saved that woman, your witness," she said quickly. "Your boss told me."

"Oh for crissakes," I groused.

"Shut up. They moved you, didn't they?"

"Because you threatened them."

"Damn right I did," she huffed, and I saw her eyes glint with anger. "Give me a hard time—fuck them!"

"Aruna—"

"As if dealing with her isn't preferable to dealing with me," Catherine scoffed. "Please."

I shook my head. "You guys can't come in here and push—"

"Do they want to be audited?" Janet asked pointedly. "I think not."

My nice and unassuming friend, one of the chief auditors in the Tax Exempt & Government Entities (TE/GE) division of the IRS, was actually the scariest person in the room. People thought she was cute and fluffy with her short curly red bob, freckles, and big blue eyes— until she pounced on you and you realized she was terrifying.

"I—"

"Mr. Jones?" a nurse said as she came into the room. "What do you—I'm sorry, but you're not supposed to have this many vis—"

"He can have as many people in here as he likes," Min instructed. "And if you call security, I'll have your job."

"Stop," I begged. "This woman puts needles in me."

"I need to speak to Mr. Jones's physician," Catherine snapped at the nurse before she even had a chance to respond to Min. "Please advise him that Dr. Catherine Benton is here."

"I don't—"

"Dr.… Catherine… Benton," she said slowly, frostily. "Do it now."

The nurse glanced around the room and left quickly.

"He won't know who you are," I said to my conceited friend. "You're very full of yourself right now."

She grunted, walked over to me, and flicked me in the middle of my forehead.

"Witch," I grumbled, but I couldn't help laughing.

"I have concerns," she replied. "And I need to know what your doctor did, because it's not in his notes and that's troubling. If he didn't do what I think, I'm going to have to wheel you into surgery in about an hour."

Min gasped.

"I really don't want you cutting me open," I said emphatically.

"You should be so lucky," said my doctor, Dr. Sean Cooper, who looked like he belonged on a magazine cover instead of walking the halls of a hospital, as he strolled into the room. "Dr. Benton is one of the top neurosurgeons in the country."

"Yes," she seconded, arching an eyebrow for me. "I saw that Miro suffered hypoxia associated with the gunshot wound to his clavicle, and my concern is—"

"Erb-Duchenne palsy," he finished. "Yes."

"And," she snapped. "How long was he—"

"I haven't updated the file, but walk with me and I'll show you the MRI we performed."

"Excellent," she said crisply, turning to follow him. "Sit tight, I'll be back," she said over her shoulder.

When she was gone, Aruna waggled her eyebrows at me.

"You guys are all bullies."

I was fairly certain the hospital staff would be really glad when I left.

I HAD been, by all accounts, well on my way to a life of crime, growing up in Pacoima, California. There was shoplifting—always food because I was always hungry—truancy, and doing the courier thing. Guys said, hey kid, I'll give you twenty bucks to take this there, and I did. I never asked what was inside; I didn't care. But I got a reputation for being reliable, and that led to getting invited along to business transactions at cockfights, gambling in back rooms, and watching as guys drank, smoked, and did lines. Soon enough, I was the one being offered a bump of coke or a drag or a drink.

I was in and out of more than two dozen foster homes by the time I turned fifteen. Enough that, with the trouble I dabbled in, I'd been caught in situations when the police came charging through the front door. What inevitably happened was the biggest, strongest men in the room ended up taking me outside and staying with me until Child Protective Services showed up.

These were the only men in my life who ever really saw me, talked to me, or seemed to care whether I was alive or dead. The savior thing, the white hat thing, the hero thing: all that imprinted on my brain. So instead of hating law enforcement, I went the other way. In fact, I decided I never wanted to be the guy getting busted; I wanted to be the guy doing the busting.

Policemen were kind, solid, powerful, and—as I aged—damn hot. I was lucky. I had it better than a lot of foster kids I knew. I wasn't raped, pimped out, or molested. My foster parents just didn't give a shit at all. I had to scavenge my own meals and clothes. It was like I was invisible. The last time I was removed from a home—because the people I was living with had a meth lab in their basement—the detective who ushered me out of the house stopped in front of my guardian and punched him in the face. As the man stared up at him from the floor, the detective tugged at the clothes that hung off my too-lean frame. I was severely malnourished, and that time, I went to the hospital. It was then I was assigned a new caseworker—my angel, as it turned out—Mrs. Perez.

She was my sixth social worker. Mrs. Benita Perez changed my last name to Jones from Chukovskaya, which was what someone thought my last name was—they were never certain, it was simply on the one slip of paper I had, with Miroslav. She did it with her pen on a form and then punched it into the computer. And with that tiny change, she gave me a redo.

"I don't like Smith, so we're going with the other easy one, yeah?" she'd said, smiling at me. "Now that you're Jones, *mijo*, let's see what else you can do besides screw up."

It shouldn't have meant or done anything, but I went from focusing on being no one's kid to being a man who was ready to grow up and do something with his life.

A week later, she'd changed my school and placed me in a home in Redondo Beach. Ten of us lived there, and it was run more like a barracks than a house, but that was fine with me. Hearing Mr. Hutchins yell "Jones" when it was time for me to come to the dinner table was music to my ears. The retired Army chaplain was like the others in that he didn't care whether I was there, but at least he actually used the money he got for taking care of me to put food on the table and clothes on my back. I chalked it up as a win.

When I turned sixteen, I got two jobs, one after school at a grocery store stocking shelves and the other at a twenty-four-hour gas station. I had the overnight shift and a lot of time to sleep and study, locked in the plexiglass bulletproof cage. No one checked how old I was, no one cared. Everyone but Mrs. Perez was surprised when I was accepted to the University of Chicago, and what financial aid didn't take care of, the scholarships she helped me apply for did. The year I graduated was the year she retired. I still sent her Christmas cards in Portland.

Until I moved to Chicago, I had never had a home, nothing permanent. The dorms were a revelation—the freedom—and the job I got at the diner two blocks from campus was nice. For once I was the same as everyone else, as every other college freshman. No one looked down on me, judged me, or treated me differently. I could recreate myself, and I did.

Having figured out a long time ago that I was gay, I went to work sleeping with any guy who looked my way. It was how I met Janet Woollard, later Powell. She came charging into her boyfriend's dorm room at six in the morning and found me naked in his bed.

She screamed.

I groaned.

Her boyfriend, Todd something, ran to the bathroom and locked himself in.

"Get your ass out here!" she roared at him through the door.

I was hopping up and down on one foot, pulling on my pants.

"Oh Jan," Monica Byers clucked from the doorway, two other girls with her, all in skimpy sleepwear I would have expected if they were Victoria's Secret models. "I guess Todd got so sick of you, he went gay."

Janet's face, the look of absolute agony on it, I couldn't take.

"Dude, I'm not gay," I said disdainfully, sneering at Monica, conceited bitch that she was. She had the total Queen Bee thing going. If you didn't kiss her ass, she was a total nightmare. "And Todd's only upset because he walked in here and Janet and I were in his bed. Guy's gonna be traumatized for life."

She was stunned.

The coven with her was stunned.

And with my lie, I kept Todd's secret and turned Janet into the bad girl she'd always wanted to be. I grabbed her hand and yanked her after me out the door and down the back stairs. On the ground floor, in the common area, I let her go. She ran around in front of me and barred my exit.

"What?"

"Todd's gay?"

"Todd was curious."

"Did you top?"

I grinned. "Baby, I always top." Which was the first truth of that day.

She put her hands on her hips and stared up into my face. "How come you lied for me?"

"Because Monica Byers is the *c* word," I explained, "and I only don't use the word in deference to you. Girls hate it, right?"

"We do, yes."

"And also, you don't deserve whatever she was about to dish out."

Her eyes softened as she extended her hand. "I'm Janet Woollard."

"Miro Jones."

"You wanna come to my room? I just got back from home and my mom loaded me up with frozen food."

"You got Hot Pockets?"

"I do, plus Bagel Bites and pizza rolls."

"How 'bout waffles? It is only like six thirty."

"I even have syrup and a crapton of soda."

"Sold."

We feasted in her room, on her bed, making trips back and forth to the microwave. Her roommate, Aruna Rao, who would meet a big Irish fireman named Liam Duffy and fall madly and completely in love with him—thus keeping her from ever returning to Dallas, Texas—breezed in two hours later.

"Hello," she greeted me.

I patted the space beside me on Janet's bed. "Join us."

And while Janet and Aruna had been friendly, they were not friends until that day when we all got sloshed on way too many wine coolers. We were inseparable after that. When I borrowed notes from Catherine Mindel in my second hour Biology class and invited her to eat at the diner I worked at, putting her at a table with Janet and Aruna, they hated her at first, and then loved her a month later when we all drove to Detroit for her cousin's wedding. We bonded, and when we got back and Min Song was Catherine's new roommate because her first one had moved out—apparently Catherine had a touch of OCD—we adopted her. Min was gentle until someone came after one of her friends. Then God help you. She had actually taken apart our Philosophy professor who belittled Janet in front of the class. He took three days off after the dressing down he suffered. Janet had hugged her so tight.

It was me and the girls, and even though we all tried to make other friends, no one stuck. So the following year we moved into a two bedroom, one bathroom house off campus. I had the sofa sleeper in the living room and got really good at having sex in cars since I had no door to lock out prying eyes. Not that it really mattered; having a house where I lived with my friends did. And they never left me. One of them took me home for winter break every year. One year Aruna decided to stay so she could be with Liam and his family for Christmas; I stayed with her and visited too. They were lovely people, and his cousin Kerry was hot and willing to let me do whatever I wanted to him. It didn't last, but it made New Year's and Valentine's Day more fun than usual that year.

When four years were over and everyone was off to either grad school, law school, or medical school—and me to the police academy—I thought maybe that was it and my family was leaving me. But Liam stepped up and put a ring on Aruna's finger, so I got to keep her close. And the others weren't about to disappear. I was the envy of every straight guy I knew: I had four smart, gorgeous, talented women all enraptured by me at any given moment.

"How do you do it?" I got asked every now and then.

I shrugged and said I loved each one unconditionally. And it was true. If any of them ever called me in the middle of the night and asked me to bring a shovel and lye and to make sure the car had gas in it, I'd be there without question. Catherine was certain I'd have to get rid of her mother-in-law at some point, but as of yet, we hadn't hidden any bodies.

"I'M BACK," Janet announced as she came in the front door, Chickie staggering behind her.

"You wore the dog out?" I asked from where I lay stretched out on my sectional. Chickie trotted over, licked my chin, and then headed into the kitchen to his water dish and, even more importantly, Aruna, whom he had a special fondness for.

Aruna had never been fond of canines, but at their first meeting, she and Chickie had bonded. The only person he liked as well as her and Ian was Aruna's husband, Liam.

"Oh, there he is," she crooned to the werewolf. "There's my angel. I missed him, yes, I did. Oh yes I did."

He was whimpering with happiness; I could hear it from the couch.

"Look what Mommy has for you!"

"Aruna, stop feeding that dog people food," I admonished.

"That's steak, yes, it is," she said to Chickie, ignoring me completely.

Lord. "Don't give that dog steak!"

"We're not going to listen to him, are we? No, we're not; no, we're not. He's a buzzkill, yes, he is."

I gave up because she was going to do whatever she wanted anyway.

"Hello," Janet snapped at me.

"What?"

"I was trying to tell you that there's no way to wear that dog out, but I bet I got closer than your partner ever has."

I scoffed. "He's very scary, you have no idea."

"He may run fast, but I run far," she quipped. "My husband can barely keep up with me."

"Speaking of your husband, isn't it time for you to go home?"

"Shut up," she mumbled, walking by me, going to the kitchen where Aruna was cooking something that smelled heavenly.

"Give the dog water," I ordered.

"He has water," Aruna informed me. "And steak."

I groaned and cast around for support.

Catherine was up in the loft, on the phone with her husband, and every now and then, I'd hear her laugh in that deep, throaty way of hers.

"So," Min said docilely, taking a seat beside my legs on the couch, curling her own up under her. "How are you feeling?"

I knew her better than to believe that docility was real. She was setting me up; it was the same way she started in court, all sweet like she was a bunny instead of a tiger. "Much better."

Her simpering smile was terrifying.

"Oh, for fuck's sake, spit it out."

"Fine. What's going on with your love life?"

Silence.

"I gotta call you back," I heard Catherine say to her husband, and she was downstairs seconds later as Janet and Aruna appeared at the kitchen door.

They hovered like vultures.

Jesus.

I pulled one of the throw pillows I was using to prop myself up from behind my back and covered my face. After several moments, I lifted it up and found my four friends sitting around me. Three perched on the coffee table, staring, and Min had not moved.

"Do tell," Janet fished.

"You guys are all so pretty," I said, just to be saying something, even though it was true.

Catherine scowled, tucking a long black lock of hair behind her ear. It had come loose from the French twist. As a surgeon, she was used to wearing it like that, up and away from her face. "Answer the goddamn question."

"You swear a lot."

"So you like to remind me," she said patronizingly. "Now talk."

"Yeah, talk," Janet said sweetly. "And if there are any juicy bits—"

"Start with those," Min prodded. "I love the juicy bits."

"What do you—"

"You know who was hot?" Aruna sighed. "His boss."

"Oh, I didn't see him." Janet sounded sad. "Tell me."

"So yummy, your boss," Aruna said, leering at me.

"He's married, you know. Didn't you see the ring?" I answered.

"Which precludes the yummy factor?" Min asked. "Since when?"

"But never mind, I digress. It's so very obvious that you're in love with your partner," Aruna said with grave certainty. "So where are you in your conquest?"

"He's straight," I announced, "like he's always been and will always be. Nothing's magically gonna change."

Aruna made a derisive noise, like I was confused. "I've met him—hell, we've all met him, but I've actually been in this very room when he's here, and the way he tracks you with his eyes…. Miro, baby, he's so not straight."

"He—"

"Or maybe he is but he just wants you," Janet chimed in.

"Fuck, that's hot," Catherine whispered.

They were all driving me nuts.

"You know, since you're convalescing, shouldn't someone go over to Ian's place and water his plants and check his mail?" Min offered brightly.

"Yeah," Janet agreed. "I mean, you've got his dog, but there must be things he needs done."

"Where is this going?" I asked, suspicious.

"Well, we're just saying that his place probably needs to be aired out or something, and since you can't do it…we will."

"No."

"Why no?" Min seemed interested in my answer. "His mail is probably piling up in his box. Someone should take care of that."

"Because I don't want you guys snooping around in there."

"Miro Jones, we would never!"

Janet crossed her heart as Aruna cackled.

They were killing me. "I'm serious. You—"

"And that way we could check and see if Ian's seeing anyone else."

"He's not."

All four of them were looking at me with bemused expressions.

"No, I don't mean like, he's not seeing anyone else, I mean he's not seeing anyone at all. His girlfriend just broke up with him."

"How wonderful," Catherine said evilly.

"You're not listening to me."

"I am," she huffed. "But now I'm bored. I want to talk about right now, and since Ian's not here and we don't know when he's coming back, what else can you do… or who…."

"Oh yes," Aruna began suggestively, "we need someone new and interesting."

"What're you—"

"Like some other hottie," Janet said, waggling her eyebrows.

"Wait—"

"And you know who was just frickin' edible," Min said, moving along the couch to stop beside my hip. "Your doctor."

"Thank you," Catherine teased. "I am, aren't I?" Janet whacked her with a pillow as she dissolved into husky laughter.

"You should ask him out," Aruna insisted. "He was really pretty."

"Oh yes he was," Min concurred.

"I'll dial the hospital," Janet offered. "Maybe he'll come over here and play doctor with you."

"He might not even be gay," I protested in desperation.

Dead silence. I made a choking noise in the back of my throat.

"Man, your gaydar is for shit," Catherine assured me. "Jesus Christ, Miro, how are you missing all this?"

"Isn't it time for you guys to go home?"

Min passed judgment: "You need to get laid."

"I—"

"You can get backed up," Janet seconded, before turning to Catherine. "Men can get sick from that, can't they? That's what Ned says."

"Your husband would say anything to make sure he gets laid."

"My husband gets laid plenty," she said, giving me far more information than I needed. "But you, Miro, how long's it been? Have you gotten any since Brent left?"

"Dear God, stop," I pleaded, rolling over onto my stomach.

"Ohmygod, no wonder he's not getting laid, look at those pajamas." Min was aghast.

"I just saw the cutest lounge pants when I was online before my run," Janet said, getting up to grab her iPad from the end table. "You know what we should do…."

"Shopping!" Catherine yelled, and she gave a war-whoop for good measure.

"I can't go, I'm convalescing," I reminded them all.

"Like you need to go," Aruna said indignantly. "When have you ever needed to go?"

"Please don't throw out anything I own now," I begged.

"No, of course not," Min promised, holding out her hands in reassurance.

Aruna put a glass of water in one and a pill in the other.

"No," I said, shaking my head. "You guys can't drug me. I've slept enough."

"Listen to your doctor," Catherine said, giving me a big cheesy smile.

"But I'm hungry," I whined.

"You can eat first, honey," Aruna promised.

I gave in, took the pain pill that would knock me on my ass, and patted Chickie, who walked over beside me and flopped down on his side. I sat up and took the plate of tandoori chicken, masala dosa, and korma salad she had made special because it was my favorite.

"Thank you," I said sincerely, and Aruna leaned over and kissed the top of my head.

"Where's mine?" Janet wanted to know.

"The rest of you can get your own damn plates."

"You are getting so hormonal," Min griped at Aruna.

"It'll only get worse," Catherine explained in her doctor voice, as if we were all having a consult.

The food was amazing; I had seconds, drank a lot more water, and then lay back down.

"I love you guys," I said as I felt my body getting heavy.

"We know, baby," Aruna sighed. "We know."

I fell asleep listening to my friends talk as they sat around me on the sectional and coffee table and ate. It reminded me of how it was before I had a job where I could die and a partner I wanted badly enough that frankly no other man would do.

CHAPTER 10

TWO WEEKS later, I went with Ethan Sharpe and Jer Kowalski—Jer was short for something I had no hope of ever learning—to visit Sharpe's partner, Chandler White. We were ridiculously happy to see him cleaning his back-up gun, a sub-compact Stainless Kimber Ultra Raptor, on the coffee table in his living room.

"Why can't he go with you guys now?" His wife, Pam, whined when she got home from work. Originally she had taken family leave time, but she went back early to escape him. That she was a high school English teacher and still would rather deal with hormonal teenagers than her husband said a lot about how annoying he had become.

"Next Monday," Sharpe said, picking up the PS4 game controller as White grabbed the other. "I'll pick him up bright and early."

As it was only Thursday afternoon, she whimpered before she went to the kitchen. They looked good on the couch together, the freckle-faced, brown-haired, blue-eyed White and his taller, darker, sleeker partner. Sharpe had told me at some point that his parents met when his father was stationed overseas in Paris; his mother had just recently relocated from Delhi, so with both being new to the city, they had fallen into friendship and love fast.

"You never know when you're gonna fall in love, Jones," Sharpe had told me. "The girl for me could be just around the corner."

I had argued that he perhaps needed to slow down auditioning women for the lead role in his life. Between him and Kohn, they were running through the lovely ladies of Chicago fast.

"We gotta go," Kowalski announced, rising from the linen-covered wing chair he'd been sitting in. "Sharpe, you coming?"

No, he was going to stay and have lunch with his partner—I understood the desire, I wished I could break bread with mine—so Kowalski had to ride with me back to the office.

"Tell me about the wolf again," he asked as he got into the black Nissan Xterra I was currently driving. The Jungle Boogie car had recently been sold at auction, so I got the next vehicle seized in a drug bust.

"Ian's dad went out of town last night, so I had no place to dump him off this morning."

"Uh-huh."

"But my friend Aruna, she called me last night and said that she and her husband could take him this weekend since they're driving out to Wisconsin for a family reunion."

"Okay."

"I guess it's at some lodge where he'll have a place to run and do whatever."

"You're not afraid someone will mistake him for a real wolf and shoot his furry ass?"

"With a big lime-green collar?"

Kowalski shrugged. "I guess. At least he doesn't have one of those douchey bandanas."

I chuckled.

"So that's why you were late getting over here, 'cause you had to drop off the dog."

"Right."

"Has Doyle's wolf been with you for the whole two months?"

"Yeah."

"Gee, Jones, I wish I had a nice boyfriend like you too."

I slammed on the brakes, which made his seatbelt tighten fast, catching him sharp and tight across the chest.

"Fuck!"

"Seatbelts work," I said drolly, rolling my head to look at him.

"The problem with you is you're way too fuckin' sensitive."

I waited.

"Fine, sorry, whatever, can we go?"

I gave him the silent treatment as we sat in traffic.

"I know you miss him," Kowalski said out of the blue.

"What're you talking about?"

"Doyle," he explained. "You miss your partner. I'd miss Kohn, if he took off too. Only your partner really knows you."

Since grown men did not whimper with pent-up need, I just cleared my throat and agreed with him. When my phone rang, I was going to answer it, but Kowalski slapped my hand.

"Where's your earpiece?"

"Probably in the other car," I snapped, answering on the second ring.

"Hey," Aruna said on the other end. "Dogs can't have chocolate, can they?"

"No."

"How 'bout yogurt?"

"Listen to me: do not feed that dog people food. I told you that before."

The tsk of displeasure was not lost on me.

"Lemme talk to your husband."

Quick huff and then, "Hey." Liam Duffy's baritone swirled over the line. "What's up?"

"I just wanted to thank you again for doing this for me."

"Are you kidding?" he said happily. "He's always so good when you bring him over, and now I have someone to run with while I'm up there, and to help look out for Aruna."

It was true. Chickie had a protective instinct when it came to women and a weird herding thing he did with kids. He was always trying to corral Aruna and put himself between her and other people. She praised him for it, and he wriggled with joy.

"I think you left me too much dog food, though."

"It's funny that you think that thirty-five pound bag will last."

"Really?" He sounded surprised. "For three days?"

I cackled before I hung up.

"Seriously, Jones," Kowalski said quickly. "Where's your earpiece?"

He was so by-the-book, which made sense, because Kohn was very similar to him. Ian was not a stickler for the rules and had worn me down in some areas so that I, too, disregarded them.

"So what's it like, trying to keep Kohn's women straight?"

"What's it like having all your bones broken following around Captain America?"

"I actually break things and get shot all on my own now."

He had no witty comeback.

We were silent for the rest of the drive in, and I made sure to pull up in front of our building so he could get out and not have to go to the garage with me.

"What?"

"You can get out, I—"

"No, man, park the car. Don't be so fuckin' sensitive."

Turning to him, the mountain of muscle in the passenger seat beside me—his biceps were bigger than my thighs, his neck nonexistent—I waited.

"Yeah, okay," he snarled. "I shouldn't give you any grief about Doyle since you're moonin' over him and all."

My eyebrows lifted, and he swore under his breath.

"Just—why don't we go to Starbucks and get some fruity coffee you like."

I snorted out a laugh, because it was only getting worse.

"Fuck you, Jones!"

Letting him off the hook, I peeled out, which he liked, and drove to the parking structure. As we walked together after I parked, I stopped and checked my boots.

"What?"

"Nothing. I just don't wanna get these wet. The bottoms are leather."

He rolled his eyes. "Jesus. You and Kohn, why do you wear your good shit to work?"

It was a very good question.

I WAS at my desk later in the day finishing up paperwork to close the Tolliver case, when my phone rang. I picked it up without checking the display, preoccupied with looking for my mouse, at a loss as to where it could be. I started rifling through my desk drawers.

"M?"

I froze. "Ian?" After close to two months, he sounded really good.

"Yeah."

"Hey, buddy," I said, smiling stupidly, I was sure. God, I was so happy to hear from him. "Are you safe?"

"Yeah."

"All in one piece?"

"I am."

"S'good to hear you." It was like I could suddenly breathe, up from the deep drowning place where I'd been struggling for air since he'd left. "Back to civilization, huh?"

"Almost. I'm in Honolulu and I'm on the next flight out for Chicago in like half an hour. I'll be there sometime in the morning, so I'll see you tomorrow."

"You should sleep in, rest up." I sighed. "Me and Becker are flying out to Tennessee tomorrow to drive a prisoner back."

"Oh, so you're working this weekend."

"Yeah, and because your old man is out of town, I sent your dog to the mountains with some friends of mine."

"Well, he'll love that. Who's got him?"

"My friend Aruna and her husband. You've met them a ton of times."

"Yeah, sure, they're real nice."

Something was wrong. "You sound weird. You okay?"

"Yeah, no, just tired."

"Okay," I said, relieved, exhaling my worry. "Well, I'm bummed I won't get to see you sooner, but it'll give you time to sink back into your life a little. I can give you Aruna's number if you want to go get Chickie before I get—"

"No, that's okay. You can bring him on Monday."

"Okay, good." I couldn't stop smiling. "I'm so glad you're back."

"You missed me, huh," he said, like, of course I had. He was so arrogant.

"I did," I confessed, because that was my place in the partnership. I said it so he didn't have to. It was how we worked. "I really did." It was so good to hear his voice, to be able to talk to him whenever I wanted. "You think you'll have to go again right away?"

"I hope not."

There were no guarantees with Ian. "Okay."

He cleared his throat. "So, you do anything more exciting than leaping off balconies while I was gone?"

"Actually," I said playfully, "I'm saving that for you. We can do that again when you get home."

Silence.

"Did I lose you?" He was in Hawaii, after all, maybe some hot girl in a bikini had walked by and he bailed on me.

"I'm sorry, what?"

"What?"

"You said you're saving that for me?"

Oh, he *was* listening. "For us, yeah. I think it should be our thing now. I'm sure the boss'll be thrilled."

"Yeah, no. That should not be our thing," he said, all serious.

"Hey, so you know, White's okay too."

"Pardon?"

"Well, 'cause he was in a coma."

"He was—what?"

"I, however, was not in a coma, merely sleeping. Don't let anyone tell you different."

"I'm—you were… what?"

"What're you doing?" Kowalski asked as he rolled his chair over to me. "You need to get that done so we can go pick up our witness."

"I can't find my mouse."

"Who are you talking to?"

"Kowalski," I answered Ian.

"Who's that?"

"Doyle," I answered Kowalski.

Kowalski motioned for me to give him the phone, and I handed it off as I checked my wastebasket. Why the mouse was in there, sitting on top of the paper, I had no idea.

"Who keeps fuckin' around at my desk?" I yelled out to the room.

The denials came fast and furious. A whole room of people who'd never even sat in my chair. Right.

"Shot," Kowalski said gruffly. "Twice. Yeah, him and White. Ching too, but you know Wes. You'd have to, like, run him over or something. He was out of the hospital while your boy and White were still in surgery."

I got the page I needed opened and started to type while Kowalski kept talking to Ian.

"He lost a fuckton of blood but he saved the witness. I think all four of them—what? Oh, yeah, Kohn, too, he was good with the diversion, gave Jones time to get the witness out."

"What was the name of the auto shop Nina and I ran into?" I asked Kowalski.

"Like I would know. Look it up."

Silence.

"What?" He was still talking to Ian. "Yeah, he's good, all in one piece except for his boots, apparently. I swear to God, Kohn's the same fuckin' way. How do you deal with all the whining about the clothes?"

I snickered as he passed me my phone and rolled away. "Hey, so—"

"Shot?" He sounded like he was going to hyperventilate. "You got shot? Again?"

"Yeah I—"

"Were you wearing your vest?"

I nearly choked. "Me? Of course I was wea—"

"Why didn't somebody call me?"

"Uhm," I began, chuckling, "how were they supposed to do that, Mr. Green Beret, sir?"

"Fuck!"

"It's fine, I'm fine, all is well with the world, except, ya know, I was stuck at home for a week and then riding my desk the next, but in all that time, I still haven't finished this paperwork. Don't get shot, it's a fuckin' nightmare."

"Miro—"

"And before that I had to go out to Elgin and—"

"You had to go see Hartley?"

"Yeah."

"When was this?"

"Before I got shot," I repeated. "Are you listening to me?"

"Yes, I'm—did anyone go with you?" He sounded pained.

"No."

"Shit."

"It's okay."

"It's not."

"Ian—"

"Have you lost your fuckin' mind?"

I was so confused. "Sorry?"

"Do you or do you not need me there?"

I couldn't see him, he couldn't see me, and so there was the possibility that we were talking about two completely different things. Like maybe I was trying to make him feel better about not being there, and all he wanted to hear was that I missed him and wanted him home. Without looking into his beautiful eyes, it was difficult to guess. "Yeah," I husked, letting the wave of aching, devouring need infuse my voice for a moment. "I need you here."

He sucked in a deep breath. "Okay, so I gotta go get on the plane, but, uhm, I'll see you in the morning, all right?"

"Ian, don't do—"

"I wanna see you!"

It took a bit for his words to sink in. He wanted to see me?

"Okay? Is that fine?" he snapped irritably.

It was so much more than fine. "Yeah, that's good."

We were both quiet a moment.

"It was weird."

"What was?" I prodded, wanting to hear whatever he was thinking about. Whenever he opened up about anything, I wanted to know.

"I kept looking at the guys that were with me and thinking: if Miro was here, he would've done this or said that or whatever."

"Oh yeah? I'm easy to anticipate, am I?" I laughed softly.

"Yeah. Yeah, you are."

"What can I say, I'm a simple guy."

"I guess."

"Hey," I said cheerfully. "My cast is off, so I can throw you around."

"What?" he gasped.

"When we square off during practice," I teased. "You had the advantage when you left, man, but I can hold you down again."

His breath hitched, and I heard it even over the phone line.

"E?" I said, shortening his name to its first syllable, which I barely ever did, but he was scaring me all of a sudden. "You didn't get hurt or something, did you?"

"No, I—"

"Remember that time you got paralyzed and they weren't sure how long it was gonna last and you—"

"That was two years ago, Miro. I barely knew you."

"Do you remember or not?" I demanded, my voice rising.

"Of course I remember—why you always gotta bring that up?"

"Because you lied to me," I pointed out.

"And I apologized!"

"Well, is this like that time or not?" I asked, my voice rising.

"Not!" he barked. "It's not like that at all."

"Okay, that's all you had to say."

He had lied about where he was, and I'd tracked him to a VA hospital in Providence, Rhode Island. I had been so angry at him for pushing me away, thinking that he had to be by himself until he either got better or didn't. I was livid that he'd thought he had to handle everything alone. He was my partner and I deserved to be thought of better. He should have known that whatever it was, I would be there. I always had his back. There should never have been any doubt in his mind.

"M?"

I coughed. "Sorry, I was just thinking about the last time you were in the hospital."

"Well, I'm sorry I wasn't there when the roles were reversed."

"It's fine," I said dismissively. "But you're sure you're okay?"

"Yeah, I swear, I'm in way better shape than you."

"I'm in great shape," I defended myself.

"Except for your shoes," Kowalski chimed in with a laugh.

"What's wrong with your shoes?" Ian wanted to know.

"They're getting wet from the snow."

He sighed heavily. "What'd I tell you about that?"

"Yeah, I know, me and Kohn both shouldn't be wearing our good stuff to the job."

He was quiet.

"You still there?"

"Yeah."

"Okay, so—"

"Miro?"

"I'm fine, I promise."

"Where were you shot?"

"Once in the right shoulder and another in my left collarbone," I reported. "But nothing serious or life threatening was hit either time. There was just a lotta blood."

"You're sure?"

"Listen," I said gently. "I'm fine, E. Cross my heart. Get your ass home and you can check for yourself, all right?"

He cleared his throat. "Yeah, all right."

"So I'll see ya when I get home from picking up—" I had to check the paperwork on my desk. "—Drake Ford."

"He sounds like an actor or something, huh?"

"Yeah, he does." I chuckled.

"Okay, well, I gotta go."

"All right, be safe."

"Always," he grunted and the line went dead.

"I think that was the most words we've ever said to each other," Kowalski commented, glancing over at me.

"Well, that's Ian, Captain Communication."

Apparently that was damn funny. Kowalski choked on his coffee.

CHAPTER 11

BRENT IVERS had lied.

He'd said he was on a business trip and only visiting the Windy City from Florida. But it turned out the new job was a bust, so he'd moved back. All of that was in a message he'd left me when, as he explained, "that coven of yours wouldn't let me in to see you after you were shot." Apparently he'd called when I was in the hospital, and after Aruna informed him I'd been hurt in the line of duty, she went on to clarify that under no circumstances was he allowed to see me. She threatened him with bodily harm, and he reported all of it in his second message. He was still ranting on the fourth one he'd left.

"He sounds nuts," Kowalski said as he dealt the cards.

I was explaining it to the table at our regular Thursday night card game, this week at Becker's house. Originally we'd held the game on Fridays, but me, Ian, Kohn, and Ryan were all single, and Friday was the night we were usually out getting laid.

"Maybe you need a restraining order," Kohn suggested before taking a long drag on his beer. "I can get one tomorrow since you'll be on a plane with Becker."

"You don't need a TRO for your ex," Mike Ryan—tall, dark, and built like the swimmer he'd been in college—explained to me. "Gimme his address and me and Sharpe'll go over there and have a talk with him. He won't bug you after that."

"Yep," Sharpe agreed from where he sat across from me.

I laughed. "I can fight my own battles, thank you, gentlemen. And it's not like that, just funny, is all."

"Yeah, it's a riot," Jack Dorsey said as he walked back into the room from the kitchen and passed Becker a Corona. "But if you see him hanging around, polishing a knife, you let us know."

I scoffed. "Absolutely. Hey, Jack, I have a question."

"What?"

"I was meaning to ask, what happened to your brother and his partner? I haven't seen either of them here in months. I miss taking money off the nice ATF agents."

He grunted. "Elliot's partner moved to this little asscrack of a town in Kentucky with his boyfriend and—"

"What?" I blurted in surprise.

"What?" he parroted.

"That guy I met, Pete… he's gay?" Holy crap, maybe the girls were right to give me shit about being oblivious. All I'd seen when I met agent Peter Lomax and his partner, Jack Dorsey's little brother Elliot, was two very alpha guys. They both came off as swaggering douchebags in the nicest way possible. It had been obvious that Jack had a good relationship with his brother, and by extension, Pete. But I had no idea Pete was gay; he hadn't pinged my gaydar even once.

"I thought all you gay guys knew each other," he said seriously.

"You did *not* just say that," Sharpe remarked dryly.

"What?"

"Finish your damn story," Ching directed.

"Well, whatever. He's gay, and so he moved to be with his partner, and so two months later when another opening came up in Louisville, my brother and his wife moved there too."

"No shit." Kohn sounded surprised too.

"Yeah, I mean, I thought for sure his wife Felicia would be upset about it, but her family ain't here, they're in Cincinnati. So it's actually closer for her to see her side."

"That sucks that your brother's not here anymore." I said sympathetically.

"Yeah, but he'll visit in the summer, and me and Sandi are going for like a week around Labor Day," Dorsey said, and he sounded okay with it. "And then he's coming home for Thanksgiving. So it won't be like it was, but it's okay. I mean, I get it, right? I love my family but I spend more time with Ryan than I do with my wife."

Sharpe nodded. "Yeah, I mean, if your partner moves, you're supposed to do... what? Just get a new one? How would that work?"

I looked around the room. I couldn't imagine Ryan without Dorsey, Ching without Becker, Kowalski without Kohn, or Sharpe without White. Or me without Ian. It was weird to even contemplate. And when one of us was away—or two as it was now, with Ian gone and White still off work—we all swapped around. Even though every single one of us would take a bullet for any of the others, your partner was the one who always had your back, who rode to the hospital in the ambulance if, heaven forbid, something happened, and he was the guy who always thought how much better whatever it was would be if you were there.

At least that was how it worked for me.

"What the fuck is this?" Ryan complained loudly from the kitchen.

Glancing over at him, I saw him holding up a thinly sliced piece of meat.

"It's prosciutto," Kohn called over.

"What is that?"

"It's like fancy super-thin sliced salty ham," Kohn continued.

"Why does it have a whole other name?"

Kohn huffed. "Why are you asking me? I'm Jewish; I don't even eat that crap."

"Just eat it," Kowalski ordered Ryan.

Ryan growled, and I would have said something, but Dorsey joined him in the kitchen to try it.

"It's good whatever the fuck it is," Ryan said, shrugging.

"I want a sandwich," I announced.

"Well, get the fuck up and make it," Ching instructed.

I snorted out a laugh, folded my 2 and 7 off suit, and got up.

"Oh, oh!" Becker said, his phone in one hand. "It looks like boss man says that I ain't makin' the trip to Tennessee."

"Then who's going with me?" I asked, glancing back to the poker table.

Everyone checked their phones and no one else had a text.

"Oh man," Ching groaned. "Tell me we don't have a newb."

Kohn cackled. "I bet we've got help since White and Doyle are both still out."

"Yeah, but White should be back next week, and Doyle'll be back… when?" Becker asked, glancing toward me.

"Monday."

"Yeah, see?" he said, looking at the others. "There's no room at the inn. We got everyone we need."

"Don't be an elitist pig," Ryan warned. "If the team never grew beyond the first guys, it would still only be me, White, Sharpe, Dorsey, and Kowalski. You wouldn't even be here. Change can be good."

We all threw food at him.

"Assholes!"

It was good to laugh with all of them, but really. Babysitting for a twelve-hour drive was not my idea of fun. I'd rather go alone.

SINCE I was flying, I had been smart and stopped drinking right after midnight, chugged water, and took Tylenol before I went to bed. So when 6:30 a.m. rolled around and it was time to get up and go to the airport, I was in pretty good shape. At the gate, I was slurping coffee and sipping from a bottle of water at the same time.

"Did you get water for me?"

Ian Doyle stood over me, dressed casually with his military backpack slung over one shoulder.

We weren't supposed to stand out in any way; we weren't marshals transporting a witness, instead we were just two guys on vacation. But there was no way for him to blend in. Even in the junker pants and military boots, the white T-shirt under the heavy wool sweater, and the duffle coat I'd bought him for his last birthday, he looked amazing. Nothing he had on went together at all, and yet, the smirk made that fact meaningless. I was weightless with happiness.

"Oh shit." I whimpered without meaning to, leapt to my feet, and grabbed him tight.

Because he was slightly taller, whenever he hugged me, he leaned heavily, giving me more of his weight than he was probably aware of. I loved it because it meant that, every time, we notched together tighter than I did with anyone else but a lover.

"You thought I'd make you have to endure a whole day in a car with Becker?"

He smelled so fucking good, like the damn citrusy soap in his bathroom and the aftershave he bought at a little place in Chinatown. Supposedly he wore it because it took care of razor burn, but I didn't care. I liked the way it smelled. It was like mint with a trace of lemon, and woodsy and smoky at the same time.

He chuckled. "Did you miss me?"

"Yeah," I whispered, realizing that for once, he was hugging me back as hard as I was hugging him.

"That's good."

He already had clear blue eyes and dimples, a smile so incredible that once you saw it you'd do anything to see it again, and a long and lean powerfully muscled frame. It was ridiculous, really, that he also smelled like heaven. To be fair to the rest of us, something needed to be wrong with him. Various women in his life had complained about everything from intimacy issues to him being crappy in bed, but I didn't actually buy that he wasn't perfect. An asshole, absolutely, but no more than any other guy I knew.

I pulled back, because any longer and the hugging might have been weird for him. I didn't want to make him uncomfortable. "So," I said, smiling like an idiot, I was sure. "You look good, no holes or nothing."

His brows furrowed.

"What's wrong?"

"Right shoulder and left collarbone?"

"What?"

"Where you were shot?"

"Oh. Yeah." I put my hand on my right shoulder. "Both went straight through, so it was no big deal. I was really lucky."

The muscles in his jaw tightened, and I slipped my hand around his throat, rubbing over his jaw with my thumb.

"It's okay."

His gaze stayed locked with mine, and then I noticed the feel of Ian's whiskers under my callused thumb and realized what the hell I was doing.

Coughing, I moved my hand. "I'll go get you some water," I announced. I didn't wait for him to say anything, bolting away instead.

When I returned to the gate, he had his coat off, discarded on the seat next to him, and was bent over, hunting for something in his backpack. As I watched, he pulled off his sweater, rucking the T-shirt up, revealing the bare stretch of skin of his powerful back.

I was abruptly bumped from behind and twisted to see a woman looking at me, mouth open, before she snapped it shut.

"You walked into me," I teased.

She bit her lip.

"'Cause you were looking at the pretty man."

A nod.

"So was I," I confessed, and she smiled at me before she rushed off.

After taking a steadying breath, I walked up to him at the same time as he pulled a dark blue Henley over his head and tugged it into place.

"What was wrong with the sweater?" I grumbled as I flopped down into my chair and held the bottle of water up to him.

"I'm burning up. It's hot in here."

"Could you not get naked in front of everyone?"

He squinted at me. "I'm not naked. I'm taking off my sweater."

I pretended to be engrossed with checking my phone for any status changes until the call came for boarding.

"What's wrong with you?" he asked while we stood in line, his backpack slung over one shoulder.

"Nothing," I said, because it would pass—the feeling I always got when he returned home. The surge of possessiveness nearly choked me every time. It was like I needed him marked or something, I wasn't sure how, or… I just needed people to know he belonged to someone and that they shouldn't think he was attainable.

"You always get like this when I come back."

I ignored the comment even though he was right. Immediately after the vicious desire to keep him—to tie him down—dissipated, I was hit with the exhaustion of having to redo all my work. Getting Ian comfortable with me, getting him to trust me, was like housetraining a feral cat. His time away always erased whatever had been built up and I was back to square one. He would come back to our world and his training would be riding him, looking for threats from every corner, and that included me. It was so tiring, the uphill battle of returning to Ian Doyle's circle of trust.

"Maybe you would have liked Becker with you better," he muttered under his breath.

"Becker keeps his clothes on in the middle of airports," I said petulantly, the only thing I could think of to say, smiling for the gate agent who scanned my boarding pass.

"Have a nice flight, Mr. Jones."

"Thank you," I said crisply, striding forward quickly, putting a little distance between me and my partner.

He caught me quickly on the Jetway, his hand on my left shoulder, his fingers digging into the muscle there. "Why're you…."

He didn't finish and neither did he move his hand, and after a moment I registered that he was using a lot of pressure to hold me still. I could feel the heat from his hand through the zippered cashmere cardigan and T-shirt, and a throb of need spurred by the rough caress went straight to my groin.

I'd never survive ten to twelve hours in a car with him if I didn't get myself under control. I should have slept with someone, anyone, even Brent, while he was gone. As it was, friendship and lust were riding me at the same time. It was a bad combination.

"You're so hard all over, M," Ian said softly, brushing against me as we moved forward. "I bet you could…."

I waited, but he didn't say more. "Could what?"

He shrugged.

"No, c'mon. Could what?"

Quietly, he cleared his throat. "I always wonder how you can move so fast and run guys down and go deep when we play ball, being as bulked up as you are."

It had been a conscious choice. When I was little, I was small, and people took things from me. They took shelter, food, and money, anything that was mine, because I was weak. Now that I was older, between the strength in my body and the gun I carried, I would never be anyone's victim again.

"It's because I'm all power, buddy," I teased, bumping him gently, wanting us to be back to how we were before he left, so desperately, but knowing it would be weeks before we would be okay. "You know that."

"I...."

When I turned, he caught his breath, and for a second, I let down my guard and gave him my total and undivided attention. I was usually so careful: I reminded myself often not to stand too close, not to turn my head so my lips accidentally grazed his ear or jaw or cheek when he leaned in to tell me something. I didn't touch him too much, I hugged him only when he left or came home or when one of us almost died. I didn't study the clear blue eyes or notice the flecks of silver in them or admire how dark they shaded when he was worried or excited or angry. When we played football, I always played on the same team so I would never have a reason to tackle him. And most of all, I never, ever, manhandled him. I knew if I ever put my hands on him, I'd never take them off. But his sharp inhale, the sound of it, wasn't like fear, but like vulnerability and need, like submission.... My hand moved before my brain caught up.

I grabbed his bicep and yanked him sideways against me. I immediately saw the confusion on his face, but even more importantly, I noted the blown pupils, the parted lips, the flush that blotched his throat, and the shiver that ran through him. And for once I didn't think about what it would mean if it was anyone *but* Ian, and instead thought about what I would do if the beautiful man beside me was a stranger.

Breathe in—

My vision blurred for a second, like the beat of my heart was an electromagnetic pulse, and everything stopped. I was frozen, trapped, aware of nothing and no one but Ian Doyle.

—breathe out

The rush of movement and color and sound was fast, so fast, but it was enough. I wouldn't have to start over with him this time, but only if I changed *everything*. I had a decision to make: Pretend I had never glimpsed any want in the man or take the leap of faith.

All of it hit me within seconds of recognizing what I had been missing when I was with him.

"Miro?"

Maybe it was a mistake, but I had to know. Because if there was even the slightest chance that Ian could be mine—I had to take it.

The people in front of us moved and he made to follow, but I tightened my grip and didn't let him.

I received a quick exhale followed by another sharp intake of breath.

God, how blind had I been?

"M?"

"Sorry," I said quickly, letting him go.

It was almost scary to realize that if I was reading him right, if Ian wanted what it seemed like he might, then this would be the very last time I wouldn't be able to touch him whenever I wanted. Everything would change, because Ian Doyle would belong to me.

BUSINESS CLASS was a few steps up from coach, so we had more leg room, more seat room, and fortunately, only two seats next to the aisle.

"You should sit by the window," I directed. "You're gonna pass out as soon as we take off, and that way I won't have to climb over you."

"Okay," he agreed, getting in after I shoved our coats into the overhead bin. We had to keep our carry-ons with us at our feet since we had our badges and guns in them.

Once we were settled, listening as the captain welcomed us aboard, explained that we'd be taking off on time, and directed us to give our attention to the flight attendants, I sucked in a breath, lifted the armrest between us and leaned into him with my whole body. All along one side—shoulder, hip, thigh, knee—we were touching. I waited— mouth dry, heart stopped, left hand clenched into a fist—to see what he would do.

"Did I miss lots of poker nights or did you guys not play?"

I turned my chin so I could look at him.

He was waiting.

"I—what?" I rasped. My voice sounded like I'd been choked to death. I needed some water.

"Did you guys play cards or no?"

Weird thought: maybe he didn't realize I was crowding him. "Yeah, we played except for the week my clan was here. Last night I took home eighty bucks."

"Impressive," he said, and he tried to smile but it looked odd, strained. "And that's nice that your friends came to see you."

"Yeah, it was."

"But they wouldn't've needed to if I was here."

"No. You would have taken care of me."

"Yes," he agreed, studying me. "You should drink some water, your voice sounds funky."

That was my cue, so I leaned forward, pulled my water bottle out of the seatback pocket where the barf bag was, took several deep gulps, and, when I sat back, gave him room.

I was so relieved he wasn't pissed that for a second I didn't register what he was doing.

"I swear I'm cooking," he grumbled, reaching up to turn on the air vent. He fiddled with it, and when he sat back, he pressed up against me, exactly as we'd been moments before. "Aren't you hot?"

Was I too warm?

"There's never enough air on planes."

I was freezing.

"And staying hydrated is important."

My throat was dry; drinking *something* was a good idea.

"Are you all right?"

I wasn't. I was terrified. But I was ready. One way or another, I would find out what I could have. I put on my seatbelt then, right before the flight attendants checked. I never put it on until I absolutely had to.

"M?"

"No, I'm good," I said softly. I let out a deep breath, feeling the calm wash over me as I closed my eyes and listened to everything going on around me. I registered people talking, bells dinging, the sensation of lifting as we took off. Most of all, I savored the closeness the man sitting beside me was allowing.

I'd had fantasies, of course. They always started off fast and hot. He would walk across a room, throw me up against a wall, and take me right there, rough and dirty. Or we'd be stuck somewhere, in some tiny little hole in the wall, like a border town in Texas or... the scenarios were always the same, with him jumping me.

He was a super soldier; he threw around guys twice his size. I'd seen him do incredible things with his body; his strength was daunting, and in combat training, he'd taken on ten men at once. His spinning high kick was really something to see. I never worried when he was with me, *never*. Even if, for some reason, we were ever unarmed and cornered by people who were, still, even then, I wouldn't worry. Maybe that was unrealistic, but he was a Green Beret. They dumped him behind enemy lines to retrieve others and that's what he did. Thus, because I knew *so well* the kind of man he was, there had never been a time when I thought *I* would be the one holding *him* down.

But he was waiting for me to do... something. It was so very obvious. The hitched breath, taking direction, wanting to be close.... I'd been missing all the clues. I was normally much better than that, and it was probably why everything with me was off, why I missed it when guys were hitting on me, oblivious to the signs and innuendo. Ian Doyle had totally jammed me up.

I had always thought that if he ever even considered sleeping with me, it would be him on top—when apparently the truth of the matter was it would be me.

"M?"

I found him smiling at me.

"The nice lady wants to know if you want something to drink."

The flight attendant was waiting on me. I'd lost time, totally checked out, absorbed as I was with Ian. "Sorry, uhm, just some apple juice, if ya got it."

"Sure," she answered, smiling at me and then looking to Ian.

"A Coke'd be good."

We both got plastic cups with ice and the cans, along with bags of pretzels.

"What're you thinking about?"

I shook my head. "You should read up on Drake Ford."

He nodded. "Gimme your laptop. Mine isn't updated since I haven't synched it with the mainframe in two months."

Leaning over, I lifted my bag up onto my lap and pulled it out for him.

"Thanks," he said, smiling. "So, this is okay, yeah? You're not afraid I'll find any porn or anything?"

I scoffed. "All my porn's on my desktop at home."

"I see. More memory."

"That's right."

He chuckled as he put down the tray table and opened the laptop. "Hey, M, your e-mail's still up."

"Go ahead and close out of it. It's frozen anyway."

"Oh, look who it is," he muttered. "Brent."

"You can't delete it, I'm not connected. But the stuff you need to read is on the desk—"

"I'm reading, shut up."

Groaning, I bumped his knee with mine. "I'm ducking him and he's getting annoyed, I guess."

"You guess? Did you read this? He sounds a little off."

"He'll be fine."

"He—oh, this is kinda… explicit."

"Yeah? Lemme see," I teased, reaching for the screen.

He bumped me with his shoulder, and I laughed as I settled back in my seat.

After a minute of more reading, he cleared his throat.

"What?"

"I wanna ask something, but maybe it's too personal."

"No such thing," I assured him, easing close so he could whisper if he needed to. "Tell me."

"Brent, he—it sounds like he… like…."

Ian was nervous. How much hesitancy, choking on words he couldn't say, and restless unease needed to be piled on before I did something? Before I acted?

"What did—I mean, do you…. Wait."

"Do I what? Want Brent?"

He nodded, clearly uncomfortable.

"No. I don't want Brent."

And that fast, he was better. Was that relief? How long had I been missing all this?

"But he clearly still wants me, or at least wants what I used to do to him." I turned my head so my lips brushed his ear as I spoke. "Brent liked me on top. I like that better, but I can do either."

Sharp indrawn breath.

"I like the control of topping. I like making someone else take me in. I get off on that."

He didn't shiver; it wasn't that gentle or controlled. He trembled.

"Ian," I said, turning into him, sliding my hand under the tray table and up his thigh—slow, so he could stop me whenever he wanted—until I reached his groin. His eyes were heavy-lidded, sweat sheened his forehead, and the dappled flush was back, spreading over his throat.

"When you come back from being away, it takes you weeks to settle down and be okay with me again."

"Oh yeah?"

"Do you know you do that?"

"It's not so easy to simply walk back into my—"

"Is there something I can do to show you that you're home and safe?"

Silence.

"Ian?"

But he couldn't say. He couldn't tell me. I was just supposed to know. Giving in to temptation, I cupped him through his pants, feeling the long, hard length under my palm.

His halting groan was all agony.

"I'm gonna think I can take what I want, if you don't say anything," I whispered.

Now there was a reason for him to remain quiet.

"Ian, this is like steel, buddy," I said hoarsely, my voice deep and low as I stroked over the cock I had seen so many times but never touched. He bucked, wanting my hand, needing the friction; his soft, low moan was the sexiest thing I'd ever heard in my life. "If I wasn't on a fuckin' airplane, I would take this down the back of my throat for you and suck out every drop."

He jolted, and I worried for a second that I'd pushed too far, scared him, been stupid, shredded three years of friendship in a rush of desire. But instead, he took a deep breath and exhaled slowly before turning to me.

"Don't be a fuckin' tease, all right?" he said gruffly. "Do what you say."

I nodded.

"And you can't—I've seen how you are, with guys. You fuck and forget or you pick the wrong ones, like with Brent."

"Yeah," I husked.

"But you can't do that with me. You gotta mean it."

"Okay."

"It can't be just whatever. I value myself more than that."

Had I been that much of a whore before Brent? "Course."

He took a breath. "I think there's a reason I'm shitty in bed."

I felt myself frowning, unhappy with him running himself down. "Which is?"

"I think it's 'cause I've never been in bed with you."

CHAPTER 12

IT WAS the longest three hours and thirty minutes my life. We had a stopover, but where, I couldn't say. No one else on the flight to Blountville, Tennessee, growled when the captain announced that there would be a slight delay with landing.

"I like that noise," he teased, patting my leg and then leaving his hand there, slowly sliding it sideways to my inner thigh.

I counted to fifty. In German.

Once we landed and were out of our seats, I mapped his frame as he walked ahead of me, like I never had before. The rolling swagger of his walk, the tight round ass, the veins in his wrists and forearms, and the flashing smile that had only ever been for me… all of it I appreciated and wanted to be mine.

I had a singular agenda. Carving out a path through the Tri-Cities airport, I said excuse me a lot and people moved for me, not the other way around.

"Why are we jogging?" he asked as I grabbed his arm and dragged him after me.

"I will kill you if you don't keep up with me."

"Like I can't keep up with you," he scoffed.

At the car rental counter beside the baggage claim, the lines were long and I couldn't take it. I pulled my badge—which I never did—announced that I was a federal marshal, and jumped to the head of the line.

"Technically," Ian apprised the woman preparing the paperwork. "He's a deputy US marshal. We only say federal marshal during a raid or something."

"Uh-huh," she said, nodding.

"And that was a dick move," he scolded me, but really, I couldn't have cared less.

Once I had the rental contract in hand, I led him out the doors to the rental cars parked in long rows.

"Where do we get the key?"

I couldn't even talk anymore; it was too far beyond me. My heartbeat was so loud in my ears, I was amazed he couldn't hear it.

Presenting the contract to the girl waiting under the canopy, I tried my best to smile, hoping not to scare her. It must have worked, because instead of running away, she directed us to the left.

"Any of the vehicles in that last row toward the parking structure, gentlemen. The keys are in them, but remember you have to drive back this way to get out."

The car itself didn't matter, only the distance between the entrance to the lot and where it was parked.

"Where are you going?" he asked as I hurried, walking fast. "Shouldn't I be the one to pick since I'm the one who—"

I couldn't wait even a second more. We were as far away as I could manage.

Rounding on him, I fisted my hands in his coat and dragged him between two enclosures, then around the side, thankful that while the partitions between every two cars were tarps, the walls and frame were metal. After slamming Ian back against it, I took his face in my hands, pulling him forward at the same time I leaned in.

I ground my mouth over his, forcing my tongue between his lips, craving his taste, his heat, all of it, everything he had to give.

I suffered a split second of terror that maybe having me all over him would be too much, but he sank into the kiss, melted against me. His whimpering moan was decadent, rich with submission and desire. The need to claim him and mark him was utterly primal, and I aggressively mauled his mouth, sucking, biting, and taking what I had to have.

His hands scrambled on my peacoat, wanting in, unbuttoning, parting, lifting my sweater, pulling the T-shirt free. His hands on my skin had me moaning into his mouth, and when he pressed his groin to mine, grinding, pushing, I realized through the haze of aching, helpless desire that I was just as hard as he was.

He lifted his mouth from mine for a second, for a quick gulp of air, and then he was the aggressor, kissing me hot and wet, tipping my head back to shove his tongue down my throat before licking the roof of my mouth, the inside of my cheek, missing nothing. I whined when he pulled away and then quivered at the sound of the low chuckle before his teeth sank into the spot where my neck met my shoulder.

I ground out his name. He must have liked it, because he pivoted and drove me backward into the same wall I'd held him against moments before.

"Shit," he panted, and I had a second to admire what passion looked like on him: swollen lips, flushed cheeks, dilated pupils, and hair spiked up with sweat. It was incredible. "I didn't hurt you, did I? Sometimes I'm too rough and—"

I lunged at him, reclaimed his mouth, my lips covering his, kissing until I felt the fear leave and only need remain. He was boneless in my arms, pliant and willing, and it was then that I yanked him sideways, switching places so it was Ian, again, with his back to the wall.

"M," he moaned softly. To hear such a sound of longing come out of the man drove me to my knees. "I—you can't."

Quickly, expertly, I got his belt unbuckled, pants unbuttoned, zipper down, and gorgeous erect cock leaking in my hand.

He bucked forward and his voice cracked. "I… Miro… I haven't even been able to get—"

"Get what," I asked before I licked over the swollen crown, then nipped and sucked at his groin.

"Hard," he choked out.

I grinned up at him. "I don't think that's an issue."

My name spilled out of him like smooth thick honey from a squeeze bottle.

Opening my mouth, I rolled forward and took the man down the back of my throat in one long sensuously smooth motion. His hands instantly clutched at my hair, and I liked that, his loss of control.

His heavy breathing, the way it stuttered every few moments, how he couldn't stop his hips from snapping forward, I savored every one of his reactions, but most of all the feel of him in my mouth, the weight on my tongue, his taste, his musky woodsy scent. All of it, of him: I could get addicted so very fast. When I wrapped my hand around the base of his cock and made the suction strong, licking and laving, he stopped forming words, only making deep guttural noises.

I tasted salty precum. He tried to move me, but I made the draw stronger instead.

He shivered and I purposely scraped my teeth along his thick shaft. The carnal growl of my name was sweet.

"You can't—M!"

He spurted hot in the back of my throat, and I swallowed fast, taking it all, loving the way his lips parted and his head fell back against the wall. I didn't let his cock slip from between my lips until there was nothing more and I had licked away every trace. He was the picture of sated lust, utterly ravished as he stood there panting, eyes narrowed to slits of blue, fly open, shirt and Henley rucked up, stubble burn on his pelvis as well as bite marks and hickeys from where I'd sucked on his skin.

When I stood up, we were eye to eye since he was slumped against the wall, still not moving. He was worrying me a little. Even though I knew he'd liked it when I was blowing him, I wasn't so sure how he felt now.

"You should put this away, buddy," I said softly, stepping in close to him, lifting his briefs up over his now-flaccid cock, tucking him in. "I don't want the whole world to see you."

"You didn't care about that a second ago."

I met his gaze. "No one saw your dick since it was buried down my throat, not to mention that there is no one out here in this cold but us."

He inhaled sharply, straightened, and took my face in his hands, then slid his thumbs gently over my cheeks, beneath my eyes as he eased me forward and sealed our lips together.

His lips were soft, the kiss tender and deep as he slid his tongue over mine. One hand pushed into my short hair, his fingers tracing the curve of my skull, finally cupping the back of my head, holding me still. Compared to the frantic mauling I had given him, his movement was sensual and deliberate.

He could kiss me forever if he wanted. The languorous attention made me feel drugged as he feasted and sucked, licked and nibbled on my lips. I succumbed easily, and when he turned me, pushed me back into the wall, I let myself be moved, bumping gently into the concrete as he deepened the kiss, not letting me breathe, only taking.

His hands slipped down the sides of my neck to my shoulders, then lower to my chest, clutching at me, touching me. I was arched against him, painfully hard and needing to be stroked, when the blast of a horn startled us.

Someone drove by on the other side of the wall, obviously having gone the wrong way to get out. I noticed then that Ian's pants were still shoved to his knees—no wonder he'd shuffled when he walked me back into the wall—so I bent and pulled them up around his hips.

"Now you're worried about someone seeing me?" He chuckled, low and seductive.

I zipped him up, still not meeting his gaze, and slid my fingers into his pants to button them. He bucked and I framed his hips with my hands, loving the fact that he was letting me touch him like this, so intimately.

"How come you weren't before?" he whispered, leaning forward, the huffs of breath in my ear and the sensation of the stubble on his cheek against the scratched-up skin on my face making me shiver.

I was terrified that I was dreaming. "I wasn't thinking before."

"Yeah?"

After I buckled his belt, he crowded close, shoved his thigh between mine, parting my legs, wedging himself tight against me.

"Look at me."

I lifted my gaze to his and saw the apprehension there.

"Don't go all silent."

He was standing in front of me, clothes rumpled and hair tousled, and I could barely breathe.

"Okay?" he murmured.

"Yeah."

His hands slid up my sides. "You gotta talk some."

There was so much to say, to ask for, and I was afraid of hoping for too much.

"Will you get in the car?"

"Sure," I answered as he stepped away. It was ridiculous, but I already missed his hands on me.

"How 'bout the silver one?"

"Whatever."

It was a Dodge Avenger, and when we got in, he made sure I was comfortable, checked that I liked the interior before he eased the car out of the parking stall. We had to stop at the gate so the attendant could check that we had a contract, ask us to confirm the mileage in his computer, and make sure we had a full tank of gas. Once that was done and we were on the street, I got my phone out to check the GPS and see where we were in relation to Elizabethton.

"It looks like it's only like forty-five miles or so away."

He grunted.

"So it's like one thirty or so here. I'm sure we can be there in an hour, easy."

"Uh-huh."

Ian wasn't really listening to me.

"Tell me when you're ready for me to navigate."

"Yep."

I sat back and got comfortable. "We should stop and get water."

Another sound of concession to acknowledge he was listening. Sort of.

Giving up, I looked out the window at the gray March afternoon, wondering how cold it was outside. The weather had been so odd, and in January, with the freaky cold snap, it had been nuts. It was probably in the thirties now, snowing a little.

Ian stopped at a Walgreens, ran in, came back out with a bag, and tossed a bottle of water at me as soon as he was back inside the car.

"Chips? Vitamin Water, other snacks? What are you, a communist?"

He snorted out a laugh but got the car moving and pulled out of the parking lot fast without even putting on his seatbelt.

"What's in the bag?"

"Nothing."

"What's wrong?"

But he didn't answer, and I noticed he was not getting back on the highway.

"Ian?"

THE STARLIGHT Motel had one of those old neon signs that looked like it belonged in Vegas, not downtown Blountville. It was three stories of mauve and pink, and when he pulled into the driveway, parked beside the office, under a carport, I wasn't sure what was going on. But he got out, forked over some cash, got a key—on one of those plastic numbered plastic tags the likes of which I had only ever seen in a movie—and then got back in the car with me.

"What're we doing here?"

I got nothing from him.

He moved the car and parked again, grabbed his backpack, and ordered me to get out and grab my duffel.

"Ian," I began, doing as he asked, closing my door as he made the alarm chirp. "We need to go and get our—"

"Shut up," he snapped, starting up a flight of stairs that had a chipped white paint railing I would not trust my weight to. It seemed more decorative than anything else.

At the top, he strode fast and reached the door he wanted, 15A, opened it, and disappeared inside before I caught up.

"Holy shit," I groaned, following him in, amazed at the pink shag carpet, floral print curtains, and the mauve quilted polyester bedspread. "This is like the hotel we stayed at in Fort Lauderdale, you remember?"

"Yeah," he said hoarsely, slamming the door and sliding the chain lock on before he rounded on me.

It was dark inside, but enough faint light filtered through the front window's drawn curtains for me to see him staring at me—his eyes glittering—tracking my movement, listening to me breathing. Like I was prey.

Sometimes I didn't pay attention when I really should.

"What are we doing here?" I asked, my voice low and rough.

He huffed out a breath as I took a step forward, closing on him.

"Ian?"

He raked his fingers through his hair and then laced his fingers together at the back of his head. It was new, the uncertainty on him, and I found it endearing.

"What's in the bag?"

"Lube."

I nearly swallowed my tongue in surprise.

"What? We need it, right?"

"If we… yeah," I stammered. "I hope you got the right kind."

"Me too."

"You could have sent me in."

"I wasn't really thinking."

I liked hearing that.

"It might not… happen, yeah?"

"Sure."

"And I maybe won't be able to… all of it."

"I know."

"But we'll still be… all right." It was both a question and a statement.

"Yes," I said with absolute certainty.

"Okay."

"You're sure?"

He licked his lips, nodding slowly.

I slid a hand around the back of his neck and drew him to me. His eyes drifted closed as I slipped my tongue in the seam of his lips. His moan was soft and sweet as he parted them for me, kissing me back, his hands on my hips.

"Ian."

He grunted, not stopping the kiss, moving me back toward the bed.

"Will you let me lead?"

Please, God, say yes.

He made a noise that sounded like agreement, but I wasn't sure, and I had to be. Breaking the kiss, I stepped sideways so I wouldn't topple back on the bed.

"Ian?"

He was staring at me intently, waiting.

I had to tell him what to do, I instinctively understood that. No wonder he'd supposedly been crappy in bed with Emma and the others, he was supposed to be the one leading and he wasn't made that way. I could see it all over him, the tremble that engulfed the hard-muscled man. He looked like he should be the one throwing me down, taking what he wanted, but instead, he was waiting for instruction.

The time for more questions was past. I couldn't ask what he wanted, I knew that. If I asked permission, I lost control, and Ian craved my dominance. He had always noticed my body, the innate physical strength in it, but he had never guessed at the leashed power inside. But I understood that a part of him wanted to be held down, wanted to be made to submit, and intuitively, he'd known I could do that for him.

It was scary. If I messed up, I not only ruined a friendship, but a partnership as well. If I'd misread him, what he needed or wanted, I wouldn't recover. If I was somehow wrong… but how could I not take the chance to have everything? Not knowing, that was worse. I was a lot of things, but a coward wasn't one of them.

All of this rushed through my head while Ian remained frozen, waiting and vigilant.

"Come here," I ordered.

He moved fast and I drew a fortifying breath.

"Take everything off."

Instantly he tugged off the duffle coat, let it drop, and then reached behind his back, between his shoulder blades, and pulled his Henley, and the T-shirt underneath, forward, up, and off. Watching him strip for me sent blood rushing to my cock, and I realized that being in control of Ian *and* myself might be more than I could handle.

"Aren't you gonna take off your clothes too?"

I cleared my throat. "Don't worry about me. Just get your shoes off."

He toed them off, sat and pulled off his socks one by one before getting to his feet fast to yank down his pants and briefs. After stepping roughly from them, he waited, hands on hips, for what would come next.

"Pull the covers down and get on the bed, in the middle, on your hands and knees."

He moved without question, and admiring him—the play of muscles under his sleek skin, the tight round ass, the powerful lines of him, his back, his thighs and legs—made my mouth dry. Every part of the man was sculpted and beautiful and scarred. He was a mess of heavy silver tissue in some places, spiderweb-fine lines in others from stab wounds and bullets, and of course the crisscross pattern on his back where he'd been flogged over and over for weeks. Scar tissue was a funny thing; under the skin it became like a root system, branching out from one place and rippling outward. On top of the skin, it became patterns, almost art, sometimes raised with how heavy it was underneath. It hurt to think of Ian being brutalized, but each mark had made him who he was now. I planned to trace each one with my fingers and tongue.

"Where's the bag?" I asked softly, trying to keep the ferocious desire in check.

He pointed at the nightstand, not moving, not embarrassed or telling me to hurry up.

I slipped around the bed fast and glanced at him as I did. His long gorgeous cock was curling up toward his stomach and drooling precum. The whole thing, my giving orders, turned him on big time.

Behind him, I shed my coat, my heavy sweater, and the T-shirt underneath, and when I unbuckled my belt, he shivered. I saw it.

"You're beautiful," I whispered, leaning forward to smooth a hand down his flank. "You know that, right?"

He caught his breath, and I smiled as another shudder ran through him.

Leaning back, I pulled my pants off, left my socks on, and climbed onto the bed behind him. When I kissed the small of his back, pulling the cellophane off the tube at the same time, he let out a low moan of need.

"I'm gonna tell you what I'm doing all right?"

He nodded.

"First I'm opening this tube of lube you got." The pop of the cap sounded loud in the quiet room with only Ian's breathing breaking the silence. "I would have liked a thicker one for your first time, so I'ma be gentle."

"I don't—just not slow."

"Why not?" I asked, curling over him, snaking my arm under him to take hold of his heavy cock and stroke him from balls to head.

"Miro!" he yelled, bucking forward into my fist. "Please."

The garbled request in Ian's gruff rumble was something I'd only ever hoped to hear.

"I have to—" He gasped as I slid one slick finger between his cheeks, his entire body clenching at once. "—you have to…."

I squeezed his cock and he heaved out a breath, relaxing at once as I slid my hand up and down his shaft, fondled his balls, and slid my thumb along the slit of his large flared head.

"Are you ready?"

"Yes," he rasped, wriggling under me.

"Ian," I said huskily, drilling my middle finger deeper, pressing against the spongy entrance, circling and then pressing steadily inside. "I want you to feel good."

"I do. Just hurry." His demand ended in a deep groan as I angled my finger forward, grazing his prostate, making him jerk in my arms. "Oh fuck!"

It was a very good sound. "Has anyone ever done this?"

"No."

"Ian, have you? Tell me."

"Miro," he whimpered, "I didn't know I would…."

"What?" I asked, stroking inside his body, relentless with my attention. "You didn't know you would what?"

"Want this," he rasped, leaning forward and then pushing back, jolting as he did it, rubbing over the spot that, from his reaction, no one else had ever touched.

I moved in and out, over and over, added a second finger, working him gently, slowly, relaxing his muscles in careful stages. His crown was swollen in my other hand, steadily leaking, adding to the slide of my hand over him.

He was sweating and shaking, and when I added my tongue to my fingers, he yelled my name.

"You're doing great," I praised softly, nibbling his ass, licking, and finally taking a gentle bite.

"I-I feel like I'm gonna break if you don't hurry."

Straightening up, I gently withdrew my fingers and released his dick. "Come, then, we can do this when you—"

"No, not like…." He released a huff of breath, almost crying out at the end, and I could tell from how rigid he'd gone that me not understanding was frustrating.

I was making him ready, opening him up, but also now killing him with my hesitancy.

"You need to stay still while I put on the condom."

"What condom?"

It was my turn to jolt. "Ian, I figured when you bought lube you bought condoms."

"Did you see them in the bag?"

No, actually, I hadn't. "Yeah, but you know I've slept with a ton of guys."

He looked over his shoulder, into my face. "Me too. Well." He shrugged. "Girls, but we get tested every six months, and I've never had sex without a rubber."

"No," I said, coughing. "Me neither."

He let his head drop back down. "Yeah, so, we're good and I trust you and you're already my best friend, so… nothing, okay? Just us."

I was going to come inside my best friend, the man I wanted more than anything. Dear God, I wanted to keep him.

"You're thinking too much."

I was.

While slathering my cock with lube, I pressed fingers back inside his slick hole, scissoring them apart, over and over, firm but gentle.

"You need to push out when I push in, you understand?"

"Yes."

"Grab your dick, Ian. Get yourself off."

"Don't need to—" He gasped. "—do anything."

"Okay," I husked as I lined my head up with his pink puckered hole.

"Stop thinking," he pleaded.

As though I could keep a thought in my head that wasn't Ian.

Easing forward, I pushed slowly inside, then stopped, waiting, letting his body get used to the invasion, feeling his muscles clamp down around me.

Ian dropped onto the mattress, arms not able to hold him, only his ass raised as I breached him, watched him take my cock inch by inch. He was so tight, so hot, and the slide was easy despite the muscles rippling around my length.

"Miro," he ground out, and the sound of him was annihilating.

He tensed against me, but my angle, the force of my weight, was too much. I drove deep with one fierce thrust, buried completely.

"Oh fuck," Ian moaned, and his voice broke, cracked, and I heard when it changed to a cry.

I was about to pull back, but his arm rose fast, his hand like a vise on my thigh, holding me still, keeping me there.

"Wait."

Of course I would; I would do anything he wanted. I was balls deep in the one man in the world I wanted my whole life to be about. Whatever he wanted, needed, I would give.

"Miro."

But I wasn't in control, and that was bad.

Leaning close, I ordered him to lift up, my low voice in his ear. When he rose, I wrapped an arm over his shoulder and across his chest, grabbing hold of his left pectoral as I braced us both with my left arm.

His head fell against my shoulder, and I stamped ravenous kisses to the length of his throat as my chest plastered to his back.

"Miro," he huffed, writhing under me as I ground my hips forward, pounded into him deep and hard. "Don't stop."

No.

No stopping.

"You have to jerk yourself off," I ordered as I sucked and licked and kissed his jaw, throat, and down the side of his neck to his shoulder. He tasted like salt and sweat and smelled like him, like Ian, and I wanted all of him on my tongue.

"I don't—you have me."

"Yes," I croaked, moving my mouth, needing to reach his back, taste there, lick there. "I have you, I won't let go."

The words were necessary and I understood that.

I eased back, put Ian on his hands, took hold of his hips, and then hammered back inside.

He yelled my name.

I did it over and over, wanting to be deeper, the need desperate, to be entrenched in him, to make it so he could never forget that I'd had him, even if he tried.

Licking up his spine, I felt his muscles clenching around my shaft, tightening fast, holding me. I reached under him and grabbed his cock roughly, tugging and squeezing, and when I felt the first stream on my fingers, I let go.

"I can't hold… Miro!"

"Just come," I demanded thickly.

He gasped with his release, as I fucked him through his orgasm, loving the feel of his silken inner walls milking my length. He shivered as I came, pulsing within his body, semen filling his spasming channel.

"It's warm," he said as I collapsed over his back.

His breathing was ragged, and I thought maybe I should move, but my climax had taken everything and I needed a second to reroute blood flow.

"Don't move, okay?" Ian murmured.

He didn't have to ask twice.

CHAPTER 13

I WAS careful when I slid free, moving cautiously and then shifting him sideways so he wouldn't drop into his own cum pooled on the sheets. I rolled off the bed, went to the bathroom, and found a washcloth and towel. I cleaned myself off, and then made sure the cloth was the perfect balance of not-too-wet and not-too-wrung-out, and moved quickly back to where Ian lay collapsed.

Gently, I parted his cheeks and wiped him up, kissed the small of his back before I returned to the bathroom and hung both towels up. When I walked out, I was caught in his deep cobalt eyes and stopped where I was.

He didn't say anything, his gaze simply moved over me, up and down and back, then locked with mine.

I cleared my throat. "Did I hurt you?"

Slight shake of his head.

"Okay."

His eyes were so dark at the moment. I had never noticed his thick and long lashes before. The flush all over him was beautiful, but even more so were the marks I had put on him standing out starkly against his olive skin.

"Can I come over there?" I asked.

"Please."

I hurried but diverted at the last moment to get to the thermostat. I cranked the heat up to 72 and then dived onto the bed. He turned his head to look up at me, and when he did, I saw the wicked, easy smile. It was enough.

Dumping him on his back, I sank over him, taking his mouth in a long, slow deep kiss, tasting him all over again, not letting him go until I felt his cock thicken between us.

"Damn, Doyle, your recovery time is amazing."

"Not usually," he murmured as I slid an arm down between us, taking hold of him, smearing the leaking precum over his crown.

"You want to put this inside of me?"

He squinted. "Is that what you want? Because you keep asking."

I never second-guessed him. It was not something that occurred in our relationship. I never checked once he said something, but here, I was doing just that. My questions were killing him, instilling doubt, and I had to remember how he was out of bed and not mess up. Normally, I asked once. I got a yes or no and never revisited whatever topic had been discussed. I needed to treat this situation just the same, as we lay there skin to skin.

"If you want something, you tell me."

"I always do."

"Okay."

"And you? What do you want?"

"I wanna be back inside you, but I think I need to slow down. How 'bout we talk some?"

He nodded, rolling sideways, propping himself up on his elbow, looking at me.

"I went to one of those clubs, you know."

"What're you talking about?"

"You *know*," he said pointedly.

I scooted closer, and he put a hand on my hip. "No, I really don't."

"A sex club."

"What?"

"A BDSM club, to be exact."

Shock tore through me, but I swallowed it down to keep it out of my voice. "You did?"

"Yeah."

"And?"

Maneuvering closer, he took hold of my thigh and lifted it over his hip so that my hardening shaft slid along his. Having the sudden urge to hold him, I didn't second-guess it and took him into my arms, tucked his face into the crook of my neck, and hugged him tight. His mouth opened against my throat; I was not proud of the mewling noise I made.

"How come you never did that before?" he asked quietly.

"Because I never thought you'd let me."

He eased free of my arms. "You should've known better."

And he was right. I should have, and would have, if I had been paying attention at all. As it was, I had been so wrapped up in my feelings that I had completely missed his.

Small things, like the way he gave everyone else space but me, how proprietary he was about all my things—from coffee cups in the office to books I loaned out—and how he never, ever, missed a chance to go anywhere with me if he could help it. Ian was my shadow, and I'd never seen it for what it really was.

"I've wanted to touch you," he said hoarsely.

"You have no idea about wanting," I replied, my voice rough.

His lip curled into a slight smile as he looked down the length of my body and watched his hand move over my chest, my abdomen, and finally lower to my swollen cock. "It felt different."

"What?"

"You."

"How do you mean?"

"Your skin, your hands… no one ever held me down before."

Big question. "And was it okay?"

"Yeah, it was okay," he groaned brokenly, shifting and settling over me, laying his head on my chest, and wrapping his arms under me.

God.

I was so done. If my life ended right then, I was good.

"You make the best noises."

"Pardon me?" I hadn't been listening.

"You do. Maybe you don't think you do, but you do."

"Not following."

"I can tell you're content right now 'cause of the noise you made."

"Which was what?"

"Like purring."

I scoffed, but he tightened his hold and I liked that. "Tell me about this club you went to. I wanna hear the story."

"Well, there was a woman at the first one I went to, a dominatrix, yeah?"

"And?"

"I let her chain me up, and she had all these paddles and whips and stuff."

"Ian, you've been hit enough in your life—tortured when you've been on missions—and you shouldn't—"

"Who's telling this story?"

I shut up but ran my hand over the raised scars on his back.

"I told her I changed my mind, and she was cool about it when I left."

"Why'd you leave?"

"Because I knew she couldn't actually keep me there if I wanted out, and it's not pain that does it for me," he said, edging out of my embrace and rising as I shifted a bit, staring down into my face. "I mean I never got off when someone was torturing me or beating the shit outta me."

I nodded quickly, swallowing my sympathy.

"I don't like to be hurt—don't wanna be."

"Sure."

He licked his lips nervously. "Is it okay if I touch you?"

It was all I had ever wanted, so *yes*, he could touch me, lick me, kiss me, bite me, hold me down, snuggle up into my shoulder— anything. Anything at all. I was simply desperately ready to accept all he offered. But the excitement and longing that roared through me would scare him to death if voiced. So I whispered instead. "You can do whatever you want."

He traced a finger down the side of my cock before leaning close to examine me. "This is impressive, Miro. Not only long, but thick. No wonder you made sure I was ready, huh?"

"I made you ready because I would never treat you any other way," I chided.

"And you liked doing it," he said, his gaze snapping to mine, daring me to lie.

As if there was any question. "Yes."

"Did I taste good when you blew me?"

"Yeah."

"I wanna try," he rumbled, bending over me, his tongue flicking over my cockhead.

"Wait," I rasped, my breath stuttering.

"Why?"

"Put your hand around me so you don't choke."

He took the direction and licked and sucked, laving me with his tongue, swallowing the precum that dribbled from the head.

"It's thick and salty, but it doesn't taste bad."

"All guys taste different," I managed to get out.

He made a face. "Like I would know."

"Do you want to?"

The half grin flipped my stomach over as he sat up, straddled my thighs. "I went to a gay club because I figured maybe that's what I needed."

Breathing was overrated, and I could hold out until I heard what he had to say.

"And I realized when I was in there that it turned me on."

"What? The men?"

He shook his head.

"The submission," I concluded.

"Yeah."

"But not to a woman."

"No."

"Because a woman wouldn't actually ever be strong enough to make you do anything."

"Not without a weapon or something."

"But that's not what we're talking about."

"No."

"The illusion of power won't work for you."

"No. It has to be real."

"Okay, go on."

"So this guy, he starts manhandling me and shoving me forward like he's gonna belt me onto this St. Andrews's Cross, and I'm thinking—yeah, he'll have to have all those buckles and shit to keep me from moving. And there's probably real ones that I couldn't get out of. But I can see that it's not riveted, so I can pull out the carpenter nails easy, flip it, do something. That wouldn't hold me."

That's what Ian did, he analyzed everything.

"But I started thinking: it would take time for me to get out once he has me in it, and he can do whatever he wants in the meantime."

"Yes."

"And that's the part I can't have. No stranger puts their hands on me, that's ingrained too deep."

"You take women home from bars, Ian. They're strangers and you fuck them."

"Yeah, but I know names, and none of them could hurt me," he explained. "Plus, I never sleep with any of them. I drive them home right after."

"Emma slept over."

"Because that lasted more than one night. And she hated sleeping over because she was afraid of Chickie."

I smiled and he grinned back.

"Tell me about the Dom."

"Well, so I gave him the go ahead to hurt me if he needed to, whatever he has to do to incapacitate me, right? He's supposed to make me submit."

Oh God. I was terrified to imagine what Ian had done. He wasn't known for his patience. "You didn't kill him accidentally, did you?"

He leaned over, hands on either side of my head on the mattress. "I put him in a sleeper hold and he passed out."

I reached up and put my hands on each side of his neck. "You're not supposed to hurt your Dom, Ian."

"I didn't hurt him," he said hoarsely, swallowing fast as I smoothed my hands down his chest to his stomach, stroking gently until I reached his hard arching shaft. "And I paid him for his time."

"I thought there was a safeword."

"Yeah, I know, but I forgot it."

"How do you forget the safeword?"

He shrugged.

"You didn't think you'd need it, that's why."

"Probably."

Only Ian.

"So," I said, toppling him over, shoving him onto his back, grabbing the lube beside me. "Tell me what you learned from all that?" I notched against him, my dick sliding over his crease. "Ian?" I asked as I flipped the cap and squeezed lube over his cock.

"What're you—"

"Tell me," I insisted, coating his cock and my fingers at the same time before snapping the tube shut and tossing it out of our way. "What conclusion did you come to?"

He drove himself into my slippery fist, mouth open, eyes closed, letting his head tip sideways. He pressed his temple against my forehead when I leaned down.

"Ian," I coaxed gently, sucking his earlobe into my mouth.

"Isn't it…. Miro," he pleaded, "I know you know."

"But you can't skimp on the words this time, you gotta say it."

He inhaled sharply. "I want to be held down by someone who could actually hurt me—"

"And?" I pried, needing more from him because it was important, because it would ground both of us.

"—but never would."

It was me, only me, and we both knew it. The only person in the world he was completely himself with, whom he trusted implicitly, was the one in bed with him. "I would never hurt you," I promised, placing his hand on his cock before I pulled away just enough so I could smear the excess lube on mine. "And you know that."

"I do."

He was safe with me, and no one else could make him feel that way because I had nurtured this relationship for the past three years, as had he. "You have to be honest."

"Yes."

"Okay," I said, pressing two slick fingers to his entrance. "Tell me if you're sore."

"I'm good."

Entering slowly, I twisted and pushed, rubbing circles until his muscles softened and gave, kissing down the side of his neck.

"You're not giving your dick any attention," I reminded him.

"What're you gonna do?"

"If it won't hurt you, I wanna fuck you like this."

Deep sigh from him. "Yeah, do that."

Slipping my fingers free, I notched against his entrance and then slid steadily forward.

"Miro." My name in his throaty whisper sent stinging heat through me, and I forgot the careful and the slow and shoved in in one long smooth glide.

The noise he made was a moan and a cry wrapped up together. It terrified me. "Ian?"

"It feels like that every time?"

The awe in his voice restarted my heart. "Yes," I answered, slipping out only to ram back in, making sure he felt every motion of my cock grinding over his gland.

"Fuck!"

I pumped in and out, lifting his leg and holding his quivering thigh in my hand.

"Kiss me." I snapped out the command, and he strained to sit up enough that I could devour his mouth.

He broke the kiss for breath, and when he did, I pulled out. His yell surprised me, and when I moved to the edge of the bed, he tackled me, crossing my wrists over my head and holding me down with one hand, the other on my chest.

"Why would you stop?"

"Put one foot on the floor," I directed, "and then lower yourself down on top of me. You're strong enough, you can do that."

He nodded, doing as I said, braced himself over me, one hand buried in my hair, the other at my side as he held me there before I shoved up inside him.

"God, Miro, I'm so full."

"It's different with this angle," I said, hands on his thighs, holding him tight as I slid out and then pistoned up into him.

His mouth fell open and there was no sound, only him obviously feeling, panting, the sensations overwhelming as I did it again and again, not stopping, wanting only to be inside him. I was lost in the action—nothing else mattered.

"Miro!"

He spurted over my chest and abdomen, and I pulled him down, impaling him on my cock as I came deep inside his body seconds later.

I checked out for long minutes, the white that exploded behind my eyes not easy to simply climb out of. Like always, though, once I became aware of where I was, I felt the weight of his stare. The deep, dark blue was really something to see.

"You okay?" I asked.

"Yeah," he said as I realized that unless he moved, I couldn't.

"I need to clean you up."

"Let's take a shower, change, and go get our witness."

"No nap?" I whined without meaning to.

"No nap," he said, curling over me. "But I'll feed ya." Again he lifted my arms above my head, this time each wrist pinned to the mattress as he hovered close. "You hungry?"

"Starving."

"Are you okay?"

"Yes," I said, unable to control my grin.

"We're gonna have to talk at some point."

"About?" I asked, almost gasping as the muscles in his ass flexed, sending a twinge of pain along my oversensitized nerve endings. Softening inside of him sounded hot, but it was actually uncomfortable.

"This, obviously."

I stared up at him and noticed his red, swollen lips, hooded eyes, and the marks all over him. No way to miss that he'd been ravaged. "Like what?"

"Like," he replied, tightening his hands on my wrists, his thighs around my hips. "Will we do this when we get home?"

He posed the question, at the same time testing if I'd let him hold me down. In answer, I yanked my right arm out of his grip, and before he could grab me again, I dropped my left foot onto the floor and kicked off, giving me enough momentum and leverage to roll him to his back and pin him beneath me. The entire maneuver was fast, jarring, and most of all, forceful. I didn't miss his sharp inhale.

"I want to," I answered before dropping down beside him and drawing him to me, sliding his leg over my hip so we were plastered together, joined everywhere. "But we don't need to say it right this second."

"I think we do."

Oh. "Do you? Want to?"

"Where would we be?" he casually asked instead of answering, even though his eyes betrayed him, flickering with concern, searching mine.

I knew him, his tells. He was waiting for any hesitation from me. I barreled forward instead. "You could hang with me at my place whenever you want, and bring Chickie. You already have a key."

"Yeah," he agreed thoughtfully.

"And I could sleep over at your place once I get my hazmat suit back from the dry cleaner."

His brows furrowed. "What's that supposed to mean?"

I grinned slowly. I had successfully restored normalcy and balance.

"It's not that bad."

"Janet and Catherine went over there to check your mail, and Cat said she wasn't going back without making sure her shots were up to date."

"Yeah, but—"

"Janet said that if I'd let her take my gun, she'd go back."

"Knock it off." He chuckled, letting his head fall back when I bumped his chin with my nose. Ian was more relaxed than I'd ever seen him, vulnerable as he lay in my arms.

I pressed a kiss to his throat.

"You'd stay there, right?"

I would sleep wherever he liked for as long as he let me. "Yeah." I just wanted to be in his bed.

He traced over the two newest scars on my body. "Don't do this again."

"I'll try."

"Try harder."

"Yessir."

WE STOPPED for a late lunch at a pancake place, badges out and strapped for the duration of the trip. I ate like it was my last meal. I was so hungry and between the coffee, orange juice, and water, the waitress wasn't sure what other liquid I could possibly need.

Ian had coffee and water and watched me hoover up pancakes and sausage, eggs, hash browns, and grits as he wolfed down steak and eggs. I paid like I always did on Fridays, as we had every day of the week accounted for and it was the only way for meals to not devolve into arguments. It used to be both of us trying to treat the other, which got old fast. Our system worked better.

After hitting the bathroom, I met Ian in the lobby, and as I yawned, shoving my coat at him while I put on my hat, two state troopers stepped in front of us. A third was hanging back.

"Help you?" Ian asked.

The trooper tipped his head at the gun holstered on my belt.

"Oh, sorry," I said, smiling, lifting my sweater so he could see the star on the other side. "We're marshals. My ID's in my coat right there."

He let out a breath, and his smile was instant as the two others joined us. "Your waitress saw the guns when you were getting up."

"'Course," I said with a shrug. "You gotta check."

He gave me a friendly nod before Ian grabbed my bicep, grunted a good-bye, and tugged me after him.

"What's wrong with you?" I teased once we were outside. I pulled on my coat. It was freezing. "You gotta be nice to local law enforcement."

"Why?"

"In case we need them."

The look on his face showed me exactly what he thought of that, and it wasn't much. "This isn't even where we need to be, M."

"Yeah, but—"

"Just come on."

Once at the car, I put my fist above my palm in the international sign for rock-paper-scissors.

"I always drive," he informed me.

"Yeah, but," I began, unable to keep from grinning, "it might be easier for you to get comfortable if—"

"Get in the car," he barked.

I tried to stifle my laughter.

"Now," he growled, getting in and slamming the door.

Once inside, I turned to him.

"Navigate already, will you?"

I pulled my phone from the breast pocket of my coat.

"Isn't that the peacoat you made me buy?"

"Yeah."

"So it's mine, but you're wearing it."

"Yeah," I grunted, checking the directions. "Okay, so you're gonna go out here and head south. You're looking for 394 to—what?"

He was waiting.

"Ian?"

Taking hold of the wool and cashmere coat, he tugged me close. "This is the weirdest blue, you know."

"It looked good on you," I said softly as he pulled the knit cap off my head. "You trying to let the cold get me?"

"In the car with the heater?" He snickered, easing me forward until his lips were a hairsbreadth from mine. "I think you'll live."

I sighed, so pleased that he couldn't keep his hands or mouth off me. "You need to get us on the road."

"Yeah," he admitted, kissing me fast, biting my bottom lip, tugging it with his teeth a second, inhaling deep, before he let me go and turned all his attention to getting us out of the parking lot.

"That's not fair," I complained, my body thrumming with sudden need. And it wasn't even sex anymore, though that was always welcome. It was more than that. I just wanted to be naked in bed with him.

"It'll level off."

"What's that?"

"The hunger."

"We just ate," I reminded him.

"I'm not talking about food and you know it."

I did, but I wanted to hear him say it. "If you're doing it right, it shouldn't."

He shook his head. "There's no way to contain that level of desire for—" His breath hitched when I grabbed his thigh and squeezed tight.

"Listen," I said seriously, meeting his gaze. "Don't speak so authoritatively about things you know nothing about."

His attention focused completely on me.

"Neither one of us has ever been in this exact place before."

He gave me a quick nod.

"So knock it off."

He didn't agree, but he didn't argue either, which I took as a win. Moments later he turned his attention from me to driving the car.

"Level of desire, huh?"

"Shut up."

I smiled. "Hurry up and get us out of the parking lot, Doyle. I'm e-mailing the boss with status."

He said nothing, just took a left out onto the street, merged too quickly, and headed for Bristol Highway by way of 394.

"How long on this?"

"Like five and a half miles," I said absently.

I directed him onto other highways until we were finally on 19E heading for Elizabethton.

"There are a lot of Christmas-tree farms here," Ian commented as we headed for the Carter County Sheriff's office.

"Yep, trees and meth are both big business here."

He laughed softly.

"Hey, do me a favor. When we get there, let me talk to them."

"What?"

I grimaced. "You always end up pissing the local guys off."

"I do not," he argued.

"You do. And stop being so defensive."

"That's insane."

But half an hour later when we had reached our destination and then gotten the run around, he was yelling.

"What the hell?" Ian barked at the deputy in front of us. "How do you release a goddamn federal witness?"

The sheriff was not in, but Chief Deputy Greg Walker was. It was the two of us and nine other men in the office. Ian was trying to get a story out of Walker while I was on the phone with Kage.

"What do you mean they don't have your witness?"

"Apparently he was released to the Bowman Police Department yesterday afternoon," I replied.

"Why?"

"He wasn't coded to be released into federal custody, but police custody."

"How?" Kage asked irritably. "Are there even local police departments there? I thought there was only one centrally located sheriff's department and then the state police."

"I have no idea, but the town's in Virginia, not Tennessee."

"Virginia?"

"Yeah, so he's in Bowman, which is in Lee County, Virginia. So maybe there, there's a police department."

"How big can Bowman be?"

"Not sure," I answered, searching it on my phone at the same time I talked to him once I put him on speaker. "But it's along US 58 right after Ewing."

"How far is that from where you are?"

"Almost two hours."

"What time is it there now, like four something?"

"Four thirty, yeah."

"All right, so get to Bowman, make contact and get a room for the night. I need status twice more today."

"Yessir."

"How's Doyle?"

"Sir?"

"He just got back, and I understand this last op went bad."

It had? That was news. I didn't usually ask how Ian's missions went, because he wasn't supposed to talk about them. But I was surprised that he hadn't said a word to me about it in this case. "Oh, I dunno."

"But he's good?"

"He is."

"All right. Give me status when you reach Bowman."

"Yessir."

Kage ended the call, and I looked up in time to see Walker pick up a phone. "You're out of line, Marshal, and I'm gonna have your badge!"

Of course. During my minute-and-a-half conversation with Kage, Ian managed to piss off everyone in the room.

"You'll be lucky to make it out of this with yours," Ian snapped.

"Your ass is mine!"

Technically, his ass was spoken for.

Ian tipped his head and gave him a smirk. "Give it your best shot."

Everyone was tense, no one moved, and I stood and waited as Walker called the sheriff.

"Sir, I have Deputy Marshal Doyle in front of—" Walker stopped and listened. "Supervisory Deputy?"

Uh-oh.

"I don't know what he—" Again Walker was interrupted. "He wasn't listed as a federal—"

I moved up beside Ian. "It's two hours."

"Yeah," he grumbled, not taking his eyes off the deputy on the phone in front of him. "Which is nothing, but still, this is stupid."

I coughed. "So our boss says that you had a rough op this last time out."

"They're all the same."

"What did you do?" I asked softly.

"Extraction."

"Did everybody come home?"

He coughed. "No."

"I'm sorry."

"We saved our target; we accomplished our objective," he said automatically, but the muscles in his right cheek were doing the *ticking* thing they did when he was tense, and his brows furrowed.

"What happened?" I gently pried.

"The intel was bad, and we got dropped into something bigger than we expected."

I put a hand on his back. "Will the guy who delivered bad intel get in trouble?"

"That guy's dead."

Jesus.

"Ian?"

He shook his head slightly to shut me up as he took a step forward. Walker had hung up the phone.

"The sheriff says that we can put both you and your partner up here, on the department, while we retrieve Mr. Ford from the Bowman Police Department."

"No thanks," Ian said snidely. "We'll retrieve him ourselves. God knows how long it would take if we wait on you."

Walker's jaw muscles clenched, as did those in his neck. He *so* wanted to run Ian over with his car. The animosity was transparent.

"We'll be going," I said gently.

"We're at your disposal, should you need us," Walker said, obviously having been charged with repeating the statement.

Ian scoffed, turning to leave. "Yeah, like that'll happen. I'd be better off with mall cops and security guards."

When I closed the door, I heard something shatter against the wall. "Your interpersonal skills are fantastic," I mentioned for perhaps the hundredth time in our partnership. He could have turned Gandhi into an ax-wielding psychopath.

He grunted, and when we were in the car, he looked at me.

"What?"

"It was a bad op, but I've been on even more fucked-up ones that have ended way worse."

"Okay."

"But what I hate now is, at the end, when it's done, I can't immediately come home."

"You have to be debriefed, right?"

"I mean after that."

"You don't just get on a plane?"

"No, we have to wait for orders to come through."

"And you don't like that, the waiting."

"No. I don't."

"How come?"

"That should be obvious," he said gruffly, starting the car.

"Tell me."

"Why you think?"

"I'd rather not guess."

"My home," he said curtly, "the job, stuff like that."

"Chickie," I offered playfully.

"And others."

"Others?"

"Yeah," he said sarcastically, "other annoying people who know better than to fish but do it anyway."

I was very pleased with him and chuckled while I checked my phone.

WE DROVE in silence except for the music on my phone. He never cared what I played which was lucky since my taste could nicely be called eclectic.

"US 23 North to Virginia," I said, getting drowsy. It was warm in the car, the heat on since it was only 28 degrees outside. "We should stop and get some Mountain Dew or something."

"Take off your coat."

It was a good idea. After mine was off, I helped him with his.

"So tell me why Drake Ford is going into WITSEC," Ian said abruptly.

"Because he saw Christopher Fisher try and burn up Safiro Olivera in an abandoned building in Gatlinburg six months ago."

"Okay."

"Apparently Ford and his boyfriend, Cabot Jenner, were running away from home at the time of the incident, and when Ford went out to get something for them to eat, he saw a man carrying what he thought was another man over his shoulder, into a building."

He glanced over at me. "Are you serious?"

"I can't make this shit up."

"Okay, so Ford, he sees something weird, follows this guy Fisher, who happens to be in the middle of committing a murder."

"Cleaning up," I corrected. "Fisher is in disposal, not killing. But yeah, pretty much."

"What an idiot."

"Who? Fisher or Ford?"

"Both, but Ford more so."

I chuckled.

"So what'd he see, exactly?"

"He saw Fisher spread out the body of Safiro Olivera, douse it with what he thought was lighter fluid, and then walk away."

"Walk away?"

"Yeah, Fisher was setting up blasting caps throughout the house with trace amounts of C4."

"How is that arson, then, and not an explosion?"

"That's how they know this guy's an arsonist, it's his signature. First, there's a small explosion inside the building, and that ends up triggering a four-alarm fire."

"Okay. So he leaves, and our boy gets on the phone and calls the police."

"Right."

"And they arrive and catch this guy in the act before he actually gets a chance to start the fire?"

"You're very good at this game."

"Shut up," he grumbled and then pointed at the side of the road. "And what the hell is with all the gigantic-ass crosses along the highway?"

"This is the South?" I offered, not sure what other reason there could be.

"Not really."

"What part of Tennessee isn't the South?"

"So… what? There's crosses all over?"

"It's roadside religious propaganda," I informed him. "Repent now."

"It's creepy, is what it is."

"Moving on."

"Fine, whatever. So Ford calls the cops; cops pick up who, exactly?"

"Christopher Fisher, serial arsonist and clean-up guy for the Malloy crime family out of Richmond."

"I've never heard of them."

"They move meth and OxyContin, dabble in prostitution and gambling. Compared to what we're used to, they're not a huge deal, but they had Fisher on the payroll."

"Who will now be rolling on them?"

"Yes."

"Which is why Drake Ford is going into WITSEC."

"Yep."

"But not the boyfriend."

"No."

"But Ford just got transferred back to Bowman, where his boyfriend is?"

"Yes."

"That sound fishy to you?"

"It does, yeah."

"Could young Jenner arrange for his boyfriend to be brought back to town?"

"Doubtful."

"But someone else could."

"Yes."

"But for what reason?"

"I dunno. How old is Ford?"

"Eighteen."

"And the boyfriend?"

"Same, just turned."

"Have they even graduated from high school?"

"Not until May."

Ian was working it out in his head. "Okay, so what do we know about Ford and Jenner? Were both sets of folks okay with it?"

"No, actually. Jenner's father has had Ford charged with everything from trespassing to car theft to kidnapping."

"Kidnapping?"

"Yep."

"How does one minor kidnap another minor?"

"Well, Ford just turned eighteen—like I told you—and there was a two-month period in there where Cabot Jenner was still seventeen."

"That's ridiculous."

"I'm not arguing with you."

"Okay, so it's safe to say that Jenner Sr. wants Ford gone."

"Yes."

"Holy shit," Ian barked. "You know what happened."

"I do now," I sighed. "The Bowman Police Department sent someone to take Ford back."

"And they have no idea who's actually coming for him—no clue who they're dealing with."

"Nope."

"Ford's in danger when the Malloy family finds him, but so is everyone else."

"Because the sooner Ford's dead…."

"The sooner Fisher is released from federal custody and no one's worried about him spilling everything he knows."

"Yep."

"Did you already let our boss know that?"

I waggled my eyebrows.

"So, you're what, catching me up?"

"Yep."

"Ass."

I laughed as his focus returned to the road.

"Where am I going now?"

"You have forty more miles on here, so sit tight. The next thing you'll be doing is looking for US 58, also known as Wilderness Road, and you won't get off that. It goes right through the center of the town."

"The town is divided by a highway?"

"Yeah."

"So what does our boss want us to do about the Bowman Police Department? Alert them that we're coming, or no?"

"He says no since we're not sure what's going on. He has the state police on alert to give us whatever backup if and when we require it, and he warned me that we're on a two-hour window of check-in."

"Like I can't handle myself."

"It's me he's worried about, Captain America," I said snidely.

"I have your back."

"I know."

He was quiet for a few minutes. "So we'll need a place to stay tonight."

"I'll find one," I said, looking up from my phone and the e-mail conversation I was having with Kage to Ian's profile. "Once we figure out what the deal is with Ford."

"Okay."

We were both quiet for a bit.

"Who's Safiro Olivera?"

I cackled.

"I'm tired, I have an excuse. But I got to it after a few minutes."

"Yes, you did."

"Tell me."

"Safiro Olivera is Leandro Olivera's little brother."

It took a moment, but then it hit him.

"Are you kidding?" he asked dryly.

"Nope. Christopher Fisher was trying to dispose of the body of the nephew of Lior Cardoso, who's the number three man in the Nava Cartel, one of the most violent drug cartels in Mexico, that just so happens to be based out of Tijuana."

"Fuck."

"That's what the FBI said."

"Why is Ford even important anymore? Fisher's dead without protective custody."

"But he doesn't know that. He has no idea who Safiro Olivera was, and neither does Orson Malloy."

"Who?"

"Malloy crime family." I snickered. "Are you listening to me?"

"Not really."

At least he was honest.

"I don't wanna talk about this anymore."

"Fine."

"New topic."

"We are a go for new topic," I said, yawning.

"How come you haven't slept with anyone since Brent?"

"What?" I asked, flustered. Christ, the places Ian's mind went.

"You heard me. Why no fucking since Brent?"

It was a tricky thing to confess, and more importantly, was that the right thing to do? Was it smart to tell him? Would I freak him out? "I haven't been interested."

"In anyone." He made it a statement.

"Yeah."

"No one at the gym."

"No."

"No one at the soccer league you play in?"

"I was shot, in case I forgot to tell you. I was pretty busy convalescing."

"I see."

"What are you trying to ask?"

"I'm not asking. I just think you're full of shit."

"Oh yeah?"

He didn't push. He went quiet instead as he drove.

CHAPTER 14

WE TOOK a turn off Wilderness Road and drove straight up into the hills. The town of Bowman was nestled close to Cumberland Gap National Historical Park, but not close enough to reap any benefits of tourists. Rockslides and landslides were prevalent, and apparently the town could be cut off at times because of those kinds of disasters. Presently, it was covered under a layer of fluffy white snow.

Driving through town, we passed huge stretches of private land. Interestingly, on one side of the four-lane road stood many houses, on the other, rolling hills, ponds, creeks running at the bottom of ravines, and huge homes. I pointed out the country club when we passed its long driveway.

"Of course *that's* plowed, but not all the side streets."

Ian chuckled.

"The rich people live over here on the right," I said playfully, "and the poor people are all clustered on the left."

"Yeah. It's not the wrong side of the tracks in this town; it's the wrong side of the road."

I snorted out a laugh. "Okay, coming up on your left—big surprise—is Willow, and that's the road the police station is on."

It took only minutes to reach it, and then we were both out, stretching in the below-freezing air, tugging on our coats before we darted into the building. We encountered a long polished oak counter and two men sitting at desks on the other side.

"Good afternoon," I called out, reaching the counter and smiling. "May I speak to the officer in charge, please?"

One of the men, the bigger of the two, got up and walked to the counter. He didn't move particularly fast, but he wasn't being deliberately slow either. I hated it when everything was a pissing contest and hoped that wasn't what my day was going to turn into.

"May I help you?"

"I hope so," I said when he put his hands on the counter. I pulled my ID wallet from the breast pocket of my coat and snapped it open for him. "I'm Deputy US Marshal Miro Jones, and this is my partner, Deputy US Marshal Ian Doyle. We have a federal warrant for Drake Ford and need him produced right now so that we can take him into custody."

He looked stunned.

The other officer rose and joined us at the counter.

"What makes you think he's here, Marshal?"

I read his name off the tag. "Because, Officer Breen, the chief deputy in Carter County explained that he was released to your department yesterday afternoon," I said flatly. "Produce my witness or I'll notify the state police and my boss will call your governor."

Ian glowered, which was making the second guy, Gilman, edgy. I tried not to appear bored. I needed something to drink and, honestly, a nap.

"Would you wait right here, please."

"You have ten minutes," I informed him.

Both men walked to the far side of the room and a glass door with the police chief's name stenciled on it, and Gilman knocked as Breen waited. Moments later, the sharply yelled order to enter was audible even from where I was. Both officers went in as Ian moved up beside me.

"Did you bring your spare, too, or only your primary?"

"For the hundredth time," I said, turning to him. "I don't own a secondary weapon. I only have one gun, no spare."

His brows furrowed.

"How can you not remember that? It's not that hard."

"You need another gun, M. Glock has that new 42. Maybe we'll get you one of those."

"You pack enough firepower for both of us."

"I—"

"Good afternoon, gentlemen."

The chief of police, Edward Holley—it said so on his door—greeted us as he strode across the floor. If I had to guess, I would have thought him in his midfifties. He was tall, with brown hair graying at the temples. He was very handsome, with deep laugh lines at the corners of his hunter green eyes and creases on his forehead that probably came from scowling as much as smiling. He had a warmth about him that came through as he stopped in front of us, the curl of his lip daring me to dazzle him.

"Marshals?"

I nodded, passing him my wallet so he could check both the ID and the credentials underneath. "Badge is on my belt."

Holley tipped his head at me. "Let's see."

Turning a little, I lifted my sweater and the T-shirt underneath.

"Miroslav Jones?" he asked, clearly amused, grinning at me.

"Long story."

"Since you and your partner are not getting out of here tonight, I'll hear it over dinner."

"Actually," Ian broke in, stepping up to the counter and taking my ID out of the man's hand. "We plan to be on the road as soon as you transfer custody. Where is our witness?"

Holley squinted at us. "I don't understand. I thought you were putting someone in our jail for the night."

"No," Ian said curtly. "We need you to turn over Drake Ford."

The chief looked annoyed. "Drake Ford is at the Carter County Sheriff's Office awaiting federal… and that's you and… shit." He groaned suddenly, turning to Gilman and Breen. "Get Lautner up here now, find out where Colby and Fann are, and do we know, is Kershaw getting ready to teach the self-defense class at the high school?"

"Yes, Chief," Breen said, wincing.

"Well, get his ass back here. You, me, and Breen need to go out to the Jenner place with the marshals and fetch Drake Ford."

The officers moved quickly, and Holley raked his fingers through his thick hair as he regarded me and Ian.

"Gentlemen—"

"Ian and Miro," I corrected.

He smiled at me as he sighed deeply. "Three months ago, I fired Dalton Abernathy from this department because he didn't really work for me. He worked for Franklin Jenner, who just so happens to be the richest man in this town, as well as three counties. You probably saw his land when you drove in: it was everything that ran along the hills on your right."

"We did."

"Well, it turned out that it was Dalton's job to keep Drake Ford away from Franklin's son, Cabot Jenner."

"Oh," I grunted. "So you think that maybe your fired officer Abernathy still has his uniform and he went with some of Jenner's men and got them to release Ford to them."

"I do."

"And so what?" Ian asked irritably. "Ford is on Jenner's land, having the shit beat out of him?"

"I hope so," Holley said with a grimace. "I hope they didn't just shoot him."

My jaw dropped. I was appalled and I knew it was all over my face.

"Franklin Jenner owns a lot of land, and his mortgage company, Derby Securities, owns the notes on many of the homes in this town. No one would convict him of anything."

"But you're not afraid of him?" Ian asked with a smirk.

"I'm blaming it all on you two," Holley answered before another man came charging into the building and across the floor.

Five minutes later, we were in Holley's Dodge Durango, followed by two patrol cars, heading back the way we came, across the highway and up the hill onto the Jenner property, driving toward the house.

"Why didn't Mr. Jenner simply go to Drake Ford's family and tell them to keep their son away from his?"

"Drake Ford lives with his mother, but she's hardly ever in town let alone home. They have a trailer down toward the highway that he pays the rent on by working at the supermarket as a checker every day after school."

"He sounds like a good kid, self-sufficient," Ian offered.

"He's a mess and a pain in the ass, but the only trouble he ever got in suddenly started when Cabot came home from boarding school last year."

"And what happened?"

"They met and that was it. Cabot told me the last time I was putting Drake in cuffs—running him off his father's property—that nothing would keep him away from Drake, not even his father's puppet."

"Oh, you're a puppet," I teased.

"Apparently so," Holley grumbled. "Let's forget the fact that the little shit was trespassing, and that the last time they stole one of Mr. Jenner's cars, and the time before that he caught them smoking pot in the stables."

"That's fantastic," I said, chuckling.

"Oh, they should be on posters of 'what not to let your kids do.'"

"But? I hear a but?"

He laughed softly. "The parents are both absent in all of this. Drake Ford has no one, and Cabot Jenner has a father more interested in his investment portfolio than in his own kid."

"Where's Cabot's mother?"

"Rehab. Again."

"Okay, you win. It's fucked up."

He turned his head to smile at me. "How old are you, Marshal?"

"I beg your pardon?"

Holley's smile was wicked, and I liked it quite a bit. "You seem a little young to be a marshal."

"Yeah?"

"I'm guessing what, twenty-five?"

"He's thirty-one," Ian broke in, his hand snaking around the right side of the front seat where I was sitting to clench on my shoulder. "Pay attention."

What?

I pivoted in my seat to look at him. "Are you all right?"

"I would have never guessed that," Holley said softly, returning my attention to him.

After passing through the outer gate, we continued up the long snow-covered driveway, passing a half mile of low wood fence before it turned into paved road that was freshly plowed. Coming over a low hill, we saw the house, tennis courts, stables, and a lot of expensive glittering cars dusted in white. It looked like Jenner had company.

We had left only Officer Lautner back at the station—Kershaw would meet him there—so that meant Holley, Gilman, Breen, Colby, and Fann accompanied me and Ian to the Jenner home. Not that I was worried. Ian and I could have gone alone, but Holley was afraid there would be trouble. I tried to tell him that Ian ate trouble, but he wouldn't hear it.

As soon as we parked and got out of the car, six men came walking out the front door of the enormous two-story log cabin with a wraparound porch. They lined the porch as the final man stepped out and came down the stairs toward us. No one moved but him.

"Chief," he addressed him. "Something you need?"

"I need Drake Ford, Mr. Jenner," Holley said quickly. "Now."

"He's not here," Jenner said, glancing at me and Ian and then back to Holley.

"Well, we need to take a look around to confirm that."

"You don't have a warrant to do that," Jenner stated, stopping in front of Ian and me.

"I do." I interrupted their exchange, stepping forward, pulling my ID out for the man. "I'm a US marshal. Drake Ford is a federal witness and as such I have the authority to search your home for him."

"You—"

"There are exigent circumstances here, sir, as I have no idea what shape my witness is in. I suggest you step aside and let me conduct my search."

"I need to see badges!"

I turned and lifted my sweater, and Ian moved his coat so the man could spot the silver stars on both of us. "It would be better if you simply brought him out here to us, because it's getting late and I'm feeling hesitant to do this alone."

"Which means," Ian explained, taking over from me, "that you will sit out here, on your knees in handcuffs until either the state police or marshals from the field office in West Virginia respond, whoever makes it here first."

Jenner had a fox's face, the vulpine features made even more noticeable by a widow's peak and the small eyes. If his son was at all pretty, he owed that to his mother.

Turning, he called to one of his men to bring up Drake.

"Up?" Ian asked.

"From the wine cellar."

It could not have been good.

"I need to see your son as well," I added.

"Oh no," Jenner barked, spinning around to face me, closing the gap between us fast and shoving me backward.

Or, more precisely, *trying* to shove me backward. I didn't move an iota.

"You don't get to see my son!" Jenner shouted in my face. "I know my rights!"

"If you did," I said casually, grabbing his wrist, twisting it up sharply so that he gasped in surprise and pain as I put him on the ground on his knees. "You would not have assaulted a federal marshal."

"What?" Jenner choked out as Ian wrenched his other arm behind him, then took the one I held and cuffed him. "You can't do this!"

"Oh, I can," I informed him, noting that not one of the men who had come out of the house with Jenner rushed over to help their boss. It was probably the whole US marshal thing that held them in check. "And I will."

"Bring both boys out now!" Ian yelled toward the house. "Or you'll all be placed under arrest for obstruction."

No one moved.

"That's it," Ian said flatly, looking up at me. "Call our boss and tell him we need the state police out here or more marshals, whoever."

I pulled out my phone and held it to my ear.

"Franklin," Holley uttered the richest man in town's first name.

"Bring both boys out!" Jenner shouted at his men.

They moved, so I ended the call which I was thankful for. It was a pain in the ass when the state police got involved. Herding cats was easier than coordinating large numbers of troopers who weren't sure who they were supposed to be listening to. Kage was good at it, but Ian had too short a fuse, and I would rather do everything myself. I had always thought directing people was easy, that being in charge was merely an opportunity to be lazy, until I actually took a stab at supervising our department baseball team. I had tried to be everyone's friend, to be understanding of schedules and times, and practice ended up being at ten at night on a Thursday because that was the most convenient time for everyone. It was ridiculous.

Being in charge meant you were not beloved, but feared, a little, and respected a lot. That was how Kage was. He wasn't my favorite person. I could never see myself sitting on his couch with his family. But he would get us our backup, and when he arrived—and he *would* arrive, bringing hell with him—everyone would be really sorry they questioned either Ian's or my authority.

"Oh shit," Ian groaned.

I snapped my head up, and there, being helped down the stairs, was Drake Ford. I knew it was him without asking; he was smiling even though his left eye was swollen shut because Cabot Jenner had his arm around him, leading him. So even though blood stained the collar of his T-shirt, various cuts and contusions littered his face, and he was holding his side as if in pain, he was in heaven. He beamed at the smaller boy, who was slender, graceful, and simply radiant. They were night and day, and I understood the attraction right then and there.

Drake was all tight muscles on a swimmer's frame. He was handsome, but there was nothing extraordinary about the brown hair and brown eyes unless you counted the way he was gazing with great longing at Cabot Jenner. Dressed in jeans and a flannel shirt and the bloody T-shirt, he could have been any boy in any small town. His boyfriend was another story.

Cabot was all boneless sensual movement, with light blond hair and big green eyes framed in long, thick gold lashes. His skin was flawless; he had delicate, sharp features with a short upturned nose and small bow lips. If I was eighteen, he would have been all I wanted too.

"Come here," I said, gesturing to them.

They moved as quickly as they could, reached me, and waited. I put my hands on Drake, checking him over. "Who hit you?"

He didn't answer.

"My father and his men," Cabot whispered for him, and when his eyes flicked to mine, I saw the tears in them.

"I need you to go upstairs and pack a bag," I directed. "Everything you want to take that you can't live without. No electronics go with us, so reset your phone, laptop, and anything else. You're walking out of your life right this second."

"What?" Jenner gasped from where he knelt in the dirt.

"Wait, now," Holley said, moving up beside me, grabbing Jenner by the bicep and hauling him to his feet. "You have no call to removing Cabot from his father's—"

"He was with Mr. Ford the night he encountered Christopher Fisher. Until Mr. Jenner is questioned, I have no way of determining what precisely was said or inferred to him by Mr. Ford. I cannot, in good conscience, leave Cabot Jenner here since he, too, is a potential secondhand witness," I explained logically. "Also, if I were to leave the younger Mr. Jenner here, and if the men looking for Mr. Ford were to show up and appropriate him, he could be used to coerce Mr. Ford."

"You—" Jenner began.

"Therefore," Ian continued my train of thought, "we have no choice but to include him in the provision for Mr. Ford."

"What?" Jenner yelled.

"We're taking your son," Ian translated, his focus on Cabot as he took hold of Drake's bicep, easing him free of his boyfriend's grip. "Go get your shit, kid. One bag only. Do it now."

He ran.

"Wow." Drake smiled at me with his split lip, his closed left eye, and blood-filled right. "I've never seen him move that fast."

"I suspect he wants to go with you," Ian surmised.

"I will get my son back," Jenner promised sternly.

Stepping around in front of him, I met his gaze. "This will be the last time you see your son, sir, unless the threat against him and Mr. Ford is eliminated. I don't think you fully grasp what you've done here, but removing a federal witness is a very serious crime."

Both Jenner and Holley stared at me in confusion.

"Have you not heard of the Malloy crime family?" Ian asked.

I got an e-mail alert and stepped back so Ian could talk while I checked my phone. The message was from Kage, and he explained he would expect status in another two hours when we would report either spending the night in Bowman or leaving with Ford. After I texted him, he sent one back, agreeing with my decision to remove Cabot as well. He would have the federal protection order changed. I tried to send him back a quick thank you, but my text didn't send. I tried e-mailing as well, but suddenly I had no connection.

"Hey," I said to Ian. "You have Internet on your phone?"

Pulling it out, he looked at it a second. "No, I got nothing."

"Chief?" I asked.

"Yes?"

"You have any bars on your phone?"

Holley checked, and when he lifted his head, he was scowling. "I don't even have emergency service. My phone's dead."

Jenner's phone, when we pulled it from his pocket, was in the same condition.

"Marshal!"

We all turned toward the house where one of Jenner's men was coming down the stairs, moving fast. When he reached us, it was like his boss wasn't there: all his focus on Ian.

"There's no electricity in the house or anywhere on the property. All we have is the backup generator."

"That's not possible," Jenner snapped quickly.

"The land line is gone as well, and we seem to have a dead zone with cell service."

"Inside!" Ian barked out the order. "Now!"

I swatted Drake's arm. "Run up to your boyfriend's room, kid, and bring him downstairs to the first floor."

He bolted, and I turned and fisted my hand in the front of Ian's sweater.

"Right behind you," he promised, giving me a trace of a smile before I let go and sprinted toward the house.

"Everybody inside!" Ian shouted. "Take cover now!"

Gilman was hurled backward as I ran by him, dead before he hit the ground.

How much clearer was Ian supposed to be?

Breen died beside his car, Fann died in front of it; both of them shot in the head. I shouted at Colby to run, but he was frozen where he stood. He died seconds later.

Jenner's man who had come from the house was running beside me but went down, hit in the back. The caliber on the bullets had to be huge—the blood spray was big. After diving toward the stairs with Ian beside me, we scrambled up and onto the porch.

"If there are any guns here," Ian yelled at the men taking cover on the porch. "You need to get them!"

A man opened his mouth to say something but dropped to the ground, sliding down the exposed log wall leaving a trail of blood on all the rounded joints.

"Shit," Ian roared, shoving me inside the open front door and down onto the polished wooden floor. I was pinned under him, his lips against my ear. "Do not get up. I'll go get the boys and bring them here. We gotta get out of this house."

"But we're safe in the house," I argued.

"We're *so* not safe in the house, M," he assured me. "It's gonna be torched."

I didn't question him, just stayed where I was as he rose and moved in a crouching run toward the kitchen.

Outside, people were shouting, and suddenly Holley and Jenner flew through the front door.

"I need these cuffs off him!" Holley yelled at me.

Clambering over to them, I used Ian's spare key that I had on the ring with mine and got the cuffs off. Another man was hit outside the doorway, and arterial spray splattered the window when he was shot in the throat.

"What the hell is going on?" Jenner screamed, terrified and unhinged.

"You removed a federal witness," I answered flatly as he and Holley joined me low on the floor. "When you did, you made what was invisible, visible. Orson Malloy sent a sniper and God knows who else to kill Drake Ford. This is all on you."

Holley turned to me, his eyes frantic with fear.

"They have us pinned down, we can't call out since they're using some kind of jammer, we're too far back from the road for anyone to notice anything amiss, and they've already cut the power and the landline." I looked at Jenner. "Do you have guns here?"

"I have a couple of hunting rifles and a shotgun, but nothing high-powered or semiautomatic."

"Okay," I said as Ian and the boys ran into the room and dived down onto the floor beside us as an explosion rocked the house.

"What the hell was that?" Jenner cried out.

"That was an RPG," Ian answered, rolling onto his back so he could talk. "You have your bag, Cabot?"

"Yessir."

"Okay. Now I need you to grab three more, hiking packs if you have any, but if not, whatever. I need bottled water, rope, a box of matches, any pairs of snow boots in the house, the heaviest jackets and gloves you and your father have, the sharpest knife you got, a hatchet, a tarp or tent, and as many flashlights as you can find."

"We have a flare gun."

"I'll take that as well as any road flares, the rifles, and all the ammunition you have."

"Okay," he said but didn't move, looking to Drake.

"Drake, help him and do it as fast as you can."

"Yessir. Let's go," Drake prompted Cabot.

They crawled quickly from the great room to the kitchen and then when they got there, stood up and ran.

"What are you doing?" Holley asked Ian.

He looked Holley directly in the eye, his voice dropping low. "They're gonna come in soon, from the road because that's the point of origin on all the fire we're taking, and when they do, we're dead. So the six of us are going out the back and up and over that hill."

"You're nuts!" Jenner yelled loudly, sounding horrified at the suggestion. "It's a lot rougher climb than it looks, Marshal. Those hills are covered in thick brush and loose rock and streams and it's going to be dark in another half an hour, so—"

"It beats being shot with a rocket-propelled grenade," Holley apprised him. "These men are trying to kill us, Jenner!"

"Why don't we hand Ford over?"

"Because at this point, Malloy's not going to let anyone else live, even if we would ever consider that," Ian said bluntly, taking hold of my shoulder. "I was thinking of taking the horses, trying for the road, but I think it's too risky."

"Agreed. The sniper, he's good, right?"

"He's hit everything he's aimed at," Ian said, meeting my gaze. "And he's using a big-ass gun with API rounds. The hole it left in the car was an inch wide."

"So you think we have military guys out there?"

"I dunno. So far there's only one shooter, but either way, we're pinned down."

"Okay, so, out the back like you said."

"Yeah. At least that way, the house will provide us some cover. The shooter's out front—that's what the trajectory tells me—and we've taken no fire from the woods. We have a small jump on them as far as timing, but that's it. We need to move."

I nodded.

He tugged me toward him. "We need to get our packs out of the chief's car first, though. I have ammo in there."

"We just got through talking about the deadly accuracy of the man—or woman—shooting at us," I said flatly. "Neither one of us is going out there."

"Miro," he began softly. "We need the bullets."

"We have Jenner's rifles and our guns, but getting more ammunition for your Glock, which won't do shit against the fuckin' sniper, is stupid."

"We need—"

"No," I snarled, staring into his pale blue eyes. Funny that they had lightened during our trip, and even this, imminent death, was not darkening them. Sex had, but not this. "I will not allow you to go out there. Do you understand?"

He shrugged, giving up as the boys called from the kitchen.

"Marshal, we got most of the stuff."

"We're all out in five," Ian directed.

I nodded before he scuttled away.

Lifting up on my elbows, I focused on the two men close to me. Outside, I could hear the men on the porch returning fire. "Chief? Mr. Jenner? Are you coming with us or staying here?"

"I'm with you," Holley said, grabbing hold of my shoulder. "But are you certain this is the best course?"

"They have a grenade launcher. Maybe the rocket one is up next. They can torch the house and then we'll fry. We need to move."

I heard a yell from outside and then glass shattering, then watched Ian race across the room, lean out the front door for a second, and then charge back to where the boys huddled together.

"I don't think you have any idea about the terrain you're headed into," Jenner said, his voice cracking. "It's very dangerous."

"We'll be fine," I placated him. "Are you coming or not?"

"Yes," he snapped.

We all rushed across the room after Ian, and when we were in the hallway beside the kitchen, I noticed that I couldn't hear anymore gunfire.

"Because everyone outside is dead, at least from what I could see." Ian said frankly, shoving a heavy parka at me. "Put this on."

It was too big—all Jenner's coats were—but we all pulled one on, along with knit hats, scarves, and gloves. Ian kept his military boots, I kept my hiking boots, Holley was okay as well, but Jenner and Drake both changed. Cabot had on Ugg boots, but they were going to have to do. He had a heavy fur-lined parka as well.

I was a good shot with my Glock, but I was not as good a marksman with a rifle. Looking at the two hunting rifles on the table, I made a decision. "How you feel about carrying the second rifle, Chief?" I asked, glancing over at Holley.

He agreed, and I picked up the gun and passed it to him, as well as the two boxes of bullets. Ian had the other of the two Remingtons, both 700 models. Shouldering the backpack, Ian stuffed two boxes of shells in another bag before putting the rifle under his arm.

"Let's go," he ordered.

I put on my pack, and so did Drake. Jenner wrenched the one that Cabot was going to carry out of his son's hands.

"It's too heavy," he barked, and I saw Cabot wince and cringe. Hard to miss that he'd been abused, probably for years. The shrinking recoil was a dead giveaway.

"Follow him," I directed Cabot, gesturing to Ian, and when Jenner tried to go after his son, I grabbed his arm, holding tight, and directed Drake to watch over Cabot.

"I will," Drake said, smiling at me and then trailing after Cabot.

Jenner wrenched his arm free but fell into line, with Holley next.

We moved silently though the house, Ian leading, me bringing up the rear, and once we were all outside, Ian ordered everyone to wait as he darted back to me.

"Yeah?"

"Don't lose me," he ordered. "Whatever you do."

"I won't."

He grabbed the back of my neck and took a breath.

"It's gonna be all right," I soothed.

"Yeah, I know, just stay close."

"Please, buddy, I've got your back."

He nodded fast and then rushed to the front and led us down the back stairs from the deck and away from the house. It was dusk, the perfect time to try to escape, and I really hoped we'd be lucky. I wasn't ready to lose Ian or have him be without me. My life was just getting started—having it end was not in my plans.

WE JOGGED until we reached the tree line and then, because there was a six-foot incline, slowed as we all scaled the snow-covered slope.

Drake held Cabot's hand, walking in front of him, making sure he didn't fall, and telling him, over and over, how great he was doing.

"Mr. Jenner!"

We all turned to see one of his men—who had managed to live after all—come running after us, rifle in hand. "We need to hand Drake over!"

I drew my gun and leveled it at him.

"Abernathy," Holley snarled. "This is all your—"

"Now, Jenner!" the ex-deputy ordered, raising his weapon.

"Drop it!" I demanded.

It was like he was so focused on Jenner that he didn't hear me, even from so close.

"Drop your weapon!" I shouted again when Abernathy didn't obey.

The second floor of the Jenner cabin suddenly exploded into flying wood and glass and steel, and only the fact that we were a good hundred yards away saved us from getting hit with flying debris.

It was a big yes on the rocket launcher.

The blast startled Dalton Abernathy, and in his confusion, I bolted forward, grabbed the muzzle of his gun, wrenched it from his hands, and used the butt of the rifle to hit him in the face. He fell back into the snow, out cold.

The crappy rifle Abernathy was using had an attached strap, so I slung that over my shoulder. I ran past Holley to stop at the top of the slope and waited for him and Jenner to climb down ahead of me. Once they were safe, I holstered my Glock and checked around, not wanting to turn my back on any more men.

Ian stood below us in a ravine, on a fallen tree in the middle of a shallow creek. "Hurry the fuck up!" he bellowed, and I could hear the frustration and anger in his voice.

"Go!" I called out.

He turned and ran with Cabot following, then Drake, Jenner, Holley, and finally me. A succession of explosions boomed through the woods as we scrambled over loose rocks, dirt, and ice, to climb the embankment. Once we got out of the ravine, the terrain changed. There was no gradual slope and no place to simply stand. The ground underneath me was solid with no give at all, and when I punched through the frozen soil, my boots kept slipping. It was slow going as we trudged through snow that was calf deep, with no open space, just pine trees growing one on top of another.

"Why didn't your fucking partner ask me if there are any ATV paths or—"

"Because we don't want anything they can move fast on," I took the time to explain. "We need to make it difficult for them to reach us."

We went silent after that, zigzagging our way up the side of the steep hill, slogging through, the men between Ian and me grunting and puffing with exertion. I was in better shape, but my jeans were soaking wet and doing nothing for the cold.

The sun had set, and between that and the higher elevation, the temperature fell even more. When the freezing rain started, Ian stopped and had everyone huddle together as he climbed one of the trees to look down at the house from our new vantage point.

"When will the missus start missing you, Chief?" I asked Holley.

He shook his head. "Divorced."

"Sorry," I muttered. "What about wives or girlfriends of your people down there?"

"It's Kershaw and Lautner back at base," he told me. "They'll start wondering where we are in another hour."

"Okay," I said gently, taking hold of his shoulder. "I'm sorry about your men."

He covered my hand with his. "Thank you."

"There was nothing you could have done."

"M!" Ian said sharply.

Moving over directly under him, I peered up through the branches.

"There's a lot of lights moving around down there."

Meaning men with flashlights. "Shit."

He looked down at me. "We've got, what, another forty minutes or so before our two hours is up and we're supposed to check in?"

Kage. "Yeah."

"Okay, so once we miss it and he can't get us on either of our phones, we'll have state troopers here in another hour."

"Let's say two to be safe." I stepped back as he jumped down, landing in front of me. "And then how many will come? Like how many cars?"

"I dunno," he huffed, and I couldn't miss the worry on him: the crumpled brows, pursed lips, corded muscles in his neck all spoke to his concern over our present situation. "More than one, because it'll be reported as an emergency."

"All right, two at the least, maybe up to four."

"And then it'll take them another few hours to get backup out here, search chopper and everything else."

"We've got the whole night up here," I surmised. "We need to find cover."

"Unless they have night-vision goggles and dogs, we're okay as long as we use no light and stay quiet."

"We have to use the flashlights or we'll walk off the side of this hill."

"No, we—"

"Missy Frain," Jenner said suddenly.

I turned to him. "Sorry?"

"Missy Frain," he repeated. "Her family has a cabin halfway down the other side. It's right on Kingman Creek that runs through the hills."

"Which is how far?"

"Up to the top of this and down the other side," Jenner replied. "Three hours easily, though I can't vouch for the state of the cabin. It's been years since I've been there."

"It's as good a plan as any," Ian agreed. "Cabot, did you find rope?"

"Yeah."

"Give it to me."

So we all had water, Ian and Holley checked the rifles—I didn't bother with the one I was carrying—and then all tied together, with my partner leading, we continued to scale the side of the hill as light rain became a deluge.

Never had I been so cold, and when I realized the clicking noise I was hearing was actually my teeth, I started chuckling like a crazy person.

"Marshal?" Holley asked.

"Sorry," I said cheerfully, nearly walking into a tree, branches scratching my face. "I can't feel my feet anymore, and this rain—I feel like we should be looking out for an ark."

I got a quick pat of encouragement as we trekked on.

Thankfully, the cabin was nowhere near as far down the other side as we were led to believe, and really, descending was so much easier than ascending that I couldn't stop smiling. The rain let up as well, changing from a raging downpour to a shower to a drizzle and finally to a gentle fluttery snow that was actually really pretty in the sky when the moon came out from behind the clouds.

Ian was amazing. Between the moonlight and keeping the flashlight beam down at his feet, he was still able to lead us without incident to the small clearing where the Frain cabin was. Or, more correctly, to the scene of what looked like had probably been a fire.

It turned out Jenner had been really generous with his use of the word "cabin."

Since all four walls were no longer intact, the cabin didn't really qualify as a structure anymore, but as most of the roof was still on, it would keep some of the rain and snow off us.

Ian untied everyone one by one, and when he reached me, he stepped close, leaning into my space.

"You all right?"

"Aren't you cold?" I croaked.

"We'll get a fire going," he promised.

"How?"

"We just needed to get away from those guys, and there was only one way to go."

"Yeah, I know," I said, coughing.

"I mean, we didn't have enough guns to repel any real numbers, and not knowing how many they had and since our first priority was to secure our witness—"

"We had to go up, I get it."

He crowded in, his lips against my ear, the warm puffs of air down the side of my neck making me shiver. "But by now, there are probably troopers on site, and I saw no evidence of anyone coming after us. There have been no lights on the side of the hill, so I'm pretty sure we're clear." I opened my mouth to say something, but he fisted his hand in my jacket. "If I'm wrong and there's guys in cold-weather gear coming up behind us with night-vision goggles and machine guns—I'll deal with it. But I'm gonna build a fire so you don't freeze to death."

I smiled. "Damn nice of you."

His grin was wide and his hand slid around the side of my neck. "Stay—"

"—right by you," I finished for him.

"Yeah." He clipped the word before turning around.

"This is so cra-creeepy," Cabot stuttered, having trouble walking, as wet and cold as he was. "Can I have a gun too?"

Drake picked him up, slung him over his shoulder, and walked toward what was left of the dilapidated cottage.

Ian went first, testing the strength of the rotting boards, and once he was confident the floor wouldn't give, we all followed him up the four steps into what had once been the great room. The stone fireplace was all that remained on one side, with the stone chimney and large pieces of what had been a roof.

"I bet this was a great little cabin," Ian said as he gathered pieces of wood into a pile.

I got up to help, but a cramp in my right calf made me sit back down hard. Ian was there beside me, fast.

"What?" he asked.

"My muscles are clenching up. I'm fine."

He barked at Holley and Drake to help him and then pulled the matches from his pack. Bending over, he did the blowing and cupping his hands around the flame and tried to get something going, but the wood was too wet.

"Maybe there's some dryer wood under the debris piles," Drake suggested.

"Not with the rain," Holley assured him.

"I'm so cold," Cabot whispered.

"Drake, you need to get his jacket off and get him in yours with you."

"I can do that," Jenner barked at Ian.

"No," he snapped back. "I want them wrapped around each other. The temperature is dropping fast, and even though it won't drop much below 25, we're all wet and it's windy and we could all get hypothermia."

I noticed Cabot was just sort of watching Drake.

"Oh crap," Ian grumbled, getting up and going over to Cabot. He stripped him out of his jacket and then shoved him at Drake, who grabbed Cabot and tucked him against his chest, wrapping his arms and jacket around him.

"Hold on to him," Ian ordered, grabbing both sides of the parka and zipping them up together. "Keep him as warm as you can."

"Absolutely," Drake promised, leaning his head on top of Cabot's.

"That's disgusting," Jenner spat. "How can you let my boy be touched by that pervert?"

"I see two kids in love, you homophobic prick," Ian snarled. "And if you don't want to look, go over on the other side of the cabin. Hope you don't fuckin' freeze to death."

"I'm going to have your—"

"Miro," Ian said suddenly, rounding on me. "Are the road flares in your bag?"

"Yeah, I think so."

"Get them out," he directed. He turned to Holley. "I need kindling, small branches off the trees, pull them off, like you're making a Christmas wreath."

"Yes," Holley said, letting Ian know he was listening.

"Keep watch," Ian told me before he took the stairs and left.

I found the flares in my bag and waited, listening to Cabot whimper, watching Jenner glare at the two younger men, and keeping vigil.

When Ian returned, he ignited two of the four flares and stacked the branches and the smaller pieces with the needles on top of them. It seemed like it took forever, but in reality, probably only thirty minutes, give or take. Once the branches underneath caught fire, the twigs ignited, and the flames got bigger and bigger as Ian added more and more wood.

"Road flare," I said, clapping him on the back.

"Forgot my training for a second there," he rumbled, his voice brittle as his eyes flicked to mine.

"Which is very human." I sighed, leaning against him, the warmth from the fire almost orgasmic. "Holy fuck, make it bigger."

He laughed softly as Drake and Cabot got close, thanking him over and over. They were able to unzip the parka, and Cabot sat between Drake's legs as they faced the fire. Ian got up and he and Holley went to fetch more branches, this time taking the hatchet Drake had carried in his bag.

I was surprised at how quickly my jeans dried out as I sat cross-legged beside the fire, and between that and the water, I felt okay. Starving, but I'd live. When Ian returned, his gloves covered in sap and smelling like pine, I took his hat off and put it on the ground beside me before taking off mine and shoving it down on his head.

"What're you doing?"

"That one's wet and covered in crap. Wear mine until you warm up. I'll go cut branches next time."

"You'll chop your hand off, I know it."

I arched an eyebrow in warning. "Your faith in me is heartwarming."

"Shut up."

It was nice. The fire was really warm, and after a while, Cabot turned, curling up in Drake's arms, and fell asleep after thanking Ian for the fire again. Drake wasn't far behind. Jenner said he was only going to rest, but he was out as well, minutes later.

"I can feed the fire," I insisted. "Why don't you try and sleep a little. If I need you, I'll wake you up."

"Okay," Ian agreed, lying down with his head in my lap. He was out in seconds.

"So," Holley said, jolting me, which was good because I was dozing. "Tell me about being a marshal."

"Tell me why you're divorced?"

He smiled. "I think you can figure it out."

I studied him.

"I really wanted to take you to dinner."

"I'm very flattered, Chief, thank you."

He grunted. "Though I would not have even entertained the thought had I known you were involved with your partner."

It didn't occur to me to deny it, to deny Ian. "It's that obvious?"

"It wasn't at first," he mused, glancing at Ian with his head in my lap and my arm across his shoulder. "But once we got here, how protective he is, how gentle you are with him—it became apparent. And," he said with a chuckle, "frankly he's a bit too comfortable in your personal space."

He always had been.

"You're very well suited."

"Thank you," I said honestly, because I would take that observation all day long. "You should try and sleep too."

"Thank you for saving my life, Marshal."

"Sorry to have dragged you and your men into our mess."

"It's Mr. Jenner's mess, Marshal, and everyone will know that come morning."

When Holley, too, was asleep, I put some more wood on the fire to make sure we all stayed warm and toasty throughout the cold, dark night. I tried not to get used to having my partner sleeping on me, but I had a sneaking suspicion the damage was already done.

CHAPTER 15

THE SOUND of thunder woke me the following morning, and when I lifted up, I realized I had been sleeping in Ian's arms. We had switched places in the early morning hours, and I had lain beside him, next to the fire. But when my eyes opened to the gray day, I saw I had used his chest for a pillow.

There was no time to say anything, though. What I had thought was thunder was actually a helicopter that landed in the clearing a hundred yards away. First one off was Kage, and Ian and I got to our feet to greet him.

"Who's that?" Cabot asked as he and Drake moved up beside me.

"Our boss," I answered, watching Kage stride toward us.

"He's big," he remarked.

"And kinda scary looking," Drake continued.

"Yeah," I agreed, smiling suddenly. "I'm really happy to see him."

"Me too," Cabot sighed.

Sam Kage reached the stairs and climbed up, stopping in front of us.

"Sir, I—"

"Good job, Marshals," he said, turning to lift a walkie-talkie to tell the others to bring a fire extinguisher.

He turned then and gestured us all down toward the helicopter. Inside, even the small change in temperature was comforting.

"Are you their boss?" Jenner snarled at Kage, the night not having mellowed him even a bit.

"I am," Kage answered flatly, scowling.

"Well, I want them both in jail for kidnapping my son and—"

"Actually, it's you who'll be going there, sir," Kage returned tersely. "Your actions led to the deaths of ten men, you kidnapped Drake Ford from federal custody, placed your own son in jeopardy, as well as an officer of the law—Chief Holley—and two of my marshals. You'll be lucky to be back outside. Ever."

"No, you—"

"I would take a moment and breathe the fresh air."

Holley, Drake, and Cabot all looked to me with wide eyes.

Well, yeah, my boss was all kinds of scary.

IT WAS a blur. We went first by helicopter to the chief's car and collected our bags, then to Drake's trailer, where he and Cabot hurriedly packed one bag of clothes and Drake's most prized possessions, including a sketch Cabot had done of him. We were then flown to Wellmont Hancock County Hospital.

All of us suffered from a bit of hypothermia, but once we had fluids and glucose, we were ready to eat. Kage culled the pack, putting Jenner in federal custody, turning him over to the FBI agents. They took kidnapping very seriously. It was sad that even then, Jenner had to spit some more poison at his son, calling him a disappointment and an abomination. Drake folded his boyfriend in his arms as the agents, more than a little disgusted by Jenner's vitriol, if the looks on their faces were any indication, took his father away.

We said good-bye to Holley, who thanked Ian and me for saving his life and hugged Drake and Cabot and wished them well. Two large Chevy Suburbans were parked at the entrance of the hospital, and Kage gave one set of keys to Ian and four plane tickets to me.

"You're all flying back to Chicago tomorrow."

"And you?" Ian asked.

"I have to fly to Arlington to bring charges against Mr. Jenner. I need your full reports no later than 0600 tomorrow morning. Do I make myself clear?"

"Yessir," I said.

"Yes sir," Ian echoed.

"And the rental car that you drove to the police station in Bowman is being returned as we speak."

Big or small, my boss never missed anything. "Thank you, sir."

Kage gave me a pat on the arm. "Good job, gentlemen."

FBI agents accompanied him, and one held the door open so he could get into the SUV. They drove away quickly through the lightly falling snow.

"Who wants food?" Ian asked.

I raised my hand, with Drake and Cabot following.

"When does a shower happen?" Cabot wanted to know.

"You want that first?"

"No," he said, shaking his head at the same time his stomach growled. "Food is definitely number one on my list."

It was the same for all of us.

"After we eat," Ian said, gesturing at the car. "We'll all get nice hot showers."

It sounded heavenly.

I called shotgun, and everyone thought that was funny, because really, who else would it have been with Ian driving?

"We should eat on the way," Drake suggested. "It's like an hour and a half to the Tri-Cities airport. That's Blountville, right? Tennessee?"

"Yeah," Ian said, fidgeting, like he wasn't comfortable in his seat.

"You want me to drive?"

"No," he snapped.

I suddenly had the oddest compulsion to take hold of his hand, but since I wasn't sure how he would take that, I just looked out the window instead.

"What do you guys wanna eat?" I asked Drake and Cabot.

"Yes," Cabot said, chuckling.

Meaning anything and everything.

"Okay," I said playfully, patting Ian's leg. "Drive."

He caught my hand and held it against his thigh, taking a breath at the same time. "Who wants a steak? I feel like steak."

Cabot whimpered.

"And all the fixins?" Drake asked hopefully.

"You got it, buddy."

I turned to look at Ian, and after a minute, he let my hand go and put his on the wheel. "You all right?"

"Fine," he answered softly.

"So get us steak, man."

Moving my hand, I checked my e-mail on my phone, and when I put my phone down, leaned sideways and took hold of the back of his headrest.

Every now and then, out of the blue Ian smiled, and I could look at him and see the little boy he must have been. It was all sunshine and happiness and heartbreaking vulnerability. The smile annihilated me and also made me almost murderously protective. So when he turned his head and gifted me with it, I smiled stupidly back.

Fucking Ian.

We stopped an hour later at a place that Yelp said was good, and at three in the afternoon, since it was just us and two older couples, we were guaranteed focused service.

The amount of food we ordered was ridiculous, and our waitress, Jill, was funny and sweet and thrilled with every new menu item requested.

Cabot ate his filet rare and smothered in mushrooms, Drake had a porterhouse I didn't think a wolf pack could have finished, Ian had a T-bone named the "cowboy cut," and I had a ribeye. We shared sides—ordered eight of them—and then had dessert.

"Someday, when Drake and I are done with witness protection, will you guys drink with us?" Cabot asked hopefully.

"Absolutely," I promised.

"And we'll be staying in Chicago, right?" Drake wanted to know. "I mean—you and Marshal Doyle are—"

"Make it Ian and Miro," Ian corrected. "After everything, I think we're done with titles, yeah?"

Drake smiled wide, and I saw Cabot looking at us hungrily as well. They were both starved for male authority-figure friendship. "Yeah," he agreed happily.

"So," Cabot hedged, "we'll be in Chicago, and you guys will check up on us and stuff?"

"Yes," Ian promised.

Nice to see the relief wash over both of them, Cabot even more so, and I understood why. His whole life had changed in a twenty-four-hour period.

"You both have to go to college," Ian informed them.

There was lots of nodding, and I heard Ian cackle under his breath.

As soon as we were on the road again, our two witnesses passed out in the back.

"Normally transport marshals don't do check-in," he reminded me.

"Yeah, but I think this is a special circumstance."

"I agree," he rumbled thickly, twisting his head back and forth.

"What's wrong with you?"

"I dunno," he said too fast.

Okay. "What do you think?" I prodded.

He shook his head.

I would have to figure it out later.

"Boss has us with a reservation at the La Quinta Inn & Suites near the airport."

"All right. I'll navigate us to there."

"Let's actually get a suite, okay? Not just a room with two beds and two cots."

"Why would you make the boys sleep apart?" I baited him, to which there was no reply.

Nothing.

"Ian?"

"Where am I going?"

"You're staying on US 23 going south. It'll turn into I-26. You'll be on it for another ten miles."

He grunted.

Something was wrong. "I was thinking that I could start typing up our incident report, since I don't get carsick."

"Good idea," he said as he checked the mirrors.

It was like pulling teeth; the man was back to being his normal laconic self. "Are you pissed at me?"

No answer, which basically let me know that he was, in fact, angry. Since I had no hope of figuring out what I'd done, I gave up and pulled out my laptop.

The thirty minutes of drive time went by quickly as I wrote the report, making sure to include the notes I'd e-mailed Kage and the ones I'd made on my phone. I talked to Aruna when she called to let me know that Chickie was having a very good time playing with the kids as well as Liam. I reported the news to Ian, who merely nodded.

"You're quite the conversationalist," I informed him.

He made a noise in the back of his throat.

"You're being a dick."

His gaze flicked over to me and then back to the road.

My phone buzzed. A text message from Kage.

"What is it?" Ian asked.

"Apparently twelve members of the Malloy crime family were murdered last night. Orson Malloy is in the wind."

"Okay, so what does that mean for Drake?"

"Nothing. While he's been in custody, Fisher's been talking, and it turns out he doesn't only do cleanup for Malloy, but for several different families. He stopped talking because he said he had a feeling that Drake might not be around much longer."

"What does the message say about that?"

"To watch out for Drake and Cabot until we get them on the plane. Once we're back in Chicago, no one will know who they are."

"Right. Does he say who he thinks might be coming after them?"

"No."

"Okay," he said on an exhale. Then after a few moments of silence: "Were you worried last night?"

"What?" I asked, turning to look at him, ignoring my laptop.

"Last night? In the woods? Were you scared?"

"No." I yawned. "You were there."

"What is that supposed to mean?"

"No, I don't mean, like, you were there, so you saw I wasn't freaked out. I mean, you were there, you were with me, and so I was fine."

"Oh."

"If you and I are together, I don't worry."

He grunted and I went back to my report.

Ian found a drugstore where we stopped for toiletries for the guys before heading over to the hotel. At the front desk, we had to wait a bit as there was a family reunion happening and a lot of people were checking in. When it was my turn, I advised the clerk that I needed a specific layout for our suite and I had checked them on the Internet.

In the room, Cabot was confused.

"There's only one bedroom."

"Right," I agreed. "Now walk with me."

We passed through a short hallway and saw a bathroom on the left that led to a bedroom. But if you walked by the bathroom, there was a couch that opened up into a bed, and on the other side of the bedroom wall, a dining room table and chairs.

"You guys will be in there," I directed. "You close the bedroom door here, and the one that leads from the bathroom, and you're completely enclosed. Ian and I are out here, and anyone who comes in has to come through us first."

"You have kind of a sucky job," Drake said bluntly. "I mean, you guys just protect us 'cause you have to."

"Normally, yes." I agreed with his summation of the facts. "But I'd protect you guys even if I didn't have to, at this point. I'm interested to see what happens."

"We're like an experiment," Cabot said, grinning at me.

"Yes," I agreed, flashing him a smile.

"I'm taking a shower first," Ian grumbled, walking toward the bathroom with his backpack. "Somebody call down and get more towels."

He slammed the door behind him, and Drake took his and Cabot's bags into the bedroom while Cabot turned on the television. Of course, the first thing he saw was his old home on the news.

"Jesus Christ, it looks worse than it did this morning when we flew over it."

The house was basically gutted. Between the grenades and the bullets, the remodeling would have been extensive. But the inside had been blasted as well. I was glad I had insisted on Cabot taking anything of value when he ran with us, because his bedroom had been completely destroyed.

"I'm sorry you won't get to say good-bye to your mother," I said gently.

Cabot shook his head. "Don't be. She never gave a crap about me. At least my father knew I was alive. Every time he hit me, at least he saw me."

I couldn't help it. He was so young, so sad, and at that moment, he needed me. Stepping in front of him, I hauled him to his feet and into my arms.

"You think I'm weak because I'm gay, and—"

"I'm gay, idiot," I told him, squeezing tighter until he broke down, going boneless against me. "Gay doesn't have shit to do with anything, and never let anyone tell you different."

His breath caught as he started to cry, his arms wrapping tight around my waist as he buried his face in my chest.

"You can get married in Chicago if you want. June would be perfect since you'll have graduated high school by then. People'll think you got yourself knocked up."

The dam broke, and the sniffling and laughing turned to all-out ugly sobbing in seconds. He had only just turned eighteen. He was still so young, had been through an ordeal, and was now basically an orphan with no one but my partner and me to give a crap about him and his boyfriend.

"You're gonna be all right," I promised. "You'll see."

He clung so hard, and I rocked him and soothed him, rubbing circles on his back. When Ian walked into the room, Drake spoke up.

"Cab," he said softly. "Baby, do you want to take a shower next or—"

Cabot tried to wedge tighter, and I motioned for Drake to go ahead.

"Did you call down for towels?" Ian asked.

"No, we didn't get that far," I said, smiling, leaning my cheek on the top of Cabot's head.

"Okay," he mumbled, crossing the room to the phone.

I stood with Cabot, and eventually he calmed. The crying became panting, stuttering breaths, and finally hiccups. I had him drink water fast, and when Drake got out of the bathroom, he smiled, big.

"Oh, there's my baby," Drake sighed as Cabot charged over to him. As he wrapped the smaller boy up in his arms, Drake looked over at me and smiled.

"Get in the shower, Cabot. Drake'll bring your towels in when we get them," I said.

He did as he was directed, and I pulled out my laptop, got myself situated at the table, and plugged it in. We had to use our phones for Wi-Fi hotspots because of all the classified data we transmitted, and once I got that working, I went back to typing up the report.

The towels arrived, and when Cabot came out looking better, definitely smelling better, and beaming at me, I told him and Drake to order room service if they wanted anything.

"Read over the report," I said to Ian next. "Add anything I'm missing, okay?"

"Sure," he muttered, not looking at me as he sat down in front of my laptop.

Something had crawled up his ass, but for the life of me, I had no idea what. But I needed a shower more than I needed to make nice with him, so I left him—sulking or pouting, I wasn't sure which—and disappeared into the bathroom.

Hot water had never felt so good. I stood under the spray much longer than I needed to, and when I finally finished, the dessert they'd ended up ordering was there. I'd forgotten how much eighteen-year-old boys could eat.

I changed into the lounge pants the girls had bought me and walked out into the living room, still towel drying my hair.

"Are you really—oh."

Looking up, I saw Drake standing over Cabot but staring at me. "Am I really what?"

"Gay," Cabot squeaked.

"Yeah," I said, smiling. "Why?"

Drake shook his head like he wasn't sure. Cabot swallowed nervously, his eyes locked on me.

They were both sort of overwhelmed, and I understood why. I was probably the first other gay man they'd met.

"Let me hang this up, and I'll talk to you guys, okay?"

They nodded in unison.

Returning to the bathroom, I hung up the towel and then checked the locks on the suite's door. When I turned to walk back, Ian was right there, having moved up silently behind me.

"I didn't hear you." I chuckled, moving by him.

He stopped me with a hand on my bicep.

"What?"

His eyes didn't leave mine, but he said nothing.

I cleared my throat. "Do you have an extra T-shirt in your bag?"

"Why, because now you're done walking around half-naked?"

"I'm sorry, what?"

"Both those boys nearly swallowed their tongues when you came walking out of the bathroom," he groused, shoving me backward. "What the fuck were you thinking?"

I was lost.

"And could those pants be any tighter?"

"Knock it off," I said playfully, thinking he was teasing.

"Are you guys coming back to talk or what?" Drake asked, coming around the corner.

"We'll be right there!" Ian yelled over his shoulder.

Drake's eyes opened wide in surprise and he backpedaled away fast.

"Why're you shouting at him?"

"I'm not!"

"Are you listening to yourself?"

"Hey, guys, we're gonna watch TV in the bedroom!" Cabot announced loudly before I heard quickly slammed doors.

"That's perfect," I groused. "Now you scared them."

"I didn't scare anybody," he snapped, clearly exasperated.

"Yeah, you did. They're just kids, Ian."

"I don't fuckin' care." He sounded angry and belligerent and mean.

"You know, you've been a surly asshole all day. What the fuck is wrong with you?"

"You!"

"Me?" I was taken aback.

"You're pissing me off."

"Why? What'd I do?"

"You shouldn't—" He stopped speaking and took a step forward, into me, pinning me up against the door, his thigh between mine, spreading my legs, hands on my hips.

I felt a throb, a pulse of want that spread down my spine and flushed me in heat. It was, for a split second, like drowning. "Let go," I said, begging him.

"Why?"

"Because you're dangerously close to being thrown up against the wall."

His breath hitched. "Yeah, okay, do that."

My gaze met his.

"Do it," he dared, licking his lips.

"Ian?" I murmured, hands on his face, easing him close. "What's going on?"

His brows furrowed.

"What do you want?"

Still nothing.

"I can't guess this time. You have to tell me."

He coughed softly.

"Please."

The muscles in his jaw corded. "Yesterday, when we—when you—" He swallowed hard. "I felt like I belonged to you."

I had treated him like that, because in bed, I couldn't hide my feelings. My desire to own him, to make him mine, was obvious. I worried about that and so worked to keep things casual and light between us out of bed. But it seemed like maybe that wasn't what he wanted—or more importantly, needed.

The way he was looking at me… the light came on.

All of his frustration, his anger, was about *ownership*.

It all suddenly made sense: his unease in the car, the fidgeting like his skin was suddenly too constrictive, acting as though he wanted to get away from me. He needed grounding. He needed to know where he belonged, and to whom.

"And is that what you want?" I asked as he smoothed his hands up my sides, his head tipping forward so his lips brushed over my collarbone. "To be mine?"

The shiver was all the answer I needed, even if he lied.

"Ian?"

He nodded, his lips parting, his teeth scraping gently over my skin. "This whole time," he said, his voice thick and full of gravel. "Right here, all along… you've been here."

My whole body tensed as I girded for what could happen, and for what I could lose.

"I don't—I mean—" He inhaled sharply. "I'm—"

"It's okay," I said gently.

"Shit," Ian muttered under his breath, pressing his face down into my shoulder, hands tracing over the muscles in my back.

"Tell me," I urged, nuzzling his temple, kissing gently, tenderly, moving my lips along his jaw.

"What the fuck is with these pants?"

Not what I was hoping to hear, but I could work with it, with the fact that he liked what he saw. Taking hold of his hands, I moved them under the elastic waistband and back over my ass before squeezing tight. "They're for taking off," I whispered raggedly in his ear.

"Miro," he choked out, lifting his head, his lips hovering over mine as he ground his rigid shaft against my thigh. "I need more."

"More what? More kissing? More sex?"

"Fuck, yeah, all that," he husked, lifting his hands from where they were down the back of my pants, one sliding up and over my hip, the other slipping around front to cup my length.

I thrust forward into his fist, and he moaned before he pressed a kiss to the side of my neck. "And?"

"I'm stuck," he said, stroking my cock, drawing it from beneath my waistband. "It's like I'm all I can be, like this is it, unless...."

The lazy touching was driving me wild. I needed his mouth on me or he had to be rougher, tug my flesh until I came. "Unless," I growled.

"You stay with me."

It took me a second to parse his words because my entire focus was on his body: its proximity, his warm breath, his hooded eyes, and his demanding hands. "Stay with you?" My heart hurt, listening to him dredge his feelings up from the deep, but I had to know what was buried in him, in his heart.

"Shit," he groaned and tried to let go of me, but I pushed my hard, leaking dick into his hand and he clutched at me automatically.

"Do I feel good?"

"Oh fuck yeah," he rumbled, pressing close to shove his own cock, straining against the front of his sweats, over mine.

"Maybe you should stay with me instead."

"Okay."

"Should I ask you to move in with me?"

"Please," he said, seemingly without thought or hesitation.

"Because then you'll know, whether we're in a car together transporting witnesses or if you're alone on the other side of the world, that you have a home with me."

"Yes."

"And when you know you belong to me, *with* me, then not being able to touch me in the car won't make you feel like you're gonna crawl out of your own skin."

His gaze met mine.

"Because when we get home, behind closed doors, I can do whatever the fuck I want to you."

"Yes," he rasped, tearing at his sweats, shucking them down enough to allow his longer, thinner cock to bounce free.

I grasped both together, tight, and he moaned like he was in pain.

"God, why haven't we been doing this since.... Jesus, Miro, you're the smart one."

Was I?

I gripped the back of his neck tight, holding him still as I slid my hand up and down our cocks, jerking us both, loving the feel of his skin pressed to mine.

"It's more than just—" He shuddered. "—this."

"I know," I soothed, then moved fast, shoving him face-first into the door, pinning him there with my bulkier frame, my chest against his back. "Don't move."

He stood silently, breathing in and out, and I pulled up my pants and left him at a run, getting to my bag, finding the lube, and noting the closed door that led from the main room to the bedroom, and then, as I passed by, that the one leading from the bathroom to the bedroom was similarly shut. As professionalism went, ours was out the window. But Drake Ford and Cabot Jenner were going to be our charges in Chicago, and since we'd first emotionally saved them, and then physically, I wasn't too worried about them saying a disparaging word about either Ian or me. But even if they did, I could have cared less.

Ian needed me.

Returning, finding him frozen where I'd left him, I shoved my pants to my ankles, then his, before kissing between his shoulder blades. Stepping out of mine, I kicked them away before flipping open the cap of the lube.

"I want to go home with you," he husked. "I want you to hold me down in your bed."

How I was supposed to manhandle him when he was baring his soul was beyond me.

"I lied, you know," he confessed when I reached around him to take hold of his dripping cock and stroke him from balls to head.

"About what?" I asked, sliding my middle finger between his cheeks.

He gasped and arched his back, pushing back into me, burying my finger to the knuckle.

"Ian? What'd you lie about?"

"I-I never dreamed about your couch, M," he croaked. "I dreamed about your bed and being with you in it."

The honesty was going to kill me.

Jesus.

"How long," I demanded, releasing his cock and gripping my own, greasing myself heavily, not ever wanting to hurt him but unable to do any more for him.

"Since the first time I slept over."

Instead of beating him, I dropped the lube beside me on the carpet and leaned forward, my mouth at his ear. "Why didn't you come upstairs and get in bed with me?"

"I was scared," he admitted, hands spread on the wall, lifting his right foot from his sweats so he could widen his stance.

Wrapping my left hand around his throat, I tipped his head back on my shoulder as I kissed along his jaw.

"Miro," he ground out. "I liked it when you came inside."

He was trying to kill me. "Oh yeah?" I asked, forcing myself to remain calm, not rushing.

"When you… when your cum was dripping out of me, and I could feel it in my ass and on my thighs… I mean, I know it happened, yeah? We're connected."

"Yes."

"Do it now."

"You're gonna take me in, do you understand?"

He nodded.

Leaning back, I took hold of the base of my cock, lined my head up with his entrance, and pushed.

"Fuck!"

His muscles clamped down tight, but I was too slick, breaching him, filling him, watching his hole swallow my cock until my balls pressed against his ass.

"Jerk yourself off," I directed, hands on his hips, as I pulled out halfway, grinding my shaft over his nerve endings on the withdrawal, and then thrust back in, snapping my hips, jolting him.

"Don't stop," he pleaded.

His hands fisted against the wall as I repeated my motion, slamming inside of him, pumping rhythmically, no trace of gentleness, only pounding, driving movement.

His sleek inner walls, the way the muscles rippled and clutched around me—he felt indescribably good, all tight, slick heat.

"Forgive me."

Like there was anything else to do. "Yes."

"Keep me."

"Yes," I promised, feeling the slow roll of my orgasm building as my balls tightened and I broke out in a sweat. "Grab your cock. Get yourself off, because I'm gonna come."

"Miro—" His voice went in and out on him, cracking. "I need it harder. Please, Miro. Make it hurt."

"If it hurts I'm doing it wrong," I growled, grabbing the back of his neck and shoving him to the carpet on his hands and knees, following him down. "Don't fuckin' move."

He cried out, voice gone, as I pegged his gland, hands on his shoulders, holding him still as I fucked him.

He went rigid under me, and I came inside of him as he spurted onto the carpet beneath him. His aftershocks squeezed my shaft almost too tight, and I wanted to pull out, but a single word stilled me.

"Stay."

So I collapsed over him instead, relinquishing all my weight, my face pressed into the back of his neck, panting into his sweaty skin.

"What if you end up hating me and I lose not only my lover but my partner and my best friend?"

"I know everything about you," I said, rolling my head to lick and suck his skin. "What's there to hate?"

"All the other women I've—"

"I'm not a woman."

"Yeah, I can tell that that since your enormous cock is buried in my ass."

"Lemme get—"

"No," he whispered, reaching back to take hold of my thigh and keep me still. "Wait."

So I stayed there, inside, taking every breath with him.

"This is good."

It was so much more than simply that.

CHAPTER 16

WHEN I helped him to his feet, I was surprised to see blood on his mouth. "What the hell?" I questioned him worriedly, wiping it from his lip with my thumb.

"I didn't want to scream," he confessed, looking at me like he was drunk. "You can still kiss me, it doesn't hurt."

"Ian—"

"*Kiss* me."

I leaned in, pressing my lips to his tenderly, and he melted against me, arms wrapped around my neck, molding his body to mine. I had missed the neediness in him, and now he was finally confident enough to let me see it.

"Don't stop," he begged when I eased free, needing air.

"Come with me."

He didn't want to shower, but I shoved him in anyway, quickly washing away sweat and drying cum, and then poured him onto the sofa sleeper where he was fast asleep moments later. I went back to my computer and finished the report for Kage, making sure it was as thorough as I could possibly make it before saving it and closing up. Then I tidied up our belongings, got Ian's computer from his pack, logged in as him, and reopened the shared document and read it again, putting myself in my partner's headspace and thinking about what to add. When the bedroom door opened, I glanced up to find both Drake and Cabot looking at me.

"It's safe." I snickered. "Sorry 'bout before, but it's new with us and still a little volatile."

They both rushed forward and took seats at the table, staring at me expectantly.

"Yes?"

Cabot cleared his throat. "I—we—" His eyes flicked to Drake and then back to me. "—have questions, if it's okay."

I stopped typing and sat back, crossing my arms over my bare chest. "It's okay, g'head."

Drake cleared his throat. "Do you top?"

"Yes."

"But he's so—" Cabot coughed, glancing over at Ian and then back to me. "—scary."

"Does the fact that I fuck him make him less scary?"

"Oh hell no," Drake answered quickly.

I stared at Cabot. "If you like Drake topping, that's great. But if you want to try, you need to tell him."

He looked startled, how wide his eyes got and how quickly his mouth fell open. "And you," I said, giving my attention to Drake. "If you want him to top, ask him. It doesn't make you any less of a man if you let him."

"Okay."

"The only reason not to trade places is if he doesn't want to and you don't want to. But if he wants your ass, and you think that sounds hot, then go for it. It's your bed; nobody else gets a say about what goes on in it."

They nodded in unison like trained seals.

"How did you…" Cabot began, inching closer to me, "get someone like him to trust you enough to let you do that to him?"

I thought for a moment. "We were friends first, and that's important."

"How did you get to be friends?"

I grinned wide. "You ever feed a stray cat?"

"Yeah," Cabot said, smiling at me. "You put the food out every day. Same place, same time. You have to be consistent."

"Yes. You never stop, even though the cat hisses at you and maybe even scratches you, and there's always the posturing, like, 'I don't need this food. I'm perfectly good out here all alone in the dark.'"

Drake looked over at Ian sprawled out on the bed, his broad, muscular back on display, as were the scars that covered it. "I would have never guessed that he was gay."

"Why?" I asked pointedly. "What does gay look like?"

He turned back to me. "Not like you or him, that's for sure."

"Like me," Cabot offered. "I look gay."

"You're beautiful," I assured him. "But that doesn't automatically make you gay. Once you guys get to Chicago, you'll see. Gay and straight comes in every imaginable variety."

They were eager to talk to me; it was all over them.

"Tell me how you guys met?" I prompted.

Drake cleared his throat and leaned forward as Cabot put both elbows on the table and stared at him with so much adoration that it almost made my teeth hurt with how sweet it was. "I was hired this last summer right before school started, by Mr. Jenner," Drake explained. "I was supposed to take care of Cabot's horses. He does dressage."

"You guys had never met before?"

"No. Cabot was away at boarding schools this whole time, but he got kicked out."

"Drugs?" I asked.

"Grade tampering," Cabot informed me. "Born hacker, what can I tell you?"

"Not a very good one, if you got caught."

"No, I'm good," he defended himself. "The guy who was fucking me at the time, he messed up and I covered for him."

"Why? You love him?"

Drake was suddenly very interested in the answer.

"No. I wanted to leave Prague," he answered, reaching across the table for Drake.

Taking the small fine-boned hand in his, Drake held it tightly. "And the first day I saw him, riding up over this rise toward the back of the property… I knew I was gay."

I laughed softly. "Nice."

"He was the most beautiful thing I'd ever seen," Cabot chimed in, his eyes all over Drake. "I wanted to climb him like a tree."

"Okay, thank you for that," I said, chuckling as I went back to my report.

"He seduced me," Drake said, patting my leg to get my attention.

"In the stable?" I asked.

"Yeah."

"You had lube and condoms in there?"

Nothing. No sound.

Lifting my gaze up from my computer screen, I took in the curious looks.

"You guys get tested?"

Cabot shook his head and Drake shrugged.

"Oh for fuck's sake," I grumbled. "As soon as we land in Chicago, you guys are going to get tested, but in the meantime, you need lube."

"We use spit."

"Oh God, no," I said putting the kibosh on that, getting up and going to my bag. Pulling out the lube I'd used earlier, I tossed it to Drake. "When we get to Chicago, we'll go to the place where I buy the one I like, but in the meantime, use that."

"We tried one," Cabot said, making a face. "But it was thick and gross."

"Well, that one's actually really slick and not as thick as I would have liked. Try with that."

They were surprised.

"Now? Just go in and have sex?"

Lord. "Sure. Do I need to put on some Sade to put you in the mood?"

They both squinted.

"Get away from me," I said disgustedly.

Cabot started laughing, and Drake walked over and patted my shoulder.

"We're both so glad we get to have you and Ian watching over us."

I sighed heavily. "You guys need to be really sure that together is what you want."

"Will we enroll in school?"

"Yes, and we'll get you both into college, too, if that's what you want."

"That's what we want," Drake said.

"We'll do all that when we get to Chicago."

"And go lube shopping," Cabot reminded me.

Good God, what had I done. "Yes."

Drake bit his bottom lip. "Can I... is it okay?"

I was making a huge mistake, but I opened my arms for him.

Rushing forward, Drake hugged me tight, his head down on my shoulder. Cabot was there quickly, waiting.

"It'll be okay," I promised.

Drake inhaled deeply, calming himself before I heard the sniffling. As soon as he stepped back, Cabot shoved his way between us, wrapping his arms around my waist, pressing his cheek to my chest and clinging even as he let out a deep breath.

I made them both feel safe, and for that I was pleased.

When Cabot was ready, he stepped back, and Drake took his hand, led him back to their bedroom, and closed the door behind them.

They'd taken the lube.

Back at the table, I added to the report, caught a strangled scream from the bedroom that I tried to ignore, and then submitted it. When I was done, I realized I wasn't tired, though it was eight and we'd had a hard couple of days. I was actually hungry again, my inner clock all out of whack. I turned on the TV, put it on mute, and flipped channels from the armchair beside the bed. Normally, to keep from eating, if I wasn't tired, I would go out for a late run, but Ian was dead to the world, so I had to stay there and protect everyone.

"Why're you up?"

Turning, I found Ian, one eye open, one closed, scowling at me. "Can't sleep."

"Why not?"

"I'm hungry."

"Order room service."

"It's too late and the boys ate all the dessert they ordered."

"You don't eat anything but pie anyway."

It was true.

"If you're really hungry, go get something or order pizza."

"This isn't Chicago."

"Oh, I am aware."

"City snob," I teased.

"Shut up."

"Go back to sleep."

"Why're you on the chair?"

"I don't want to crowd you."

"For crissakes, M," he mumbled, moving the sheet on the sofa sleeper that was going to render us both paralyzed by the morning. "Crowd me, be all over me."

I smiled.

"Come here," Ian ordered.

I turned off the TV, put the remote down by the lamp before I flipped the switch, and crawled into bed beside him. "Oh wow," I said, snorting out a laugh. "You can feel every spring in this, can't ya."

He chuckled, sliding a hand around the back of my neck, drawing me down beside him, into his waiting arms.

I settled over him, parting his legs and lying between them, my head over his heart. His fingers trailing through my hair was so soothing, my eyes closed in seconds.

"From now on, just assume that I want you right next to me."

"Okay."

"Good," he whispered, slipping an arm across my back, holding tight as he continued petting me.

I smiled as I exhaled out the last of my day, more content than I ever remembered being.

CHAPTER 17

OUR FLIGHT was at nine fifteen in the morning. I made sure everyone was up early to shower so we could grab breakfast. After dropping the car off, we walked through the terminal and stood in the line for law enforcement. Security checked our IDs, tickets, our warrants, and then our firearms. I only had one, Ian his two, and then we were on our way.

In the boarding area, I left to go to the bathroom, leaving Ian with the boys. When I was washing my hands, I caught a peek at myself in the mirror, and it startled me. I was smiling like a goof, and now I understood why everyone from the waitress at the Cracker Barrel to the ticket agent to the TSA agent had been so accommodating. They all thought I was lobotomized. I looked like I was drunk.

Ian.

It was all his fault. He was having a ridiculous effect on me, making me feel like I should whistle while I walked. God, what would I do if he ever said he loved me?

"Fuck," I groaned, grabbing hold of the sink, almost clunking the face of the Rolex Daytona Catherine had given me last Christmas against the porcelain.

"You all right?"

Snapping my head up, I glanced into the mirror and saw a man in a three-piece suit standing behind me.

"You look like you're gonna pass out."

Pivoting slowly, I faced him. "No, I'm good, thanks."

He took a step sideways. Not closer, but not away either. It was a circling motion I wasn't crazy about.

"I appreciate the concern."

"Of course," he said softly as a janitor walked into the bathroom pushing a supply cart and holding a Heckler & Koch P30 with a suppressor attached.

"Don't move, Marshal."

Fuck.

The first man took a step forward, and I grabbed the butt of my gun.

"Don't fuckin' move," the janitor said, lifting his weapon, two-handed, and holding it on me.

"You better shoot me," I warned, not pulling my gun from the holster, but ready to. "Because I'm not giving up my gun."

"Marshal."

I turned from the man covering me, back to the man in the suit, who pulled a Beretta 92FS from a holster inside his suit jacket and aimed at me.

"I am Rahm Daoud," he said. "And I only need to confirm something quickly, Marshal, and then I will be gone."

"Those are not my orders," the janitor snapped. "The plan is to kill one of the marshals and let the other live."

Daoud was silent as he stalked slowly closer to him. "Yes, but as I advised your employer, killing policemen, marshals, FBI… brings trouble no one needs."

"Leandro said that—"

Daoud's action was a fast, scary coiled-snake striking movement. One second the janitor's gun was trained on me, the next it was wrenched violently sideways before the janitor was forced to fire into his own chest.

I rushed forward but was brought up fast by the Beretta aimed at my face.

"Stay where you are, Marshal."

Stilling, I watched as Daoud let the man sink to the floor before he released his hand, bending it gently across his chest. As he was wearing driving gloves, his prints would be nowhere on the murder weapon.

"This man worked for Leandro Olivera," Daoud explained, his lip curling into a sly, sexy grin. Honestly, if he wasn't about to kill me, I would have been a fan. He was stunning, with his dark flashing eyes, dimples, glossy black hair, and dark tanned skin. He looked like one of those hot Portuguese soccer players, and he moved with the same fluid grace.

"And who do you work for?" I asked, my eyes never leaving him.

"Lior Cardoso," he answered, and the way the name rolled off his tongue sounded really pretty. "You know the name?"

"I do."

"So you understand his interest in making sure the men who killed his nephew and then tried to cover it up were punished."

"Sure."

"But Leandro is a hothead. Thus we have this mess, instead of simply you and I having a quick conversation in the men's room."

I waited.

"And perhaps more."

I scoffed. "I seem easy, do I?"

Daoud's mischievous grin would have done things to my insides if a shyer, sweeter, more seldom-seen version from Ian didn't already have me enslaved. "You look good."

Flirting took the fear factor out of the equation. "What does Lior Cardoso want to know?"

He lowered the Beretta and replaced it in the holster under his coat. "The boy, Drake Ford. He will testify that Christopher Fisher was about to burn the body of Safiro Olivera?"

"Yes."

"There is no question of identity?"

"No."

"Good," he said cheerfully, "then that is all I need, Marshal."

"So, what?" I pried, taking a step toward him. "Cardoso was waiting to hear if it was true before he moves against Malloy?"

"He already moved on Malloy, as you very well know."

I did, so I made the next intuitive leap. "Lior Cardoso has Orson Malloy."

"Yes," Daoud said, moving toward the door.

"But he was waiting to do whatever until he had confirmation."

"Yes."

"Did Fisher work for both Malloy and Cardoso?"

"Yes."

"That's dangerous."

"Deadly, actually, at least for Christopher Fisher," Daoud said, putting more space between us.

"So can I expect that you'll be paying Fisher a visit?"

"Perhaps," he said huskily, edging away faster.

"Will we find any piece of Orson Malloy?"

"It's doubtful."

"And Drake Ford?"

"Drake Ford is in protective custody."

"So is Christopher Fisher, and I know you know that," I said, taking a step toward him.

"We have no problem with Drake Ford," he informed me. "And soon Drake Ford will be able to get back to his life as we will kill every Malloy that wants him dead."

"You—"

"I enjoyed meeting you, Miro Jones," Daoud said silkily. "Let's pretend we had an interlude and you wait the appropriate few minutes before emerging after I leave."

"You know I can't do that."

"Then I'm going to kill you."

"You can try."

He grunted. "So cocky. I truly wish we could have met under other circumstances. I think we would have got on well."

"We still can, Daoud, just gimme your gun."

"Sadly, like you, I cannot be parted from it."

I watched his eyes, and the second I saw his gaze shift, I grabbed my gun.

He darted around the corner as I yelled out the order for him to freeze. Flying after him, reaching the entrance, I ran to the right far enough that the bullet he fired at me grazed my left bicep instead of embedding itself in my heart.

His expression, the begrudging respect paired with the head tip before he turned and ran, was infuriating.

He tore through the terminal, gun in hand, and I followed, arms and legs pumping, gaining ground, as we flew past the boarding area where Ian and the boys waited. I didn't slow to say anything, knowing he would stay and protect them.

Airport security joined in the chase; they ordered us both to halt, which, of course, caused neither of us to slow even a little.

I was too close behind Daoud for him to stop, turn, and fire a second time, and shooting over his shoulder at me would slow his momentum. If he faltered even a little, I'd have him, and he knew it as well as I did. He screamed at people to get out of his way, and they made a hole that he and I charged through.

It was not a big airport, and when we ran past security, I yelled "Fire!" to get attention and held my gun up, which caused the expected eruption of shouting.

More people started to chase us as Daoud bolted through the automatic doors, and I was seconds behind him, running straight out into the middle of the street and almost getting hit by a car—screeching tires, blowing horns as people slammed on their brakes to miss us. I sprinted down the median after him before stopping suddenly and hitting the pavement as a barrage of bullets strafed the road.

I saw him get into the passenger seat of an SUV that tore away, but not before Daoud waved.

"Fuck!" I roared, getting to my knees, not missing the fact that there was no plate on the car.

Sirens, armed men and women all converged on me, and I was ordered to drop my weapon and put my hands behind my head.

Laying my gun down gently, I laced my fingers over the top of my head and waited. The first guy who reached me almost put his foot on my gun to kick it away from me.

"You touch the gun, and you'll buy me a new one."

He stopped—they all stopped—and then someone noticed the badge on my belt.

"Oh fuck."

My sentiment as well.

Fifteen minutes later, I was talking to the head of airport security and individuals from the sheriff's department, and getting my arm bandaged up by two EMTs.

"How long's it been since you had tetanus booster, Marshal?"

"Like a month ago," I informed her.

"Get shot a lot, do you?"

"Pretty much," I said, wincing as she cleaned the wound.

"Miro!"

I groaned, leaning around her to see Ian charging through the terminal, Drake and Cabot in tow. From the bellow I'd been treated to, the hard set of his jaw, and the tight bunch of his fists, I got the idea I was in trouble.

Pushing through bystanders, he reached me and dropped down to one knee beside the bench I was sitting on. "What the fuck?"

"There was a hit man for the Nava Cartel in the bathroom."

"What?"

"I—"

"There's a dead man in there now," someone chimed in.

His eyes flicked to my arm. "Jesus."

"It's a graze."

"It's on the same side with your heart."

I grimaced.

"Again!"

"Yeah, but—"

"Miro!"

"I got a name," I said quickly, hoping to get him to change the subject.

"You got whose name? The hit man's?"

"Yeah."

"How?"

What was I supposed to say? "He was kinda flirty."

"Flirty," he repeated flatly, and I watched, utterly riveted, as his eyes went from their normal pale icy blue to deep, dark cobalt.

"Wow," I said, grinning without meaning to. "You have it kinda bad, you know?"

His eyes narrowed to slits.

Crap.

He moved to get up, but I took hold of his wrist and held tight. "Don't leave me."

"Oh, I won't leave you until I kill you," he promised, smirking. "Now I'm gonna call your boss. I hope you live."

That wasn't nice.

BECAUSE IT was my day, Kage was flying into the Tri-Cities airport to rendezvous and fly back to Chicago with us. We had, of course, missed our plane, and with the latest development, he wanted to be on site. He would have been leaving Arlington today anyway, but now he was backtracking to help us transport our witnesses home because I was, technically, out of commission. Even though I told him I was fine, he was coming because he, too, wanted to hear what I had to say to the sheriff's department, FBI, Homeland Security, and airport security. Press swarmed everywhere, and law enforcement sequestered us in the lounge, since no one was supposed to see our witnesses.

Ian alternated being on his phone with working on his computer while Cabot and Drake watched television until Cabot fell asleep on his boyfriend.

"So it sounded like, from what you said," Drake began when I crossed the room to check on him, "that the cartel people don't want to hurt me."

"Yep," I sighed. "That was my understanding as well."

"How come, do you think?"

"I think if you hadn't seen Safiro Olivera that night, he would have been burned up and no one would have ever known what happened to him."

"So now his family knows what really happened to him."

"And that way they can grieve."

"Well, good, that's important."

We were quiet a moment as I studied him. He had such a good face, strong and kind. "So your life will probably go back to normal faster than you think. Maybe you and Cabot can go back to Bowman and—"

"No sir," he said implacably. "Cabot and me, we're going to start our life together far away from all that."

"You're really young, Drake. You realize that this—you and Cabot—might not end in a fairy tale. You might not last."

He thought a moment, his gaze surfing the room before landing back on me. "Maybe. I mean, I'm not stupid. I know we're really young, both of us just turned eighteen, and it's not gonna be easy. We're gonna have to go to school, and even though school will be taken care of, we hafta eat, right?"

"Yes."

"And Cabot, I mean, he's never worked a day in his life. He doesn't know about anything, so that part's kinda scary."

"Sure."

"But I love him like crazy, you know? And when you love someone like crazy, should you stand around being scared that something might not work out, or do you do something about it and take a chance?"

He was right. And because he was so young, he could look at his situation and see it for what it really was—time to take a leap of faith. I had to do the same.

Leaning forward, I patted his knee. "You're right. Just do the best you can."

His face lit up. "Thank you, Miro."

I got up and walked over to Ian, who was back on his phone. When I was close enough, I overheard him say "Emma," and so I hesitated.

"No," he sighed, raking his fingers through his hair before he turned around to look for me. I could tell because his gaze swept the room, and then he tensed before he noticed I was right there.

I saw him take a quick breath and settle, and it hit me, like I'd been shot. He needed me to ground him, to tether him, so he didn't float away. I would do the best job of it ever once we got home. We had to talk on the plane. There was so much to say.

"I can't," Ian said gruffly into his phone. "It looks like I'm gonna be tied up for the foreseeable future."

And he was. With me.

CHAPTER 18

ON THE second leg of the trip home, there were six seats for us, two in first class and four in business. We sat in twos, Kage and White—who was back from leave—up in the fancy seats, and then Cabot and Drake, and me and Ian. I had been really happy to see Chandler White striding up to me beside Kage, looking all hale and hearty.

"What did you say?" he teased.

"I'm being all corny 'cause I'm so happy to see you back on the job."

He gave me a gentle pat on the shoulder. "You're a sap, Jones."

And I was, but having the team back together meant a lot to me. Like the four women in my life who loved me, they were my family.

We played musical chairs with the seating because my boss wanted to talk to everyone. I thought Cabot was going to come out of his skin when it was his turn to go sit with Kage.

"He's just gonna ask you some questions," I promised when he walked back to me instead of forward to sit with Kage in the last row of first class, where they had actual glass salt and pepper shakers.

He nodded, inhaled quickly, and strode forward and sat down.

"What's he asking him?" Drake wanted to know, leaning up over the seat.

"He's looking to get an accounting of what happened at his father's house," I explained. "I wrote a report, my boss is only corroborating it."

"Yeah, okay," he said worriedly. "But he won't take us away from you and Ian, right?"

White did a slow pan to me from where he was sitting now beside Drake.

"Shut up," I snapped at White before returning my attention to Drake, who appeared terrified. "It'll be fine."

"My mother never gave a shit about me and I never knew my father. Cabot's folks were the same. So you and him," Drake said, tipping his head at Ian, "are as close to people who give a shit as we have."

I would so hear it from White later; the smirk told me so. "Yeah, kid, I know. Don't worry about it. It'll be okay."

Ian leaned forward and put his hand up over the back of Drake's chair, and Drake immediately grabbed it, squeezed, and then let go.

"Take a breath," Ian directed.

"Okay," he said, then turned around in his chair and got comfortable.

I had never put the armrest down between Ian and me, so once both Drake and White were facing forward, Ian slid his hand down my thigh.

Turning to him, I saw the scowl. "What?"

"You got shot at again."

"Yeah, well," I croaked, realizing I had to have a very serious conversation with him. "That's gonna keep happening since I'm a federal marshal."

His brows furrowed and the scowl changed to his normal glower.

"Stop," I ordered, sliding my fingers through his on my thigh, flattening his hand, holding it pressed tight against me. "Listen."

All his focus was on me, and he waited, calming simply because I was touching him. Who knew that, all those times when Ian was bouncing off the walls, all he needed was for me to reach out and hold his hand?

"You're gonna live with me, yeah?"

Boom.

That fast, his eyes darkened with heat. "You said I could."

"Well, then I gotta tell the man sitting in first class."

I don't know what I expected, but Ian thinking a moment and then nodding wasn't it.

"Ian?"

"Yeah," he said huskily. "Good. So that way he'll stop asking you if you want a new partner and leave it alone."

"You knew about that?"

"'Course," he said as I moved my hand, letting him go.

"How come you never said anything?"

"Because you always talk for both of us."

"You know if I didn't love you, I'd kill you," I grumbled, getting up after seeing Kage had finished with Cabot.

I passed the younger man, gave him a quick pat on the back, and was almost to the seat beside Kage when it hit me.

I went almost light-headed with the realization of what I'd said to Ian Doyle.

Holy shit.

"Jones?"

Looking down at Kage instead of back toward my partner, I flopped into the seat beside him.

"I actually wanted Ford next, not you."

My gaze met his, and I noticed, as always, that meeting his stare was not that easy. He was an intense man, and being his entire focus was slightly unnerving.

"Jones?"

I took a settling breath and jumped. "I'm gay."

Nothing.

"Boss?"

"Yes, Jones," he said, sounding so very bored.

"You heard me, right?"

"I did," he said patiently.

I cleared my throat. "Ian, he—he's gonna move in with me."

He squinted. "And?"

"I—we—thought you should know."

"Because?"

"Well, I mean, you've gotta be thinking, if we're in a relationship and it goes south, what does that do for your partnership?"

"Why would that concern me? It should concern you."

"I—"

"If things go south, you're the ones who have to deal with the fact that you're partners and stuck together. I'm not getting how that's my problem?"

It was all so… composed. Kage was acting like it was no big deal, like people came out to him at work every day. All of it perfectly normal.

"So you're okay with—"

"Is there anything else, Jones?"

I coughed. "No sir."

"May I speak to Mr. Ford now?"

"Yessir."

"Excellent," he said sarcastically as I stood up slowly.

I couldn't stop staring at him.

"I'm aging here, Jones."

"Yessir," I muttered, turning and leaving, making my way back to where Cabot was sitting beside Drake. "Hey, Drake, my boss would like a word."

He was frightened; it was there on his face.

"It's no big deal, I swear."

He got up, White took his spot, and I flopped down next to Ian. Immediately, his hand was on my thigh, gripping tight.

"So?" Ian prodded.

"Your boss could care less."

His smile came slowly as I shook my head. "I knew it."

"You knew what?"

"That Sam Kage was not the kind of man who cared about us outside of work."

"What?"

"You know what I mean."

"He cares about the kind of job we do, not about who we do away from it."

"Yeah," he said, grinning as he let his head bump against the back of his seat.

"So," I said, clearing my throat. "What'd Emma want?"

He turned to look at me blankly. "What?"

"I heard you say 'Emma' when you were on the phone back at the airport."

"Oh, no, that wasn't Emma. That was Jocelyn, a friend of hers."

"And? Don't make me dig."

"She, uhm," he began, his voice low and rough, "wanted to have dinner to make sure I was okay."

"How sweet," I said curtly.

He took my hand in his, lacing his fingers through mine. "But I can't have dinner with her. I'm busy, right?"

"From now on, yeah."

He squeezed my hand for a second.

"You like me saying that."

"I do," he growled, and the sound slithered right through me to my cock.

"Jesus," I mumbled, shifting in my seat, my jeans suddenly very tight.

"Call Aruna when we land and see if she and Liam can keep Chickie one more night."

"Okay," I agreed, my body heating fast.

He leaned into me, his mouth on my ear. "I wanna move all my stuff in tonight, but we'll just go to my place and get clothes for tomorrow."

"Sounds like a plan."

"All I wanna do is sleep in your bed."

He'd be lucky to do any of that.

"I wanna be there, like, now."

"You have no idea what you're getting into."

"Yeah, I do," he said softly. "I'm yours."

They were magic words.

ONCE WE landed in Chicago, we walked through one of the many enormous terminals toward the security gates, then down to baggage claim, where we could get a cab back to the field office to process Drake and Cabot.

"Daddy!"

We all looked up as a beautiful little dark-eyed, dark-haired girl came charging toward us. I was wondering where her father was when I saw Kage drop to one knee and hold out his arms. She flung herself into them, hugging him tight, her smile huge.

His daughter?

Christ.

Would it kill the man to have pictures on his desk? And I got it, we were marshals, and you didn't want scary people perusing snapshots of your kids, but still. It was a lot to take in, Sam Kage as a father. He let her go and took her hand, didn't turn to introduce her to us, nothing. They walked together, him looking down, her looking up, as she chattered to him about their cat that was now pink, something about food coloring and an experiment gone wrong and cupcakes. When the doors slid open and we walked outside, she waved crazily, and a boy, older, maybe nine or ten, ran up and stopped, wrapping his arms around Kage's waist, leaning for a second as the scary man who led our team bent and kissed the top of his head.

I wondered which kid was adopted as both children left him, his son with his duffel, his daughter with his laptop bag, running to the curb where a van idled. The side door slid open sideways, and then, from the driver's side window, a head popped out. And you could have knocked me over with a feather.

Not a woman.

Sam Kage did not have a wife.

The kids climbed into the back, and the door closed as Kage reached for the stunning blond man beaming at him. He cupped his face in his hands, leaned in, and kissed him. It was quick, but tender and a revelation to witness, because holy crap, who knew Kage had it in him? When the other man ducked back inside, Kage opened the passenger-side door and got in. They didn't leave, though; the man popped his head out again, looked right at us, and waved.

"Glad to see you again, Deputy White."

My teammate waved back, Kage raised a hand, and the van was gone seconds later.

I rounded on White. "You fuck!"

"What?"

"How come you never told me our boss was gay?"

He bristled. "What does it matter?"

"Because I'm gay, asshole," I barked.

"Oh yeah," he huffed, relaxing from his combative stance. "I forgot."

And that was nice, that to White it didn't matter one way or another who I slept with—I was simply another member of his team. But still! Kage was gay?

"Does everybody know but me?"

"I don't think anybody knows but me, Sharpe, and now you and Doyle."

"How does Sharpe know?"

He squinted at me. "Everything I know, my partner knows."

"Right. Sure." Processing. "He's gay?"

"Yep."

"How did you find out?"

"I had to take some surveillance photos over to his house like three years ago now. It was right before you started, actually."

"So how long?"

"How long what? How long has he been gay? How the fuck am I supposed—"

"No. How long has he been with his husband?"

"Oh, he's been in a civil union with Mr. Harcourt like fifteen years or something, but in June they're gonna have a big party."

"Oh really?"

"Yeah."

"And you know this how?"

"I was with him when he was talking to that friend of his, you know, the homicide detective who has that billionaire boyfriend—what's his name?"

"I don't remember."

"Well, that's how I know."

I had to absorb. "Sam Kage is gay."

"So am I, get over it," Ian said, walking around me toward the curb to get a cab.

"See, now, I figured Doyle was gay too," White yawned as he looked for his wife's car in the sea of vehicles.

"What?" I managed to get out, certain I was having a heart attack.

He shrugged. "I mean, how he looks at you all the time? You'd hafta be blind to miss that shit, right?"

Oh dear God.

"And how you're always in his space and you're the only one he lets do that—I mean, I was pretty sure you guys were, yanno… together."

I needed to sit down before I passed out. Leaning over, I put my hands on my thighs and took steady in and out breaths before I hyperventilated.

"What the fuck's with you?"

"Nothing," I croaked.

"Oh, there's my wife," White said, smiling as he waved. "You guys wanna ride or—"

"No, we're good," I rasped, my mouth dry. "And you shouldn't want Ford and Jenner near your wife anyway. They're witnesses, or did you forget?"

"No, smartass, I didn't forget."

"Well, technically they shouldn't have seen Kage's family, either."

"Yeah, but there's grades of witness," he reminded me. "And your boys are classified as friendly and long-term. You know that."

I did know that.

"So," he asked again. "Ride or no?"

"No, we're good. You go home. I'll see ya tomorrow."

"Okay, I'll see ya," he said, chuckling, patting me on the shoulder before he dashed to the curb.

A gentle hand touched my back, and I turned to find Cabot there, looking concerned, Drake with him, holding both of their bags.

"You okay, Miro?" Cabot wanted to know.

"Yeah, buddy, I will be."

His smile was blinding.

"Guys!" Ian yelled from the curb.

We all hurried.

CHAPTER 19

AT THE field office, we sat with Ryan and Dorsey as they performed the intake paperwork, going over the massive document that made Cabot Jenner and Drake Ford formal members of WITSEC. They went through where the boys would stay until an apartment was procured, how they were both officially now graduated from high school, and when they would go with me to the University of Chicago to get them both enrolled for the fall quarter.

"He went there," Dorsey said, indicating me with a wave of his hand. "So he's the best one to take you guys over."

It took hours, like always—Ian and I had done it for others—and when I got up to go to the bathroom and get drinks for all involved, Kohn caught me in the hall.

"What?"

"White says you and Doyle are, like, together?"

I groaned.

"No, man," he said, smiling, bumping me with his shoulder. "Nobody cares."

"Maybe not you and White and—"

"Sharpe," he teased.

Of course Sharpe already knew; White probably called him from the car. "Becker will care, so will Ching."

"Nope," Kohn assured me, shaking his head. "You and Doyle, we're family, yeah? We've all got your back. You know that."

I stared at him.

"Don't be a dick, Jones," he said irritably, walking away. "We never cared when we all knew it was just you."

God, could it really be this easy? In our self-contained little group, no one cared? And it wasn't that Ian and I were going to make a general announcement, but if the guys in our unit were okay with us, what else did we really need?

"Hey, you gotta come back in. Ryan's digressing and we could be here all—what's wrong?" Ian asked, walking around in front of me.

"Everybody knows."

He shrugged. "Well, yeah, I told White I was gay at the airport. News travels fast with him. You know that."

"White never let it slip about our boss."

"That's 'cause he's our boss. But you and me are fair game."

"So Ryan and Dorsey know?"

"Uh, yeah," he said, chuckling. "Dorsey just said to Drake and Cabot that they're lucky that they have gay marshals watching out for them, so we can run 'em down to Halstead."

"He did not."

Ian smirked.

"Fuckhead."

"And you're surprised, why?"

"Ian."

He grunted.

"Are you sure you're okay with all this?"

"I get to sleep with you, right?"

"Yeah."

"Well, then, I'm good."

I took a breath, and he took the cans of Pepsi out of my hands and walked back into the room. My plan was to follow him, but my phone rang, and seeing it was Liam, I answered.

"Hey," I greeted him. "Is it okay if—"

"Miro," Liam said.

"Yeah. Who else would it be?"

"Did Aruna call you?"

"No," I said, and then a jolt of fear ran through me. "Is she okay?"

"Yeah, we both are, but we're here talking to the police."

"What? Why?"

"Dude, we got carjacked."

One of my dearest friends had her life threatened? "Holy shit," I choked, bolting from the room, on the way to the elevator. "Where are you guys? I can be there in—"

"No, it's—"

"Is Aruna all right?" I demanded, rushing down the hall. "Are you all right? Did you—"

"No, listen. Shut the fuck up and stop moving. Don't do anything but listen."

I froze where I was.

"I meant to say, we were *almost* carjacked."

And that made all the difference in the world. "Maybe *start* with that next time, dickhead."

He grunted instead of apologizing and then gave me the rundown. The way he explained it, he and Aruna had stopped at a light on their way home. Liam rolled down the driver's-side window to give money to a homeless guy on the street, and when that guy stepped away from the car, another thrust a gun in Liam's face.

Aruna screamed, and before a demand could be made, Chickie shoved between their seats, scrambled over Liam's lap, and launched himself at the window in a fury of ferocious snarling and snapping jaws.

"Miro, he scared the fuck outta that guy. He dropped his gun and ran."

I took a breath. "You're both okay."

"Yeah," he said hesitantly. "We called the police and they came to get the gun. They're hoping that the prints or serial number or something will lead them to the guy."

"Well, that's good."

"Yeah, it is."

"So do you need me there or no?"

"No, we're good."

"So then what's going on, 'cause you sound all weird. Are you freaking out?"

"The cops are here taking our statement, and they're all treating Chickie like he's the second coming, ya know?"

"Sure," I said, trying to figure out why he sounded so odd. "What's wrong?"

He cleared his throat. "Aruna… she—she really doesn't wanna give Chickie back."

"I'm sorry, what?"

Liam coughed. "Aruna. She wants to keep Chickie, and I gotta tell you, how protective he is of her, how much he loved all the little kids this weekend, and my uncle, who's a vet, he says that Chickie is actually not a wolf at all. He thinks he's malamute and Caucasian Ovcharka."

"I have no idea what that is."

"Well, he thinks that's why he's so big, plus he's got a really even temperament."

I laughed into the phone. "Liam, Ian's not gonna give you guys his dog."

"Who better than a family to have him?"

"Liam—"

"Gotta go, talk to you later," he said and then hung up.

I called Aruna, but all I got was her voice mail. Switching to text, I let her know that she couldn't keep something that didn't belong to her.

She sent back one word. *Hah.*

I tried her again.

"What?" she said irritably, finally picking up.

"You can't keep Ian's dog, but I will let him stay until I get off tomorrow night," I told her.

"I might move."

"I'm a US marshal, I'll find you."

"But Miro," she whined.

"No."

"He loves me."

"You're gonna have a baby. You're gonna be too busy to take care of a werewolf."

Another whimper.

I laughed. "I'll see ya tomorrow night."

"Fine," she said and hung up.

I stood there a second and then walked back to the office and into the room to listen to more of the intake paperwork. Cabot was nodding off; Drake had his chin in his hand, staring blearily at Ryan, who was reading in a monotone voice as Dorsey and Ian had their arms crossed, heads back, resting their eyes.

"You look weird," Ian interrupted, which woke everyone up.

"Well, that's because Liam and Aruna are trying to keep your dog."

His smile was fast. "Yeah, I figured that was coming."

"What? You did?"

"Yeah, I mean, who volunteers to take somebody else's dog with them to the mountains? Come on."

"You're not gonna give them Chickie, are you?"

"I dunno," he said thoughtfully. "I have to think about what's best for him."

"Really?"

"Sure. For instance, where would he go every day?"

I didn't even have to think, I knew already. "He'd stay home with Aruna or go to the fire station with Liam."

"And when Liam's home, he'd take him with him wherever he went, right? Plus when Aruna has the baby, when she goes out, who better to protect her and the baby than demon dog?"

"But he's yours."

"What are we talking about?" Ryan wanted to know.

"Doyle's wolf," Dorsey informed him.

"Oh, okay."

"You have a wolf?" Cabot asked.

"He's a dog," I said, clearing it up.

Ian's phone rang, and after checking the caller ID, he got up and left, taking the call outside the room. I wanted to know who called, but more than that, I wanted to be done.

"Have them start signing," I told Ryan. "Let's give them their document packets and get this show on the road already. We're all wiped out. Please."

"We need food," Cabot begged.

"Just gimme a pen," Drake pleaded as well. "I'll sign whatever you want."

"I bet this is a form of torture in some countries," Cabot insisted.

"But you guys need to be apprised of—"

"Miro and Ian are gonna take care of us," Drake explained to them. "We'll be fine."

Ryan and Dorsey looked up at me.

"Let it go," I groused.

"Awww, you and Doyle are parents," Dorsey said snidely.

Ryan grinned. "Mazel tov."

"You guys are such assholes," I grumbled.

But large plastic document pouches slid across the table, as well as two binders.

"Make with the signing," Dorsey directed.

By the time Ian came back an hour later, we were done.

There was so much to do in the first days and weeks of new witness relocation. Social Security cards were already in the packets along with birth certificates, but Drake and Cabot had to get driver's licenses, enroll in school, and be placed in jobs. All the things that fell under setting up a new life, Ian and I would make certain were done. We would be with them the whole way, from finding a furnished apartment to buying supplies for their new abode to purchasing clothes and school books and all other essentials. We'd set them up and then keep tabs. Ian and I had done intake many times. It was the part of the job I loved the best, helping people pick up the pieces of their lives to start anew. I was looking forward to watching over Cabot and Drake.

As the four of us walked to the elevator, I asked Ian who was on the phone.

"My father," he said, hitting the Down button.

"And?"

He coughed. "He was upset I hadn't gotten a hold of him."

"And?" I prodded. It was like pulling teeth.

"He wants us to come to dinner next Sunday," he said, leading us all to the car. "I said I'd check with you and get back to him."

Inside, he punched the Lobby button before I took hold of his arm.

"Look at me."

He complied instantly. "You told your father what?"

"That you would be there too."

"And?"

He shrugged. "He said that was good, since I'm better when you're around."

"He did?"

"He knows I don't care what he thinks anyway, but he's fine with us."

"Us?"

"He said he always figured we were a thing."

I was at a loss.

"I guess it's what people think when they see us."

"Yeah?"

"Yeah. We seem like we're married."

I had to lean on the wall for support.

WE PUT the newly made Drake Palmer and Cabot Kincaid in one of the federal safe houses in a secure high rise downtown. There was a doorman who let us in and a guard at the front desk, a key fob had to be swiped to push the button for the elevator and then again inside to enable the buttons. On each floor you punched in a code to get into the condo and disabled an alarm inside with another code. It was a whole process that had to be followed, because to get out, all the same steps had to be repeated.

"I'm already confused," Drake whined.

"I got this," Cabot said, taking the direction sheet Dorsey had given them with the numbers he'd filled in that were entered specifically for our two newest guests.

Ian thought he could make a break for it without being hugged, but he couldn't. They were crazy about him.

We left them with their money allotment for the evening, told them they were free to go wherever they wanted but that sticking around downtown might be best. I suggested Navy Pier, and they were excited to go and check it out.

"You'll both be back in the morning?" Cabot asked as he hugged me.

"We will," I promised and passed him his new phone with numbers for me and Ian programmed in.

He was very pleased.

AS WE drove to Ian's place, he mentioned again how much he was not loving the Nissan Xterra. He had said it earlier when I led him to the car parked in the garage at work.

"This is such a comedown after the Jungle Boogie car."

I chuckled. "Yeah, I know."

"Hey."

I glanced over.

"Are you gonna tell the girls about us?"

"Of course." I sighed. "And they'll be ridiculous about it."

"What do you mean?"

"When I was recovering at home, they wanted to know what I was doing about getting what I wanted."

"And you wanted what?"

"That should be fairly obvious."

"Tell me."

"You, idiot. I wanted you."

His smirk was ridiculously sexy every single time. "Yeah?"

I was not going to feed his ego anymore and instead checked my e-mail as he parked outside his apartment building. When I was done, I grabbed his phone, which he had left in one of the cup holders, and checked his e-mail. I was surprised to find a letter from a lawyer on which Brent Ivers, my ex, was the subject line.

The trunk opened before I finished, and Ian threw in a garment bag and a large duffel. I held his phone up so he couldn't miss what I'd been up to.

"Why are you getting threats from a lawyer?"

He slammed the trunk shut, and came around the side of the SUV and got in. He took hold of the steering wheel and squeezed tight.

"You threatened Brent?"

"No."

"It says you did."

"All I conveyed to the man," he said, smiling evilly, "was that if he came within five hundred feet of you, I'd fuckin' shoot him."

Oh for fuck's sake. "Are you kidding?"

"Don't look so fuckin' pained," he groused, starting the car, shotgunning out into the street, as usual. "I told him not to call or text or send e-mail, either."

"Or the same punishment would befall him? Gunfire?"

He narrowed one eye like he was thinking.

"You can't do that. The lawyer filed a TRO against you. That doesn't look good."

"I give a shit."

"Ian—"

"I'll end him if he comes near you again," he said flatly. "Make no mistake."

"I can take care of myself, yeah?"

He pointed at my arm where the bullet had grazed me. "I beg to differ."

"That's different and you know it."

"Do I?"

I reached over and slid my hand around the back of his neck.

"It's nice that you care."

"It's more than that."

"I know."

"Okay."

"Can we stop and get burgers at Shorty's? They're still open; it's only eleven."

He made a noise in the back of his throat.

"Are you salivating?"

"Yeah, I think I just swallowed my own spit."

Why that was so hysterical I had no idea, but I lost it, and listening to me laugh, tears rolling down my cheeks, made him smile like he hardly ever did, his whole face cracking wide open, dimples popping, laugh lines crinkling, and deep sigh of contentment emerging.

"Fuck, I love it when you're happy."

Which was the nicest thing anyone had ever said to me.

At Shorty's, a dive off of Harlem Avenue that was only a shack with a stove in it, the cashier being the same person who passed you your food, I ordered while Ian stood behind me. Two picnic tables were the extent of their seating, but it hardly mattered, as most people took their food to go. Everyone grabbed their burger there after being at a club all night, and on Friday and Saturday it was fun to see the cross-section of cars, fashion, and people all standing in line. As it was a Sunday night, it was us and a few hookers, some college kids, and four women.

After we ordered, we waited, leaning against the side of the building.

"You know what I can't get outta my head," Ian asked, leaning close to me, his voice in my ear.

"What's that?"

"You with your lips wrapped around my cock."

Instantly my body flushed with heat, but my words stayed cool. "Liked that, did you?"

"Yeah," he said huskily, leaning in to press a quick kiss to the side of my neck.

I covered it with my hand, feeling oddly like I'd been branded, and watched him swagger over to the window to collect our food. He smiled at the women at the table, and I saw them all check him out, following every fluid movement until he reached me.

"You know each and every one of those girls wants to take you home, Marshal," I informed him.

"Yeah, well, I only go home with you."

I coughed. "What's with you being all sweet all of a sudden?"

He shrugged, grabbed my hand, and tugged me after him. The looks we got, first surprise, then smiles, were nice. But as he led me to the car, I understood. I had said where he would be—I'd laid claim—and because of that, he felt safe. He needed me to say what he could and couldn't do; it was how he knew he was loved.

I couldn't put my finger on the exact moment when I fell in love with Ian Doyle, but at some point, having all his attention became what I *had* to have. And even if he decided tomorrow that he didn't want me anymore, the short time when I was all he saw would be enough.

"What're you thinking about?" he asked as he made a U-turn in the middle of the street, nearly getting us killed before he got us in the correct lane.

"Nothing."

"Something, you got all quiet."

"I just hope this works for you for a long time."

"What's that?"

Was he kidding? "Us," I said simply.

"You lost me."

"I want this, you and me, to work out."

"There's no question about that," he said, making a face like I was ridiculous. "You're the only one I've ever wanted."

Only Ian made my heart stop and start with such frequency.

"You made what I needed okay."

I couldn't have said a word if my life depended on it.

"So it's for you to say if you ever want me to go away. I'm in."

He was so matter-of-fact.

I'm in.

There would be no more questions for him, no second-guessing, no hesitancy.

"You know I love you. What else do you need?"

To him, it was obvious. He knew where he stood. I cleared my throat. "Nothing. I don't need anything."

"So we're good?"

"Yeah," I said hoarsely. "We're good."

He grunted and turned onto my street, then parked the car a block from my Greystone. He could have parked in my assigned space, but my truck was there.

I carried his duffel bag, he his garment bag, and I kept the burgers inside my jacket to try to keep them warm. Inside my apartment, we both hung up our coats in the entryway closet, and then Ian crossed quickly to the stairs and went up to my bedroom. I cranked up the thermostat to seventy and dropped the burgers on the coffee table and my bag and his on one end of the sofa before I went to the kitchen to get a couple of beers.

When he came back down, I had our burgers split as we always did so I got half of his hot-as-hell Four Horseman burger and he got half of my To Thai For burger. Fries and onion rings got divided up as well.

"Oh thank you." He almost cried, and I laughed as he came around the couch and flopped down beside me, leaning sideways and kissing me.

It was quick, and then he had his hands full, tearing into his food.

I stared at him a moment, hit with a sudden wave of normalcy. Us eating together; the TV going on as we checked basketball scores; him shoving fries into his mouth, sucking down a beer, grabbing for a napkin, and bumping me with his knee.

This was how it would be every night. At work, nothing would change, but here in my house behind closed doors or out with friends, it would be like this. Ian Doyle would be in my space, with me, living, breathing, building a life.

"Eat," he ordered with his mouth full.

I swallowed down my joy so I could.

I cleaned up afterward while he carried our bags upstairs, and threw things in the laundry, our stuff together, as he hung up his suit in my closet.

"Christ, I'm so happy to be home," I said happily, taking a seat on my bed, unlacing my boots and letting them clunk down on the floor. "I swear I'm never—Ian?"

He was standing next to the railing, staring at me but not moving.

"Come here," I suggested, patting the space beside me on the bed.

Rushing across the small room, he shoved me down, climbed on and straddled my hips, holding me still.

"Something you want, Marshal?"

"Miro," he croaked. "This bed is—oh."

I wriggled under him, gripping his thighs and pressing my quickly hardening cock up against his crease. "This bed is yours, too, from now on. You understand?"

"Yes," he huffed, arching his back as his eyes closed and his mouth fell open.

"I'm yours too."

His lashes fluttered open, and his gaze locked with mine. "Swear," he said, his voice hoarse and full of gravel. "You and me."

"I swear," I promised, reaching up for his face.

He bent into my hands, letting me ease him down, his lips parting the moment they touched mine.

"Miro," he breathed into my mouth.

He tasted like beer and salt and Ian, and when I rolled him to his back, I deepened the kiss, mauling his mouth as he wrapped his long legs around my hips and ground up against me.

God.

Ian, in my bed.

"Jesus," I moaned, shoving away from him before I came in my jeans just from thinking about it.

He smiled as he panted under me. "You like having me here."

I couldn't speak, instead rolling off the bed and stripping fast. He sat up and did the same, as rough as I was, tugging off his clothes. Grabbing the lube from my nightstand, I turned and found him stretched out, waiting.

"I wanna see your face when we do this."

He nodded and reached for me.

I pounced on him, taking his mouth, parting his thighs so I could move between them, raising his knees so his feet were on the backs of my calves. His cock was pressed between us as I devoured him, missing nothing, giving him bruising kisses until he had to turn his head to gulp for air.

"Kiss me again," he pleaded.

I sat back, flipped open the cap of the lube, and as I slicked my cock, his eyes narrowed to slits of feverish dark blue.

"Miro."

"I need to make you ready."

"No," he insisted. "I can't wait—don't want to."

Tossing the lube aside, pressing against his entrance, he bowed up off the bed, wanting me.

"Pass me a pillow."

He handed me mine and I shoved it under him, changing the angle as I pushed gently forward, slipping inside. He grabbed hold of my biceps, slid his legs up my thighs and locked them around my hips.

"I'm gonna go slow and—"

"You know, sometimes I'll notice you walking beside me, and I'm so proud."

I dropped my head forward, needing to be buried in him but holding back, keeping my entry slow, steady, feeling his muscles ripple around me.

"And now… it'll be more, 'cause I know you're mine."

"Ian," I ground out.

"I need… Miro… c'mon, man, just take what you want."

I thrust hard, as deep as I could, and he yelled my name before coiling his arms around me.

I was wrapped up in him.

"You have to move."

"Then you have to let go."

"No," he rasped, lifting for my mouth.

Jesus.

He didn't want to let go of me?

"Miro," he said, thick and dark. "Show me—"

That I loved him? Wanted him? Needed him? What did he have to see? Feel? Taste? Hear?

"—your heart."

But I had. For three years, every day, I had shown Ian Doyle the depth of my love.

Unwinding his arms from around my neck, I curled my fingers into his, marrying our palms, and pressed both hands down onto the mattress.

"I love you, Ian," I rumbled, my voice gritty with feeling as I stared into his eyes. "Don't ever doubt my heart."

He squinted fast but it didn't work: a stray tear leaked out and ran down his temple. I caught it with a kiss before I drove into him, desperate to make him feel my love.

"Do you believe me?"

"Yes," he said, sounding broken, crackly. "Always."

Our hands fused together, both of us holding as tight as we could, him lifting, meeting every rolling thrust, and me trying to anchor him, his knees spread wide, my mouth slanting over his, laying claim to every piece of Ian. Heart, mind, body, soul—all mine.

I ground into him, the motion slow and sensuous, and he took me, his muscles holding me tight as I pushed and pushed deeper, taking as he gave until he went stiff beneath me in his release, pumping hot and slick between us.

"Miro," he panted, trying to free his hands, wanting them on me.

His orgasm twisted his muscles around my cock, and the heat between us, the rhythm and the slide, all of it tore my climax from me. He shivered as I filled him, and then harder when I kissed him, rubbing my tongue over his.

It took long minutes for us to be able to speak, much less move.

"You okay?" I asked when I finally unsealed our lips.

"Oh yes," he murmured.

When I eased free, I was going to dart to the bathroom and grab a washcloth and a towel, but he wrapped me in his arms, hugging me tight.

"We should take a shower." I chuckled into his sweaty hair, nuzzling, kissing his temple, his cheek, tightening my hold on him instead of letting go.

"Yeah," he agreed, not moving, sliding his leg between mine. "You know, I think I might be ready to tie you down."

I smiled, loving the feel of all his skin all over mine. "Oh yeah?"

"Yeah," he growled, and God it was sexy.

"Anything you want."

"Anything?"

"I belong to you, right?"

"Yes, you do," he said, and the confidence in his voice sent a warm buzz through me.

"Okay, then."

"How do you feel about rope?"

The laughter bubbled out of me. I could not ever remember being happier.

"I promise to untie you," he swore, kissing my throat, his hands starting to roam. "Maybe."

Like I cared. Between us was trust, friendship, the whole shebang. And now, most importantly, love.

"I've got you," he whispered into my ear.

It went both ways.

MARY CALMES lives in Lexington, Kentucky, with her husband and two children and loves all the seasons except summer. She graduated from the University of the Pacific in Stockton, California, with a bachelor's degree in English literature. Due to the fact that it is English lit and not English grammar, do not ask her to point out a clause for you, as it will *so* not happen. She loves writing, becoming immersed in the process, and falling into the work. She can even tell you what her characters smell like. She loves buying books and going to conventions to meet her fans.

A Matter of Time Series from MARY CALMES

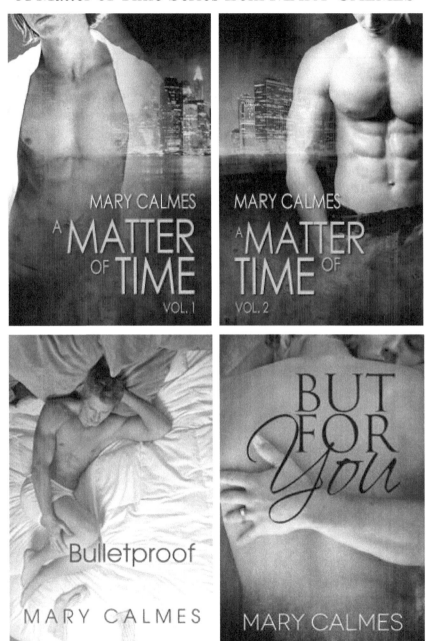

Also by MARY CALMES

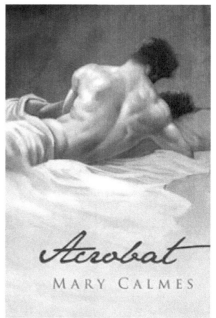

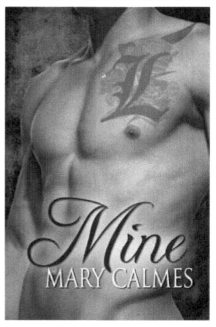

http://www.dreamspinnerpress.com

Also by MARY CALMES

http://www.dreamspinnerpress.com

Change of Heart Series from MARY CALMES

CHANGE of HEART
Mary Calmes

TRUSTED Bond
Mary Calmes

HONORED Vow
Mary Calmes

CRUCIBLE of Fate
Mary Calmes

http://www.dreamspinnerpress.com

CPSIA information can be obtained at www.ICGtesting.com
Printed in the USA
LVOW01s0707220614

391100LV00002B/38/P

9 781632 160645